A Stable 1

by

Harriet J Kent

© *Harriet J Kent* 2012
Revised edition 2017

Chapter One

Leya Martin hopped around frantically as she placed her highly-polished black leather boot into the stirrup iron and gingerly mounted the young horse, Del. Her heart was pounding. She tried to swallow but coughed. Her mouth was bone dry. She eased herself into the saddle and felt the cold, wet feeling of soaking leather between her legs. Her bottom was drenched in a second. Del moved sideways as she reached for the other stirrup and placed her foot on the iron. She adjusted the girth for the umpteenth time, just as Manna constantly instructed her to. She moved her hands gingerly along his neck and gently patted it in reassurance for Del but mainly for herself. She tried to swallow again but made a gulping sound.

She moved him into an active walk. He responded instantly. She looked around, trying to focus on the cross-country course. Leya's vision was hampered by the driving rain. It lashed hard against her face, driven by the howling, relentless wind that enveloped the entire field. It was devoid of any form of shelter, bar the copse. The wind scooped at the trees, like an enormous, invisible hand. It made them lean and arch with its power.

She heard a voice beside her. It was her friend, LB.

"You'll be fine, hun! Don't be scared. It's only a few little jumps." LB, dressed in smart trainers and fashionable skinny jeans, smiled up at her from beneath her pink hoodie. Her brown hair was fashioned into a short, boyish cut. She was as soaking wet as Leya.

LB wasn't that interested in horses but she was keen to support her friend, particularly as this was the first time Leya was riding one of Manna Jacob's promising young eventers at the local riding club competition. Manna had high hopes for Del and was giving Leya the opportunity to ride him around a novice course. Manna had told Leya it would be the ideal competition to introduce the young horse to cross-country and, perhaps, in the future, he might make the grade as an event horse. Manna was also competing with another young hopeful, the six-year-old Irish Sport Horse Figaro. She was already out on the course.

Leya turned Del into the wind. In protest, he moved swiftly backwards and dug his hooves into the rain-soaked, sodden ground. LB, who was standing behind him and sending a text on her mobile, leapt out of the way, straight into a pile of droppings, previously deposited by Del. She groaned and looked down at her white trainers where a green mass oozed around her feet.

"Oh man! I only bought these a few days ago!" she whimpered. She indicated for Leya to hand over her riding crop so she could attempt to scrape off a large clod of muck. She winced in disappointment and frowned. "They are gonna be stained for life! I'll lose my swag, wearing shitty trainers!"

Looking down at what LB was trying to achieve, Leya yelled, "LB! Don't do that! I need to use that stick!" She grabbed the crop back off her friend. "Don't make such a fuss! They'll clean up; it's only muck! Why you didn't wear welly boots, I don't know!"

Sighing, she turned her attention to her horse.

"Come on!" she hissed at Del. "We've got to go... now!" She squeezed her legs against his Del's wet body and urged him forward into a trot. "We've got to do this... trust me! We need to warm up. Oh, why I am doing this? The whole competition should have been called off. Come on," she pleaded.

She slammed her legs on. Her spurs brushed against his sides and Del obeyed. He moved into a hesitant sideways trot into the collecting area.

A voice called out from the distance, "It's a bit hairy out there. No one has gone clear yet! The course is a real sticky bitch! Glad *I'm* back safely!"

Another voice sounded the death knell. "It should be cancelled. No one can ride a decent round in this. It's atrocious out there!"

Ignoring the doom and gloom, Leya blinked away the rain from her eyes and tried to breathe. In, out, in, out; her nerves were in shreds. Del was very excited at the prospect of his first competition and was understandably on his toes. The wind made him shy at the smallest possible object, be it a stray leaf or a plastic bag. Everything was a threat to him and he was desperate to take flight.

Leya cantered Del in a circle. She was shortly called into the start box. She walked Del around and waited for her countdown... *three, two, one... go!*

"Next to go is Leya Martin riding Delaware!" boomed the loud speaker to the handful of spectators who had braved the foul weather. Del, spooked by the noise launched forward and sped off, cantering sideways and looking all around him.

"Shit! Why am I doing this?" Leya asked herself as she and Del approached the first fence of straw bales, designed to encourage the horse over a simple low jump. Del took one look at the bales in horror. His eyes were on stalks: he reacted like he had never encountered straw in his life, let alone eaten it or laid on it in his stable. He believed the bales to be alive and tried his very best to run out. Leya turned his head at the last minute and he leapt over them from a near standstill, his head on a level with the bales as he refused to take his eyes off them. He jumped at least six feet into the air in an unsightly fashion. Leya was thrust onto Del's neck and she forced herself back into the saddle.

Del thought it was great fun and proceeded to canter sideways in banana fashion to the next fence, the drop. Leya gathered the reins to collect Del as he skidded to a halt at the edge of the grassy bank, which was already churned up by the many hooves that had passed through before them. Del momentarily looked at the other side, his head bent down low. He cat-jumped, again from a standstill. Again, he threw Leya onto his neck and she found herself in between the saddle and his withers. She blinked away more rain from her eyes and cantered on towards the next fence, the rider frightener! This was so-called because the upturned wooden pheasant feeder appeared larger and wider than it actually was. Leya was feeling less nervous and they cleared the feeder with ease. Del had settled down and wasn't pulling quite so enthusiastically.

He jumped the next two jumps, the rustic upright and the hurdles, very cleanly and then they galloped on towards the open ditch. Leya hated water jumps but she tried not to transmit her nerves onto Del. She closed her eyes tightly as the jump loomed large and daunting in front of them. She felt Del take off and breathed a huge sigh of relief as he safely reached the other side. Losing his balance momentarily under the slippery ground, he faltered. Leya patted his sodden neck, still holding firmly on to the reins.

She looked for the next jump. It was under the cover of the copse, the 'in and out'. The wind blew fiercely into Leya's face as they rounded the course towards the raging foliage. Spatters of mud flew around them as the turf had been so badly cut up by previous competitors and was beyond boggy. The trees were thrust from left to right by the incessant wind. Del strengthened his speed and decided to gallop erratically, unaware of exactly where he was being asked to go. He wasn't happy about galloping into a black hole, which was the impression the thrashing trees gave him. Leya put her leg on and collected her reins; she half-halted Del to prevent him from running out. He slowed to a canter and pensively entered the woods. Once in, he saw the in and out and gallantly jumped over it. He landed in a sticky mud bog, disguised by a pool of water the other side of the jump, but cantered on enthusiastically.

"Good boy! Well done, Del!" Leya praised him as they upped a gear.

They galloped towards the coffin. Del was performing very well and Leya's confidence was boosted. As they approached the fence, a dog became loose from its owner and ran on to the course, directly in front of them. Del spooked and his concentration became fixed on the dog. Leya took hold of Del and tried to detract his attention but it was too late. Del wasn't listening to her and decided he didn't want to jump the coffin. The dog was much more interesting. He ran out at the jump, much to Leya's annoyance. She swiftly turned him, cantered in a circle and headed back at the jump. Del wasn't interested. He fought against Leya and planted his feet at the take-off and skidded to a halt. Again she turned in a circle but made the hasty decision to carry on to the next fence. She was becoming weak with exhaustion.

Del's momentum and enthusiasm immediately evaporated after the coffin. He had switched off. He decided he'd had enough jumping for one day. He refused the following two jumps and, in an attempt to please his rider, with one last effort, decided that he ought to jump one more fence, albeit the wrong way! He approached the jump with much gusto and stopped dead at take-off, launching Leya spectacularly into the air like a puppet. Del watched with interest as Leya landed in a heap amongst copious amounts of mud and brushwood. The steward's flag was raised, and a whistle blew in the distance: they were eliminated.

Leya was angry with herself and distraught. She shook her head in annoyance, got up and picked off hedge cuttings from her sodden, muddy clothes. Her back was hurting and she held on to her side and winced. She grabbed hold of Del's reins and limped solemnly off the course and back to the lorry park. She untacked him, placed his cooling rug over his soaked back and threw the tack into the lorry compartment. She dreaded Manna's reaction. Del put his head down to the ground as far as his lead rope would allow and proceeded to eat a circle of grass around him as he stood tethered to the lorry.

Manna returned to the lorry, riding Figaro. She was elated.

"Guess what? We went clear! Fig was brilliant! Took the jumps like a stag! Really gutsy, good boy! Shouldn't you be walking Del round, to cool him off? How did you do, Leya?" she asked cheerfully and leapt off Fig's back.

Leya took a deep breath.

"Not so good. He ran out at the coffin, there was this dog—" Leya began but Manna interrupted.

"But you got him over it, didn't you? Tell me you got him over it, Leya?"

"Well… ummm. No, I didn't. I couldn't get him—"

"Oh, Leya you idiot! You *know* what I've told you. It is *so* important to get the horse over a fence that they have previously refused! Especially as he is a youngster! It's the golden rule of riding! And you blew it! Will you *ever* learn anything? I am really disappointed in you. Why don't you just think for once in your life? You could have seriously ruined Del's eventing chances! Thinking he can refuse a jump and being allowed to get away with it! And he won't even qualify now!"

Manna angrily dragged a sodden Fig to the other side of the lorry. She was clearly furious with Leya. Leya shrugged her shoulders. She shook her head again in dismay. As always, Manna was on to her like a ton of bricks. It was never the horse's fault, it was never the situation: it was always Leya's fault. She felt utterly deflated. Leya didn't get the opportunity to tell Manna that she had fallen off and hurt herself.

"Hey!" LB returned to the horsebox. Her trainers were covered in mud and she had yanked her jeans high above her knees. Her legs were scalded by the wind and rain and were in shades of mottled red. "That was really bad luck, man! That woman with the dog should be shot! Still, as I said, it's only jumping."

She walked past a fuming Manna and promptly climbed into the dry cab. She placed her MP3 player on her lap, fiddled with the earpiece and started nodding her head to the music.

Manna went on to win the class and was presented with a beautiful silver salver and a glossy rosette emblazoned with '1st' in large gold letters. As she collected her prize in the collecting ring, Leya reluctantly congratulated her. Manna smirked at Leya.

"Perhaps, one day, you might win. On the other hand, judging by your performance today, perhaps not!" She sauntered off to the lorry with the salver tucked under her arm. "I want those horses taken back to the yard now. Can you drive the lorry for me? I've just met someone who has a horse she wants me to have a look at with the possibility of training it. I'm getting a lift with her. I'll be back later on."

Leya interrupted her, "But, Manna, I can't…"

Manna scowled back at her, "Look, just drive the bloody horsebox, will you! Surely you can manage that?" She waved to her prospective client who was waiting in a 4X4 and turned her back on Leya.

"Okay. LB, help me load these two, will you? LB!" she yelled, making her jump. "Come on!"

LB removed her earpiece, clambered down from the lorry and thrust her hands into her pockets.

"So where is Mrs J going? Ain't she gonna drive the lorry?"

"Apparently not." Leya wrestled with Del as she tried to fasten travel boots on to his legs. "She is going to see someone about training their horse. Asked me to drive it back for her."

"But that's cool, innit?" LB held on to Del's head collar. He tried to nudge her away from him.

Leya held her side. Her hip and lower back were throbbing and she felt nauseous.

"I don't have much choice in the matter. Right, walk him round in a circle, turn him and walk him straight up the ramp. Watch your feet!"

"Why, in case I get shit on my trainers again?" LB remarked in sarcasm. "Cos as far as I'm concerned, these trainers are just shit now anyway! Wasted!"

"Walk him up the ramp!" Leya was getting impatient.

The rain pelted against the back of her head as she untied Fig and led him up the ramp. LB had tied Del up to a ring positioned on the side of the lorry where he began to munch on the hay net. Leya fastened the wooden partitions, making sure both horses were secure.

"Okay, let's get out of here. I've had enough for one day!"

Leya started up the lorry and it boomed into life with a plume of smoke. They inched out of the churned-up mud. The wheels spun in the last few strands of grass, but they were soon out of the field and heading for home.

LB reinserted her earpiece. Leya could hear the music above the drone of the lorry's engine and rolled her eyes.

"Can't you shut that thing off?" she yelled.

LB jumped. She turned, clearly startled. She pulled at the earpiece and looked at Leya.

"Don't get the arse with me just cos you messed up! It wasn't my fault you missed the jump. Blame the dog, man!"

"I can't bear that noise you're listening to. It's really irritating!" Leya crunched into third gear and the lorry lurched. Her passengers were thrust forward as she did so.

"Take it easy, man, or you'll be wearing those horses!" LB looked at the road ahead. "Don't worry about Mrs J, she'll get over it. You may be in for a hard time for the next day or two, but chill!"

"I wish I shared your optimism. It's easy for you to say; you don't work for her," returned Leya, concentrating on the road.

"If I worked for Mrs J then I wouldn't mess up with her horse," LB announced and looked out of the side window.

"Yeah, right! You can't even ride! So that would be something else to see. You wouldn't last a day there!" Leya retorted.

"Wanna bet? I reckon I could get the gist of this riding lark and go round those jumps clear, man. It would be wicked!" LB flicked her index finger against her thumb as she spoke. "I certainly wouldn't take no rap from a dog! You gotta get over it, Leya. Move on!" LB smiled and resumed fiddling with her earpiece. The endless *thump, thump* racket of the music continued.

Leya was fuming. She reached across and lunged at LB's MP3. LB grabbed Leya's arm and they wrestled against each other.

"You are really pissing me off! Give it to me!" yelled Leya "Just… give… it… oh nooooooooooooooo!" She looked at the road and screamed. "Oh shi—"

A tractor and trailer had pulled out in front of their lorry. It was fully laden with large, round straw bales. Leya slammed on the brakes and the lorry skidded violently sideways. The horses were thrown from one side of the box to the other with uncontrollable force. Leya could hear the sickening thud of their hooves as they desperately tried to regain their balance. She closed her eyes as the lorry swerved, mounted the grass verge and launched into the air. LB was screaming and trying to hold on in what seemed like slow motion. The lorry began to tilt, teetering momentarily on the edge of its tyres before it slammed down onto the road, landing on its side. The sound of metal scraping the road and splintering wood rang out as it eventually slowed and ground to a halt.

There was an eerie silence as the bodywork of the lorry creaked. Its wheels continued to spin in mid-air, squeaking intermittently, before they too became silent. Leya had been thrown sideways and ended up suspended from her seatbelt across LB's lap. Still encapsulated by her seatbelt, she fumbled across to turn off the engine. She blinked and focussed on LB who was lying in a crumpled heap between the passenger seat and the footwell. The earpiece was lying on the floor; the music continued to play. LB wasn't moving.

Unclipping herself from the seatbelt, Leya inched her way up to the door and pushed against it. It was a difficult manoeuvre but she managed to clamber out. The tractor driver met her. His face was white and his expression was one of horror.

"Are you all right?" he choked. "Didn't you see me? You couldn't miss me! The tractor isn't exactly small, is it?"

Leya couldn't concentrate on what he was saying. Her concern was for LB.

"Can you ring for an ambulance? It's my friend, she's in there. She isn't moving." Leya pointed to the footwell.

"Yes, course I will. I think we'll need the fire service as well, don't you? Are there any animals in the back?"

"Oh my God!" Leya, through shock, had momentarily forgotten the horses. She suddenly remembered. "Yes, two horses. Oh no! I don't think I can bear to look at them. Can you check them for me, please? See how they are?" she pleaded with the farmer and dragged him to the back of the lorry.

"Can you get the ramp down for me? Oh! It's all twisted!" she screamed.

The farmer made a 999 call and reported the accident. He then attempted to open the ramp on the lorry. It was jammed and distorted. Leya indicated towards the groom's door. She stood aside as he carefully released the clasp. What met his eyes made him gulp in horror.

"You don't want to look in there, love, it ain't a pretty sight. Best wait till the fire brigade gets here. They'll be able to deal with this. We do need to call a vet. Like *now*! Who's your vet?" he urged.

"Er, Mike at the Malsham practice. He's an equine vet. But they're not my horses! His number is on my mobile," wailed Leya in confusion. She reached into her pocket and handed her phone to the farmer. "They are Manna Jacob's horses. They're only young; only babies!"

"Best wait here, love," the farmer gravely repeated.

It seemed like an age before the distant peal of a siren pierced the silence of the road and its carnage. It was an ambulance. It drew to an abrupt halt and two paramedics emerged. They ran to the scene. The farmer gave his account of what happened as Leya sat in shock on the wet grass verge. Her hands covered her face. She felt a gentle, warm hand on hers.

"Come on, love, let's have a look at you. Can you tell me your name? Can you remember what happened?"

Leya looked at the paramedic and closed her eyes. She didn't speak. The second paramedic joined them and whispered to his colleague, "We need the fire service for this one." He indicated the twisted remains of the lorry where LB lay trapped.

A second sound of sirens filled the air as two police cars arrived. One officer cordoned off the road with cones and tape. He placed a blue *Police Accident* sign a little distance away from the lorry. He spoke briefly on his radio before walking over to where Leya was sitting.

"Hello. Can you tell me what happened?" he asked. "Just to put us in the picture?" he added.

Leya blurted out what she could remember before breaking into sobs. "It was my fault. I was trying to stop her… LB, my friend, from making the racket on her MP3 player. I was irritated by it, it was so loud, and then, I looked at the road and there was the tractor. I couldn't avoid it!" She sobbed and held her head in her hands. "I should have told her. I should have *told* her that I couldn't do it!" she wailed.

"Couldn't do what?" the police officer probed.

"Drive the lorry," Leya whispered. "I shouldn't have driven the lorry, but she didn't listen to me! She was too angry with me. Too concerned about her new client. Angry with me for messing up on the cross-country. She made me do it!" she yelled. "And I didn't want to!"

The police officer nodded in silence as he made notes. "Are you telling me you aren't insured to drive this vehicle?" he calmly asked.

"No. I'm insured okay. I tried to tell her, but she wouldn't listen!"

"So, why couldn't you drive the lorry?" the officer pried.

"Cos my back is really killing me. I fell off the horse around the cross-country course, onto one of the jumps. I really hurt my back. But she wouldn't listen. She was too wrapped up in her own glory and her own self... as usual. It's always about her! Her! Her!" Leya blurted and thrust her head into her hands.

"Who are you talking about?" asked the officer.

"My boss, Manna Jacobs, at Littlebridge Stables, Malsham," Leya replied in a muffled tone. She didn't take her hands from her face.

"Right. Okay, let's check these horses in the back. The farmer says there are two horses, is that right?"

"Oh please let them be all right!" Leya wailed. She shook in fear.

"It's okay," reassured the officer. "We'll sort them out. Stay here please whilst we go and have a look at them."

Leya closed her eyes in despair. The body of the lorry lay silent with only the periodic creak of settling, splintered wood. The farmer, who was standing by the groom's door, met the policeman. He bent forward and lowered his voice.

"It isn't good, officer. One horse is alive, but I'm not sure about the other one. I can't see him moving. He's pinned beneath the partition; the other horse is lying on top of him. And... look." He pointed to the side of the lorry where a trail of blood steadily trickled through the wood and onto the road.

"Has anyone called for a vet?" the officer asked.

"Yes, I did it straightaway. I spoke to the local Malsham vet. The young girl gave me his name. He's coming over now."

Sirens pealed through the silence once more as the fire service arrived with two engines. Briefed by the police, they immediately attended to cutting LB from her tangled metal trap. Cutting equipment made short work of the solid frame of the horsebox and they deftly removed the windscreen so they could provide easy access for the paramedics. The drone of the equipment shocked Leya as she remained seated on the verge. LB was gently manoeuvred into a position where the paramedics could safely remove her from the lorry and place her on to a flat orange board. Her head was taped, to prevent her from moving. She was given painkillers intravenously and the two paramedics, aided by three firefighters, gently carried her to the waiting ambulance. She was whisked away with the sirens blaring and blue lights flashing into the distance.

The chief firefighter made his way over to Leya.

"The ambulance has taken your friend to Malsham General Hospital, to A&E. She's in safe hands now. Try not to worry," he reassured an ashen-faced Leya. "We're dealing with the horses now. The vet has arrived and he's assessing them. We should know what's happening soon. Stay here, and I'll come and find you once I know what the score is."

"Can you stay with her?" he asked a female police officer who had just arrived at the scene. She nodded and sat down beside Leya, who was staring at the ground.

The vet emerged from the groom's door. He looked gravely at the chief firefighter.

"Not good," he sighed. "The horse underneath is dead, crushed by the weight of the other one. I've checked for a pulse, but there's nothing. The other horse is badly injured but he should survive. I've sedated him to stop him from thrashing around and causing more damage to himself. But we need to get him out of there. I'll arrange for a horse ambulance to take him back to the practice. He's going to need surgery. He's impaled on a piece of wood. It's gone through the top part of his chest, so we need to act fast. Can you brief your guys, please? And we are going to need the knacker wagon. Can you ring Malsham Hunt for me? I'll give you the number. As far as I know they still take fallen stock. We need to remove the body as soon as possible."

The fire officer nodded in silence and indicated to his crew to gather round as he explained the situation.

"Has the owner been informed of all this?" asked Mike.

The police officer moved towards him.

"Yes, Mrs Jacobs is apparently on her way now. She'll be here in a few minutes."

Leya sat in silence. She was in deep shock. Not long afterwards, she could hear a familiar voice but didn't register that it was Manna who had arrived at the scene. She could hear a gasp and a deafening cry as Manna was informed that Del was dead. She listened to a lonely blackbird's afternoon lament. It was the end of the day and he was saying goodnight to it. Leya blinked away a tear as she thought of Del. The female police officer had already broken the news to her that he was dead. Leya began to sway backwards and forwards. Her arms crossed her chest as she held on to her body. She heard the noise of machinery, cutting into the bodywork of the lorry. She heard the knacker wagon's winch as it lifted Del's body on to the flatbed with its high sides so you couldn't see or smell the stench of death. She rocked backwards and forwards as the vet worked to release Fig, who was heavily sedated. She listened as Manna screamed when Fig was cut free. The piece of wood remained firmly in his chest.

She didn't even register when she was led to a waiting police car and taken to the hospital to be checked over. She was in a parallel world, which was being acted out in slow motion. It was a parallel world which she hoped she could stay in for the rest of her life.

Chapter Two

"Shouldn't you be going?" Natalie Roberts whispered as she pushed against the masculine frame that peacefully slept beside her in the antique pine double bed. She repeatedly nudged him until he woke up. The bedstead squeaked and groaned as she moved her fingers under his arms, then onto his ribs until she received a response.

"Why? Wh… what time is it?" He slowly moved beneath the faded blue gingham duvet cover, delicately lifted his head and hovered it above the pillow, eyes blinking awake, trying to catch a glimpse of the clock radio that sat on the bedside cabinet.

"It's time for you to go!" she replied and pushed his warm body towards the edge of the bed.

"No, Nats," he groaned. "I don't wanna go!"

He placed a protective arm around her shoulders and pulled her close to him. Opening his eyes, he took in the new morning. He blinked against the weak sunlight that had infiltrated the large, Victorian bedroom. It had been decorated in primrose yellow emulsion paint, about the same time as the sheets and curtains were purchased; everything was now faded, tired and in desperate need of new touches. Stray and age-old cobwebs hung haphazardly from the ceiling, with resident dead flies encapsulated in webbed tombs around the curtains. The light fitting was coated in dust like camouflage netting. He smiled at Natalie as he recalled their night of passionate lovemaking. He fondly kissed her on the forehead.

"*You*," he sat up and wryly smiled, "are even *more* gorgeous in the morning." He carefully moved a strand of blonde hair away from her hazel eyes.

"I know, so you keep telling me," Natalie interrupted. "Now... out... you go!" She gently shooed away his slumbering advances.

"Okay, you win," he conceded, and reached out for the black moleskin trousers that lay on top of the duvet. They were in exactly the same position where he had thrown them the night before, crumpled but warm, alongside a checked shirt that also held its fair share of creases.

He tried to organise his exit from the comfortable bed. He found great difficulty in achieving any sort of motivation. He complained loudly as he placed his feet on the bare floorboards. He stretched his arms upwards above his head, yawned and ran a hand lazily through his tousled hair.

"Ooh, it's a bit nippy!" he remarked. He clutched his sides and rubbed them vigorously until he felt warmth running over his body.

He walked to the window, blinked a couple of times and then took in the view towards the downs. He could make out some sheep grazing in the distance. They looked like early morning mushrooms scattering the fields, fresh for picking. He looked to the sky where the sun had climbed midway and set a warming, yellow hue over the valley. A pheasant in the leaf-filled copse rang out its warning trill with much flapping of its wings. He smiled at the late spring scene and started to pull on his clothes amidst yawns and stretches.

Natalie lazily stretched her body in preparation for another day. She lifted her hands high above her head, exposing evenly tanned breasts. He stopped dressing and gazed at her slender, toned body and then moved back towards the bed, entranced at her appearance.

"Why do you *always* do it?" he questioned and beckoned towards her breasts, urging them to move forward towards him.

"To tease you; I know what you're like," she coyly replied. She moved seductively forward and dragged him back onto the bed.

"I thought I was supposed to be going?" he softly mentioned as Natalie slowly unbuttoned his creased shirt. She fumbled with his trouser zip.

"I've changed my mind," she coaxed and lay back in the bed, awaiting his advances, which didn't need to be awoken.

They passionately began to make love. Natalie drew him close to her body, writhing beneath him. She draped her legs expertly across his back as he gently guided himself into her. She grabbed his head and drew him further into her as he kissed and probed her mouth with his tongue. She groaned in rapid anticipation. He lay back on the bed and caught his breath. His chest rose up and down revealing a mixture of rippling, well-toned muscles. Natalie smiled and kissed the top of his head. She athletically swung herself over his body and leapt off the bed.

"Told you, you should've *gone*, but instead… you *came*!"

She grabbed her pink bathrobe that hung precariously on the back of the bedroom door and breezed purposefully out of the now sun-filled bedroom, swinging her robe in her arm.

"Do you want tea or coffee?" she called from the bathroom.

"I think I need a shower first," he called back. Glancing at his watch, he noticed it was nearly 8 a.m. "I'll have a coffee, then I must dash; I need to be somewhere soon."

"Somewhere nice, I hope," she called from the shower amidst echoing, splashing sounds of intense running water that pounded over her.

"Littlebridge," was the response.

"Shower's free so you can cleanse your infidelity!" she teased.

Natalie Roberts, an attractive widow, looked considerably younger than her age, even though her complexion was weathered through years of exposure to the elements. She was confident, outgoing and passionately fond of the opposite sex. Her explanation to those who questioned her youthful looks was that she ate sensibly, worked out regularly and had a lover whom she seduced at least three times a day. Fun-loving and young at heart, Natalie was the life and soul of the social scene, and popular amongst friends and acquaintances of the neighbouring farming and equine fraternity. She was ambitious, bossy but level-headed and spent her days trying to run her farm, albeit on a much-reduced scale since the sudden death of her husband, Sam, earlier that year.

The man arrived downstairs and slumped down into the large red armchair by the bottle-green Aga, which nestled in a large brick alcove of the kitchen. Natalie passed him a mug of black coffee and smiled. She leaned back on the wooden work surface, sipping her tea from a baby-pink floral-encrusted china cup.

"Are you going to the show at Malsham on Sunday?"

"The dressage? No, not if I can get out of it," he answered amidst gulps of coffee. He glanced briefly at the headlines on the front page of the newspaper. "There might be a chance we could slip away. What do you think?"

"I think that if there is even the slightest chance, we should take it. Anyway, it's not like you to miss a horsy event, is it?" she whispered over her cup and seductively added. "I think we should slip away, don't you?"

"I'll text you with a time."

"Great!" Natalie glanced at the pile of letters on the kitchen table and sipped her tea.

"Bills?" he queried, knowing the exact response that he would receive.

"Probably, there always seem to be lots of them." She continued to nonchalantly drink. She looked away as she did so. "I'll look through them later, when I have time."

Running the farm had not been easy since the untimely death of her forty-two year old husband, Sam. Natalie had been left with a string of debts and favours, and a daughter who was halfway through university, studying law. Sam had suffered a fatal heart attack. It had been a dreadful shock, leaving Natalie in denial. Her daughter, Calico, had taken his death so badly that she hadn't been able to bring herself to return to the family home. She had decided instead to throw herself into her studies and made various excuses to stay with friends during the holidays. This had deeply upset Natalie.

As with most mothers, Natalie had invariably had differences of opinion with the Calico since she'd hit her teens. Sam, the mediator, had always managed to smooth things out between them, usually in Calico's favour. Calico knew that life would never be the same without him and that she would struggle to get her own way in the future with her mother. Her solution to this dilemma was to stay away. Natalie hoped that bridges would, in time, be rebuilt, and that one day they might be able to pick up from where they had parted. She secretly knew this would take time with a lot of talking and understanding. Not just from her, but also from Calico. Give and take would be the key to their much-needed reunion.

"You know, I could—" he began.

"I don't need your help," Natalie interrupted, slamming her cup into the sink; a small piece of china chipped from the rim. "Look, it's my problem. *I* need to sort it out, it's up to *me!* Oh damn! That's my favourite cup!"

She angrily tried to find the missing chipped piece by thrusting her hands into the washing up bowl without success.

"Okay, but you don't need to be a martyr, Nat. It won't achieve anything, will it? The bills will still be there. You can't bury your head in the sand forever."

"I'll find a way, I always do. But, thanks anyway. Look, I'm sorry for snapping at you… it just irritates me, all this bloody hassle since Sam died!"

He stood up, gathered her into his arms and gently kissed her on the cheek. He stroked her hair away from her eyes.

"I'd better go. We'll speak soon, okay? Take care and call me?"

He closed the door slowly behind him and stepped into the concrete exercise yard that was littered with a mixture of weeds, nettles and bindweed. Natalie watched him get into his 4x4 and, with a little encouragement, the old beast burst into life with a graceful puff of black smoke from its diesel engine. She watched it amble up the unmade, bumpy lane, lined with leafy elm trees. It reached the narrow road and chugged its way towards Malsham.

Natalie pushed herself away from the kitchen work surface and shuffled towards the pile of letters. She flicked with distaste through the first batch. She noticed most were final demands. One letter, however, immediately caught her attention. The envelope had her solicitor's name and address emblazoned in crimson across the top. She placed the other letters back on the table, giving her full attention to the one she still held in her hand.

"I *know* I need to open this one," she murmured to herself.

She turned the envelope over and, with apprehension, slid her fingers beneath the seal to reveal the contents. She slowly unfolded the letter and, as she did so, a slip of paper fluttered onto the floor, printed side facing downwards. Nell, her aged tortoiseshell cat, twitched briefly as the slip landed near her wicker basket. It wasn't loud enough to wake her completely from her peaceful nap.

"Right!" Natalie prepared herself. She sat down and began to read, holding her breath as she took in its contents.

'Dear Mrs Roberts,

Re: The Estate of Mr Samuel Edward Roberts - Deceased

Further to our previous correspondence, please find details of the final settlement of your late husband's estate of which you are a beneficiary. I apologise for the extended delay, which was due to unforeseen circumstances. Please also find enclosed my account in respect of work carried out, which I hope you will find reasonable.

Yours sincerely,

A & A Solicitors, Malsham.'

Natalie placed the letter on the table and neglected to read further. She balanced awkwardly on her chair, leant down and picked up the slip of paper. It was a statement, which indicated the amount of money that was left in the estate with a place for Natalie to sign in agreement of the amount. She stared for what seemed like hours whilst her brain took in the amount: £1,557,500.24! What a magical figure! She stared first at the slip and then at the letter, which she scanned several times to make sure she hadn't made a terrible mistake. She checked the address on the envelope: yes, it was addressed to *her* and *her* alone. She glanced at the solicitor's fee account and started to laugh.

"Oh Sam, you've saved me! You won't know how much, but you've saved me! Oh!"

She lowered her head into her hands, her hair spread across her face like a golden veil, and broke down into tears. Tears of relief, disbelief, sadness and every other emotion her body could muster. She sat up with a start thinking of Calico. She took hold of the statement again and carefully re-read it.

"How come you had *so* much money and I didn't know about it?" she asked out loud, as though she was anticipating a reply from her deceased husband.

Nell stirred in her basket making it creak and shift. Natalie looked about her and tried to find a reason for her husband's wealth. She realised there would be *more* than enough money to ensure Calico would be able to stay on at university to complete her degree. This was one of the subjects Natalie needed to talk over with her, and now she would now be able to do it with renewed confidence and adequate financial backing. She reached across the table, wiping her tear-stained eyes swiftly with her bathrobe sleeve, grabbed a handful of the letters and threw them up high into the air in glee.

"Get stuffed, the lot of you! You bastard bills! You won't ever cross my path again, hear me?" she whooped and watched the letters cascade from the air and scatter to the floor, like large square-shaped snowflakes in slow motion.

Her heart beat very quickly and she felt her face redden. The realisation of a better and more comfortable life began to sink in as she got up and started to dance around the kitchen, accidentally kicking against Nell's basket. The sudden thwack made Nell jump up in fright and disappear rapidly into the hallway. Sitting at a safe distance from the noise, Nell licked her foreleg and yawned in disgust at being rudely awoken. Natalie glanced back and apologised.

"Sorry, babe, I didn't mean to frighten you!"

Clutching the letter firmly in her hand she swung it above her head and gyrated like a native engrossed in a frenzied tribal dance.

"Yes!" She punched the air in delight. "I *will* survive!"

When she had marginally composed herself, Natalie wanted to share her news and who else should she phone first but her best friend, Manna Jacobs, at Littlebridge Stables. She grabbed her mobile, scrolled down and found Manna's name. She waited, hardly daring to breathe. She found it impossible to contain the excitement that welled inside her like a volcano about to erupt. She reached Manna's voicemail and sighed in frustration.

The next phone call she made was to her bank manager. He was in a meeting, so Natalie begrudgingly left a message with one of the call centre operators. She prayed that he would get the message to call her and that a note wouldn't be left lying in limbo as an email from Mumbai.

She wanted to get on with the next stage of her life now that she was able to envisage a positive future. She tapped the kitchen table impatiently with her fingers. A few minutes later her mobile phone rang and Natalie jumped with a start. She snatched up the phone.

"Hello? Manna! Oh Jude, hi. What… oh shit! How terrible! Oh no! I'll come over now! Bye!"

Natalie glanced at the morning paper that was propped against the side of the Aga. '*Promising Malsham Eventing Horse Dies*' was the headline. She shook her head in disbelief. Her own glory evaporated as she took in the tragic news. She had so desperately wanted to tell Manna her own news. She had wanted to gauge her reaction and revel in the congratulations that Manna would have surely have showered upon her. After all, it wasn't every day that the sniff of £1.5 million dropped through one's letterbox.

She walked across to the Welsh dresser and stopped to look at a photograph of Sam, dressed in his tweeds, that was proudly displayed in a silver-plated frame. She smiled fondly at the photo. She reached for a corkscrew and retrieved a bottle of chilled Chablis from the fridge. She triumphantly poured herself a glass and glanced again at the photograph. She raised her glass in a personal toast.

"Cheers, Sam! God bless you, and Del too. You were a sweetie. What a waste of such potential." She gulped a mouthful of wine. "And God help you, Leya!"

The phone rang again. Swallowing quickly, she took the call before the answerphone kicked in.

"Hi, Neil. You got the message then! The bank's communications *are* good today! Yes, I need to see you… tomorrow afternoon? Yeah, that will be great. I'll see you at three o'clock at the Malsham Branch. Bye!"

She quickly jotted down the appointment with her bank manager in her well-thumbed diary. She picked up the slip from the solicitor and placed it against the page where she had written the time of the meeting.

Half an hour later, Natalie arrived at Littlebridge in her 4x4. She drew up in the concrete yard. The air felt tinged in sadness as she walked towards the house. Manna, the successful horse trainer and semi-professional rider, stood in the doorway of her Georgian home. Her slim body was hunched, her hair uncombed, her eyes red with crying. Natalie put her arms out and greeted her with a silent hug.

"Come on, let's go in. Where's Callum?" Natalie led Manna to the kitchen. "I need a drink," she added, looking around for alcohol.

"But it's still morning... isn't it?" Manna observed. She was still in shock. "I thought you were giving the *vino* a miss."

"No!" Natalie sat down with two glasses and a bottle of red wine retrieved from a cupboard. "In times of tragedy, it's this stuff that gets you through. Here, have a sip." She poured the wine and handed a glass to Manna who sat, shell-shocked, staring at the table.

"I don't really want to drink it. I haven't slept a wink. I just keep thinking of poor Del and Fig. My lovely young boys... struck down, so young... so young." Manna continued to gaze at the table. Her hand reached out for the glass and she took a reluctant sip.

"How is Fig doing?" Natalie gently asked and put her arm around Manna's shoulders.

Manna sniffed and sighed. "Mike phoned me last night to say that he got through the op okay. The wood had pierced his chest but it's mainly muscle tissue damage. Thankfully no broken bones. But he will take time to heal. Mike said he's going to keep him in the equine hospital for the time being, to monitor him. It's going to be ages before he can get back to some sort of normality. But at least he's alive. Not like my lovely Del. I shall never forgive Leya for this. Never! That bloody girl has ruined everything!"

"That's a bit harsh, isn't it? She didn't mean to do it. She's only young, Manna. You shouldn't have made her drive the lorry in the first place. Why did you?" Natalie probed.

"Because I had a client to see, there and then. I couldn't miss the opportunity. But I suppose even that won't happen now. People will think my yard is incapable of transporting horses safely, thanks to Leya!" She gulped the wine and reached for the bottle to top up her glass.

"So what happens now?" Natalie asked. She held her breath.

"Now?" Manna simpered. "How should *I* know? I suppose I will have to deal with the police. They keep phoning up and wanting to ask loads of questions. Callum is fending them off for me. But I don't know how long for."

"What do they want to speak to you for? Surely they will pursue Leya with the dangerous driving thing?"

Manna shrugged her shoulders. "Yes, they probably will, but they are on to me because the silly bitch told them she couldn't drive the lorry. She told *plod* at the scene. She said she hurt her back when she fell off Del. Blurted it out, apparently, according to them. So, my life is going to be sheer hell now and I don't have time for all this!"

"Not necessarily. It was an accident. What about Leya's friend? How is she?" Natalie continued her barrage of questions.

"I don't know and don't really care!" said Manna callously. "All I know is that I have one dead horse and one that is ruined. I can't think about anything else!"

Natalie decided to cool off her interrogation. Manna was going to be answering enough questions with the police. She decided the time was right to tell Manna her own news.

"Well, in amongst all this tragedy, I have some news. Take a look at *this*!" She thrust the letter into Manna's hand and waited for the reaction. "Read it to me! I need to *hear* it spoken out *loud*!"

Red-eyed and exhausted, Manna looked at her friend incredulously. She reluctantly agreed, took hold of the letter and began to read aloud. "Okay... Dear Mrs—"

"Yes, I know *that* bit!" Natalie interrupted. "Go on, the next bit! Keep reading!" she instructed and bounced heavily up and down on her chair like an impatient child, making clouds of dust appear.

Manna read the letter out and Natalie slumped back on the chair, drew her legs up to her chin and closed her eyes. Manna stopped reading when she reached the sum of money.

"Wow, Nat!" Manna dropped the letter and stared at her friend in disbelief. "Now that's a turn up for the books. Did you know anything about it?"

Natalie shook her head.

"No! If I had known, I certainly would have enjoyed trying to spend it. At least so Sam could have had the pleasure of seeing me blow it, or maybe not..." She broke off in reflection, then burst out laughing. "Bloody hell! I expect he's spinning in his grave now. He couldn't stand me even buying a new pair of knickers at M&S let alone letting me loose with £1.5 million!"

"Oh, Nat! That's a horrible thing to say!" Manna appeared shocked but secretly knew that Natalie was telling the truth about her late husband. Sam Roberts had been obsessed with making money, and lots of it. He had never spent a penny if he could help it. He built up investments and reinvestment portfolios. It was part of his *secret* game. He had dabbled in the stock market and in gilts. His gambles had paid off. He had never told Natalie of his *business ventures* and had led her to believe that they weren't that well off and that they had to live on the breadline, hence the farm being rundown and overgrown and running at a loss. Sam's philosophy was that if a house looked unkempt, then one would never be pestered by burglars, con artists or hawkers because the impression of a neglected property meant the occupier wasn't worth much in monetary terms and would be left alone.

"So, what are your plans then, Nat?" Manna took another slug of wine.

"Seeing Neil, you know, the bank manager, tomorrow afternoon to have a chat and decide. But do you know the first thing I'll do? I'm going to get rid of all my debts!" She smirked in distaste as she remembered the pile of unopened letters strewn across her kitchen floor. "And I'll make sure that Cally gets through university with a 2-1 or whatever the blazes you call it! A pass, graduation… you know! There's certainly enough cash to pay her student fees now!"

She drained her glass until dry and indicated with outstretched fingers towards the bottle for Manna to refill her glass. Manna declined.

"No thanks, Nat. I've had enough. I need to have a clear mind. I'm going to visit Fig. Look, I am *really* pleased for you, really I am. You deserve a break. Sam came up trumps, didn't he?" Manna picked up the letter and read through it again.

"He certainly did, Manna!" Natalie smiled as she thought of her eccentric late husband. "You'd better go. Hey, what about lunch sometime?"

"Yeh, love to. Just let me get this morning out of the way. Oh… have you read *all* of this letter?" asked Manna, pointing at the final paragraph.

Natalie looked at her in an odd fashion. She ran a hand through her hair and poured another glass of wine.

"What bit? I don't *need* to see anymore bits."

"I think you really ought to read this last paragraph," Manna warned.

She looked concerned so Natalie grabbed the letter from Manna. She scanned the last few sentences and her face dropped.

'Please be informed that Mr Robert's business partner is being sent a copy of this letter...'

"Business partner? Business partner? What does that mean? How could he have had a business partner? He never said he had a bloody business partner! What does that mean?"

Manna looked at her friend.

"It means whoever this business partner is they will be entitled to a percentage of the estate. I think you need to get in touch with your solicitor immediately. Get an appointment to see him and find out exactly what is going on. Look Nat, is this news official or should I stay *mum*?"

"Please, don't say anything, not for the time being. I need to get my head around all of this. Promise you won't say a word?" Natalie looked at Manna, her expression serious.

"Not a word, I promise. Take your time, see yourself out. I'm off to the vet's." Manna got up from the table and rubbed Natalie's arms in reassurance. Natalie felt she could trust Manna not to gossip.

Natalie watched as the light blue BMW convertible swiftly disappeared in a dust cloud out of the yard into the distance. She poured herself another glass of wine and thought about the pile of bills. She picked up Manna's copy of *Horse and Hound* and flicked through the pages, not really taking in what she was seeing or what the letter had said. She felt Manna was genuinely pleased for her and that made her happy.

'All I need to do now,' she thought, 'is to get my hands on all that lovely money.'

She leant back in the chair, closed her eyes and thought of her impending fortune, but with growing annoyance at the *business partner*. She reached for her mobile phone and dialled her solicitor's number.

Chapter Three

Jude Armstrong was engrossed in mucking out the third stable that morning at Littlebridge. It was a large and extremely well-kept equestrian establishment, home to a number of liveries, competition horses and riding school hacks. Littlebridge was on the edge of Malsham, nestling beneath the vast expanse of downland that sheltered it from the prevailing winds. It was ideally positioned within close reach of a maze of bridleways. It was a draw to many holidaymakers during the summer months. They loved to hack out in groups to drink in the beautiful scenery that the surrounding countryside was able to liberally offer.

Manna had run Littlebridge for many years and was regarded as an excellent riding school instructor and useful horsewoman who thrived in training difficult horses for competition. She was committed to getting the best out of every horse that passed through her yard. Even down to the most fun-loving little ponies that inevitably could cause a few upsets to their unsuspecting young riders. Manna's life revolved around horses and she'd been fortunate enough to be able to realise her dream career with them.

Jude had always worked with horses since leaving school. She lived on site in the grounds of Littlebridge and kept her own horse, Berkley, at livery there. Manna insisted it made good business sense for Jude to live-in at the yard, ensuring there was always somebody to watch over the horses if she had to go away on business or to competitions. Manna had provided Jude with an aged caravan, or *mobile home*, as she referred to it as it sounded more upmarket. It was remotely located in one of the lower paddocks, away from the prying eyes of the local planning office. Manna hadn't bothered to apply for permission to erect the caravan as she hoped it was out of sight and therefore out of mind. Warm and dry, it was not exactly a contemporary home but it did have an array of retro built-in 70s furniture and suitable plumbing for a toilet and shower. Jude was content with the arrangement as she was not a lover of housework and, being covered in horse-smelling clothes and the obligatory dung for most of her life, it didn't matter where she resided. She lived alone, and hence lived how she wished to without having anyone tell her to keep it tidy. She cleaned up when she couldn't get through the door!

Her attitude to her work was much more fastidious.

"Have you mucked out Othello?" Jude called across the yard to Leya, who was busily chatting on her mobile phone. "Leya! Get off that phone! Come on, we've got loads to do. Manna will be back in a minute!"

"Sorry, gotta go, bye, seeya!" Leya ended her call and placed the phone in her gilet pocket. She looked across to Jude and smiled. "Hey! That was LB."

Jude stopped what she was doing. "How is she?"

Leya closed her eyes.

"She has a broken collarbone and she took a bump to her head. But it isn't life-threatening. She's able to talk okay. She doesn't remember much about the accident, thankfully!"

"Well, that's something I suppose. Are you sure you're all right to be working? It's only been a few days since the accident. I mean, with the way Manna is at the moment, you aren't exactly her favourite person."

"No, I don't suppose I am. But I have to work, Jude. I can't sit at home worrying about things. My back still hurts like crazy but I need to be doing something."

"How are you getting on?" Jude continued to walk across the yard to another stable needing to be mucked out.

"Yeah, okay. Othello is done. Do you want me to give him his feed?" Leya asked, twiddling a strand of hair.

"Leave him tied up outside his stable and give him some haylage. Manna's riding him later on. You know what she's like. Life always goes on. She won't want to hang about waiting for him to digest his food," Jude replied. She grabbed the wheelbarrow and pushed it towards Othello's stable. "Oh, and finish mucking him out properly this time, with him *out* of the stable, then groom and get him tacked up, okay?"

"Yep, will do," replied Leya as she reached for Othello's head collar and unfastened the bolt on his stable door.

Leya had worked at Littlebridge for nearly a year. She had decided to take a gap year before going to university and had hoped that by working at a livery yard she would get enough experience to progress onto working at a racing stable.

Leya was a dreamer, and only felt the need to pull her weight if Jude nagged her. She lacked initiative but Jude hoped that this would come in time with experience. The accident had, however, dented her confidence.

"Come on, big guy, breakfast." Leya opened the door.

Othello walked slowly out, gazing into the morning sunlight. He blinked as he saw the net of haylage Leya brought towards him. He was Manna's dark bay Irish Sport Horse. He stood an impressive seventeen hands high. His glossy coat shone like a conker newly prised from its shell. He had won many eventing competitions in his career. He was in peak form and in amazing condition, the result of good balanced feed and being turned out in the lower paddock for two hours' grazing and two hours' work per day. When evening time came, offerings of the previous season's best meadow hay to munch on were presented to him, which he duly accepted with typical equine greed.

Manna had a good track record of success with Othello and she rewarded his abilities with first-class schooling and an enviable lifestyle that any horse could ever wish for. She had invested in a horse spa, which relieved aching muscles, strains and bruising and was even used to prevent laminitis. Jude wasn't intrusive enough to ask Manna how much the spa had cost. Leya had asked, so she could brag to her friends about the 'state of the art' facilities at Littlebridge, but had been told to mind her own business.

Ariel was Manna's other experienced competition horse. A leggy liver-chestnut thoroughbred mare, she stood at sixteen hands. She whinnied as she saw Othello eating his haylage and having his feet picked out simultaneously.

Jude walked over to Ariel carrying her feed.

"Are you riding Ariel today?" Leya asked, as she began to groom Othello.

"No, I'm riding Nelson later. You can ride her out with me when we've finished mucking out. She could do with some more exercise."

"Course, no problem," Leya replied.

She looked at Othello, who was licking the bottom of his empty feed bowl. He was ever hopeful of finding any remaining morsels. She dragged the bowl away from him, rinsed it under the tap that hung precariously on the wall then placed it back in the feed room after swinging it enthusiastically from side to side to remove any excess water. She continued to groom Othello who looked about him, enjoying the massage with the body brush.

The shrill sound of the phone rang out in the yard. Leya threw down the brush and ran to the tack room. She snatched the phone and announced, "Hello, Littlebridge

Stables," in a bright and cheery manner. "Hi, Natalie, she should be back from the vet's soon. She's visiting Fig. Yes, he's doing well. Then I think she's schooling Othello. Shall I get her to ring you when she's finished? Right, okay then, yeah, see ya, bye!"

Leya returned to Othello, who was trying to pick up the brush up by its handle and had nearly succeeded in doing so until Leya grabbed it from him. She continued to brush his body, then his legs.

"Who was it on the phone, Leya?" Jude called out.

"Natalie. She said she'd ring back. If you see Manna first, can you tell her?"

"Can you write it down in the diary, so Manna will see it? You know she likes her messages put in there."

Jude continued to work her way along the line of stables that were mucked out daily and skipped out during the afternoon. This was a daily task that was time-consuming, but essential. Jude was always pleased to see the line of stables clean with fresh wood shavings or washed-down rubber mats within them. She stopped for a moment and lifted her cap off her head and re-tied her hair. She was never without her baseball cap and faded brown-leather half-chaps, winter or summer.

Her life as head stable girl had evolved entirely from her love of horses. She had no time for men: a couple of failed relationships, though brief, didn't really fulfil a commitment. She could devote so much more to horses. Past suitors soon realised that they could not compete with the equines in Jude's life. She didn't have the time to meet guys anyway, always working long hours and sometimes into the night if Manna was due to compete with her horses. Any spare time she had she used to care for her own horse and bestow much love upon her Jack Russell terrier, Tag, who monitored Jude's every move.

The only men that crossed Jude's path in a typical week were Manna's husband Callum, George Trippit, the handyman who worked at Littlebridge, and the local vet or the blacksmith. The choice was not exactly mind-blowing. But this was the way Jude liked to live her life: uncomplicated, without challenge, malice and totally independent. She could never envisage herself pushing a pram or attending mother and toddler groups. She would much rather attend a horse show any day.

She did go out on occasions accompanied, or rather encouraged, by Leya, Manna and Natalie if they decided on a girls' night out. Invariably, Jude would elect herself driver for the evening so she couldn't be persuaded to drink and unlock her personal life to her friends by way of endless drinking sessions. She didn't feel it necessary for people to know in depth the person beneath that baseball cap. As far as she was concerned, it was none of their business.

The sound of a car drawing up in the driveway forced Jude to look up from her chores. Manna got out. The wind took her hair and it billowed out over her shoulders. She called out to Jude.

"Hi! Is everything all right?"

"Yes, all good." Jude walked over to Manna's car. "How's Fig doing?"

Manna made a face. "He looks really sorry for himself, poor love. He has a huge bandage over his chest, but Mike says he is making really good progress. Is Callum around, do you know?" Manna coiled a strand of her hair around her finger.

"Haven't seen him in the yard yet," Jude answered. She balanced the fork and broom within the wheelbarrow so they didn't fall out.

"Right. I'll get changed. I'll be in the school if you need me. Can you get Leya to sweep the yard? With this wind blowing all the straw about, it looks like an American ghost town with tumbleweed!"

"I'll get her to do it in a moment," Jude said and continued walking towards the muckheap where she deposited the contents of the previous night's stables onto the pile of steaming dung.

Manna soon returned in a crisp white shirt, beige-checked jodhpurs and long brown leather boots. She looked like a fashion model. She beckoned to Leya from across the yard for her to bring Othello over. She had fastened spurs to her boots and was pulling on her leather gloves when Leya met her at the gate.

"How is he today, Leya? " Manna coolly asked, as she always did every morning.

"He's fine." Leya patted Othello on the neck as she passed the reins to Manna. "Do you want a leg up?"

"No thanks." Manna leapt agilely into the saddle, checked the girth, and readjusted the length of the stirrups. "Carry on helping Jude, will you?"

Manna urged Othello forward into a purposeful walk. Leya closed the gate to the school with no mention of the accident. No mention of how Leya was feeling. Nothing. She turned to watch Manna begin her schooling. Leya smiled. It was a dream watching Manna get the best out of her horses. The ease with which she warmed up and then carried out her transitions, from forward walk to working trot, circling without any visible effort on either rein, moving forward into a collected canter, circling again on a twenty-metre circle, then into a figure of eight and back to trot. She instructed him back into walk again, to rein back, forward again, this time into sitting trot and changing legs through the centre, into rising trot and then into a forward working canter again. She made it seemed effortless. It encouraged Leya to think that one day she might be lucky enough to be in a position to be riding an expensive event horse and running her own yard too.

Her daydream ended abruptly when she heard Jude calling her.

"Leya! The yard needs sweeping!"

"Okay, I'm on it!" she replied, turning on her heel and walking swiftly back to the yard.

She took hold of the broom and began to vigorously sweep, making clouds of dust arise like a sandstorm in a desert. Every so often she would stop and hold her back. She still felt stiff from her fall. She didn't draw attention to the fact she was still suffering. She hesitated as she passed by Del's empty stable and sighed.

"I am so sorry, Del, so very sorry," she whispered as she held on to the stable door. Tears filled her eyes.

"I'm putting the kettle on, do you want a cup?" Jude called out. She was attempting to keep Leya occupied.

"Yeh, please… Oh Tag, get off the broom will you! Go away!"

Leya's frantic sweeping had enticed Tag to rush out of the nearby straw barn. In *typical* Jack Russell fashion she had proceeded to grab the end of the bristles and shake them like a rat, along with a certain amount of excited growling. It prevented Leya from completing her task, particularly as the wind was picking up even more. She felt that the exercise should be abandoned until the situation got a little less complicated!

Jude saw Tag enjoying the game and laughed to herself. The little terrier had been a great companion ever since she had bought her as puppy just over a year ago. Feet thrust forward with no intention of letting her prey go, Tag's hairy white body, with splodges of erratic brown markings on her head, was pulling for all it was worth against the exasperated efforts of Leya, who was trying to regain control of the broom. Jude soon decided Tag had had enough, or rather that Leya had. She called out to her.

"Tag, enough now! Drop it! Drop it!"

Tag obediently stopped shaking the broom and sauntered over to Jude in a smug manner with her tail erect like a ship's rudder, in full belief that she was victorious in her attempt to *kill* the broom.

"Come on, pups. Come over with me now." Jude laughed at Tag and patted her head before the terrier, tail still aloft, ran towards the barn once more in search of rats and mice.

Half an hour later, Manna had finished her schooling and was leading Othello back to his stable as Leya appeared from the tack room with a tray laden with cups of steaming coffee and placed it on the lid of a grooming box.

"Which one's mine?" Manna asked, as she tied Othello up outside his stable. She secured him in his head collar and handed the bridle to Jude. She removed her gloves and hat and ran a hand through her auburn hair as it tumbled across her shoulders once more. She was hardly perspiring at all, unlike Othello who, when untacked, looked as if he was still wearing his saddle.

"Here you are." Leya handed Manna a dark blue mug.

"Thanks. Could you flick Othello over with a brush and put him back into his stable and put his sweat rug on?"

"Sure, this one?" Leya grabbed a large, blue-checked rug which was hanging over the partition wall.

"Yes," replied Manna not looking.

Leya untied Othello and led him into his stable where she rugged him up. He began to dig a large hole with his foreleg in the freshly-laid golden wood shavings within his stable.

"Othello was a good lad," Manna told Jude, who stood at the stable door with a mug in her hand. "He should be ready for the dressage at the weekend, bar anything happening between now and then," she added, shooting an icy glance in Leya's direction.

"Surely we can't have any more bad luck. You ought to touch a piece of wood!" Jude soothed.

Manna reached for the door and proceeded to pat the doorframe.

"Am I safe now? Or should I grab a handful of shavings and stuff them in my bra for safe keeping?" she added sarcastically.

"You *know* I'm superstitious, I can't help it," Jude admitted as she slowly sipped her coffee.

"You'll be telling me not to walk under a ladder next," Manna joked, pushing her hair back over her shoulder. "How many people have we got booked for lessons today?" she asked as Leya returned.

"There's one booked at four o'clock and one at five," Leya replied, looking down through the yard's diary.

"Is that it?" Manna asked in surprise at the lack of people.

"Perhaps they're away on holiday," Leya announced. She snapped the diary shut, making a plume of dust and strands of straw arise from its pages.

"At least it gives me more time to concentrate on Othello and Ariel, I suppose," Manna mused. She drained the last of the coffee from her cup. "I'll be in the house if you need me. See you later."

Leya looked after Manna as she strode over to the house. She turned to Jude.

"It makes me really on edge that she hasn't said anything to me about the accident. It's like she is trying to avoid talking about it. I think that makes things worse." Leya felt uneasy. "And I hate walking past Del's stable. I keep thinking he will look out of it…" She broke off.

"You know what she's like. Same as she always is, she blocks things out," Jude replied.

"To her it's like nothing has happened, isn't it? She hasn't even asked about LB!"

"She won't, because it doesn't concern her directly."

"Do I say anything to her about it? About Del?" Leya kicked at a lump of muck that was pitched on the edge of her boot.

"I wouldn't, unless you're fed up with living. Let her deal with it in her own way. She'll come round; she always does. Just bear with her, Leya."

They watched Manna walk back to the large Georgian farmhouse that was positioned at the edge of the driveway. It was maintained to an extremely high standard with enviable lawns surrounded with regimental staddle stones at its perimeter. Handyman George Trippit, who momentarily leant on a shovel resting his back, tended the garden with extreme care. George was employed by Manna to carry out tasks that ranged from lawn mowing to building new stables, from mending fences to driving her horsebox to shows. He acknowledged Manna with a tip of his tweed cap and carried on with his morning task of trimming back the rosebushes, buddleias and a host of assorted shrubbery that adorned the gardens.

A slightly-built man of pensionable age with a mass of greying, once-brown curls, his eyes appeared to smile as he spoke. He had a perpetually tanned face from spending all his waking hours outside, and it was marginally lined with a certain mature, distinguished air. He clacked away with the shears as he busied himself amongst the shrubbery. George was impeccably polite to everyone and was always complimentary, especially to Manna, whom he loved to please. He had just one weakness: he was a dreadful gossip!

Jude and Leya believed George had a soft spot for Manna, as he would never hear an ill word said against her. He always tried to attend the local shows, some of which were held at Littlebridge, on the chance that Manna would need his assistance for something. They had nicknamed him *Randy the Handyman*, a name that was periodically used to refer to him by but never to his face. Leya nearly gave away his alias when, one day, she had casually asked him for something and only just stopped herself in time from calling him *Randy*!

Manna leaned very heavily on George and was guided by his knowledge and wisdom. If ever she needed an opinion, she always turned to him before her own husband. George had a mind full of facts, figures and dates: in fact, anything she needed to know. He was an active member of the local pub quiz team at The Black Sheep, Malsham's oldest pub, and his knowledge of the breeding habits of the ruddy duck or the native language of Equatorial Guinea was legendary!

George lived with Beryl, his long-suffering wife of twenty-five years. Beryl loved him dearly and was the perfect, adoring wife. George brought the money into the household and she looked after him: that was their deal. Beryl was in denial about, or at least diplomatically turned a blind eye to, George's addiction to the females of the species. Lunch dates out with her girlfriends or monthly talks at the WI kept her active and made her forget that George found women irresistible. Theirs was a marriage of independence, or rather, in George's case, convenience. He spent most of his time at Littlebridge, busying himself with tasks even when he wasn't needed. It had a draw on him like a magnet and he was at his happiest when he was there.

George stopped for a brief respite from his pruning and gazed at the large sycamore maple tree that stood in the far corner of the garden near to the orchard. It was early summer and the air had a noticeably warm feel about it. The birds had changed their chatter. George loved the Canadian sycamore tree with its large leaves and beautiful canopy of deep crimson that spanned at least twenty feet.

He breathed in the aroma of the gardens. He had worked for Manna for five years, ever since he took redundancy from a factory job in Culverton. George loved the outdoors and held a passion for country pursuits, including beating on alternate Saturdays and following the Malsham Hunt on Wednesdays, when he could be sure there would be no sign of the ever-watchful *antis* whom he detested with a hidden vengeance. He still blamed them for the hunting ban.

He sighed to himself as he finished pruning the rosebushes. He pushed his cap to the back of his head and wiped his forehead with his hand. He collected up the assorted foliage and plunged it remorselessly into the petrol-driven garden shredder, which ably transformed the long, woody spines into neat chippings. George wheelbarrowed the remains over to the bulging compost area, which was full of every recyclable waste product one could imagine since Manna was a keen environmentalist. Tag also contributed to the compost by depositing piles of steaming poo, usually across the lawn much to George's disgust!

Manna walked towards the porch that was festooned in climbing white jasmine, with Tag at her heels. He was hoping for a chance to get into the kitchen to sleep in front of the Aga. Manna turned and called out to Jude.

"Tag's here with me, if you're looking for her."

Jude smiled and called back. "As long as you don't mind her getting under your feet, Manna."

"How are you getting on pruning those roses, George?" Manna called from the backdoor. "Would you like a cup of tea?" she added, removing her riding boots on the bootjack.

"Yes please, Mrs J," returned George. He always referred to Manna by this name. "That'd be grand!" A smile crept across his face.

"Come on up to the house in a minute then," Manna replied as she picked up her boots and disappeared inside.

George was immediately spurred on by the opportunity of taking tea with his boss. He leapt into top gear and scuttled about enthusiastically, collecting up any stray buddleia branches. He offloaded them into the shredder, which gobbled them greedily into its mechanical jaws and spewed them out onto the lawn. George switched the shredder off and walked up to the house, removing his gloves as he strode. His pace quickened with each step.

He frantically kicked off his boots at the door, removed his cap and made his way into the kitchen. Manna was on her phone, talking avidly as she walked around the table in a circle. There was a cup of freshly brewed tea. Manna indicated to him to sit down at the table where a plate of his favourite chocolate biscuits was waiting to be devoured. She finished her telephone call.

"Please help yourself, George," Manna said and noticed that he already had and was tucking into a second biscuit.

"Thank you Mrs J, very kind," he spluttered, showering crumbs in all directions. He fastidiously tidied the corners of his mouth with his sleeve.

"Have you finished the gardening?" Manna probed.

"Almost. I just need to trim back the bay tree so it's all ready for the summer. It's pretty much up together, Mrs J," he reported back.

"Great. In that case, can you have a look at Othello's stable? He kicked out at the wall the other day and some cement has come loose: it needs patching up."

"Not a problem, Mrs J. Be happy to do that," replied George, between slurps

"Oh, and I was wondering if you might be able to drive the horsebox for me on Sunday to Malsham Show?" Manna asked and emphatically batted her eyelashes at George.

He felt his face instantly redden and was compelled to accept.

"Yes, I can do that. No problem, Mrs J. You sure you are okay to do the show, you know, with all that's gone on with Figaro?"

Manna didn't respond and George looked awkwardly down at his cup.

"Well, you just let me know what time and I'll be there," he smiled weakly at her, hoping she hadn't noticed how red his face was.

"Course I'll be okay. Life goes on, doesn't it? Trouble is, you won't be used to driving the replacement lorry, will you? But it's the qualifier show and I am taking Othello and Ariel, so I need to be there. Callum is away at some sort of meeting; probably at a pub." She sighed.

Manna smiled at George as he took the last two biscuits from the plate. Tag was underneath the table and placed a paw on his leg, to remind him she was waiting for a titbit. George didn't let her down.

"Here you are, Tag!" He offered a piece of biscuit down beneath the table. Tag obliged by snatching it. She chewed it once and swallowed, then waited for another piece. "That's all there is," George confirmed to the terrier, who was eagerly licking her lips in anticipation. "No more, it's all gone!" He presented both hands in the air in surrender and to indicate the lack of biscuit.

Tag returned to the warmth of the Aga, grumbling as she sat uncomfortably on a pile of old *Country Life* magazines.

"When you've finished, George, put your cup in the sink and take Tag with you. I need to make some more phone calls."

"Right-o, Mrs J. Say hello to Natalie for me *when* you speak to her, as I bet that's who you'll be calling next!" he guessed as Manna walked towards the stairs. She turned, smiling, and went back into the kitchen.

"Surely I'm not *that* predictable! If you must know, I have to speak to the wretched policeman who keeps pestering me about the accident." She paused as she recalled Del's lifeless body. "Then I'll phone Nat!"

George smiled sympathetically. He thought about Natalie. He hadn't seen her since he had inappropriately clasped her bottom with his roughly chapped hands at The Black Sheep at the last Malsham Hunt Supporters' party. Natalie had not been impressed by his greeting and had swiftly slapped him across the face!

Manna soon phoned Natalie, brushing hair from her face as she paced around the hallway. "Hey, Nat! What time do you want to meet for lunch at the Sheep? I think I'll be alright to come after all. I'll meet you at yours. Yeah, that will be fun!" Manna really wanted to know if Nat had spoken to the solicitor and found out any more about the mystery business partner – she was quite sure that Nat would tell all over a meal. "I need a shower so I'll be over in about an hour."

Manna decided to walk the distance to Heyrick Heights as she felt the need for peace and fresh air without the hassle of driving, and it was a warm day. She had changed into a pretty tangerine shift dress, which she accessorised with her comfy tan flats, a chunky amber necklace and a cream cashmere cardigan. With her Dior sunglasses perched on top of her head she breathed in the air as she sauntered along the lane. She thought about Del. She was finding it hard to accept what had happened and hoped that lunch with Natalie would cheer her up.

She was halfway down the lane when she saw Callum's car parked in the yard. She checked her watch, it was just before one o'clock.

"Hi!" Manna called out.

"Hi! Wow, you changed quickly!" Natalie commented as she took in Manna's feminine look. "Callum's in the barn looking at my old Massey Ferguson. Reckons he's got someone who might want to buy it or restore it or something."

"That's promising. Does he know about our lunch date?"

"Do you think we ought to invite him too?" Nat glanced about for her battered handbag.

Manna looked pensively towards the barn.

"It would be nice for a girly chat, you know," she urged.

"Ok, better make your excuses," Nat indicated to Callum, who had appeared from behind the barn accompanied by his young black retriever, Kier.

He walked towards them. Tall, and slender, Callum Jacobs was a quiet, serious man. His sense of humour was droll, not unlike his dress sense, but somehow he was able to keep anyone who met him amused with his conversations and exceptionally dry wit. He ran Littlebridge from behind the scenes and kept a firm check on Manna's frequent overspending. He rarely complained but made diplomatic suggestions and guided Manna when he thought she needed it. He dropped hints if he felt she needed a reminder to be careful. He wasn't an emotional man but held an air of sophistication.

He came across as a silent romantic. He acknowledged Manna and walked towards her.

"You look, uh, rather nice." Callum kissed Manna on both cheeks. "Having lunch then?" he surmised.

"Yep, no stopping us socialites is there!" laughed Nat. "Let me know about the man, if he wants to have a look at the old tractor?"

"I'll give him a ring when I get home. I'll see you later, Manna." Callum got back into his car. "Do you ladies need a lift to the pub?" he casually asked, his eyes studying the two women as they deliberated.

"No, we'll walk, thanks," Manna decided.

Nat looked at her in horror.

"But it's at least twenty minutes away," she protested and looked to Callum for support.

"Better get in then hadn't you, you lazy cow!" He leant across and unlocked the back door. "Come on, you two! Kier get in as well!"

Kier responded by bounding into the back of the car and making himself comfortable by climbing all over Natalie.

"Thanks, Callum," Nat smiled with relief. "My poor old feet couldn't take all that trekking. Oh Kier, get off! I don't want to be ravaged! Not before lunch, at any rate!" She pushed him gently away from her face and wedged him firmly on the back seat beside her.

"We can walk back afterwards, can't we Nat? Walk off our lunch!" Manna got into the front passenger seat and slipped on her seatbelt. She smiled as she caught Nat's scowl in the rear-view mirror. Although she was in good health, Nat hated walking anywhere.

As they drew up outside the pub, Manna looked over to Callum.

"Thanks, love. See you later this afternoon. I'll be back in time for the lessons. The girls are hacking out with Ariel and Nelson, so you'll have a bit of peace for a while," Manna informed him.

She leant across and kissed him on the cheek while Natalie waited for her at the pub door. She jumped about on the spot to encourage Manna to hurry up. She was impatient and hated to be kept waiting, even for a few minutes. Manna walked over and they linked arms. Waving Callum off, they waltzed into the bar, pulled up two barstools and nestled themselves into a comfortable position to begin their chat. Over a couple of gin and tonics, they began their gossip with hoots of carefree laughter amidst the buzzing public bar.

"So, have you spoken to your brief yet, Nat?" Manna started enquiringly and sipped her drink.

Chapter Four

Jude and Leya had mucked out the remainder of the stables. All the horses had been fed, watered and turned out.

"Leya, you ride Ariel and I'll take Nelson," said Jude. "When we get back, we'll sort out who is going to ride what this afternoon for the lessons. We'll check which horses Manna wants to use. We shan't be out that long, no more than an hour at the most."

They tacked up and mounted their respective horses and clattered noisily out of the concrete yard, along the lane to the nearby bridle path that led towards the downs. The yard was conveniently located in the middle of perfect riding country without the need to use the constantly busy roads that rattled with heavy traffic and inconsiderate drivers. Jude shortened her reins and encouraged Nelson into a steady trot as they made their way towards the downs. Their hooves clicked in unison on the tarmac surface. Ariel became impatient and wanted to go faster. Leya held her back. Jude called back to Leya when she saw the mare shy for the third time since leaving the yard, "Keep her on an even rein, Sit into the saddle and don't hold her too tight as she'll try and fight against you. Make sure you haven't got your leg on, half halt on the inside rein…"

Leya looked annoyed.

"I *have* ridden her before, Jude. Believe it or not, I *can* ride. you know!"

"Yeh, but just watch her, she's a bit mare-ish today, probably due to come into season," Jude indicated as Ariel was enthusiastically on her toes. Her energy levels were high.

Ariel trotted with a very forward pace and her hindquarters edged towards the middle of the lane. Her neck was arched and she mouthed the bit into a creamy lather.

"Get her onto the bit, Leya. Leg on now... make her work *for* you, not *against* you," Jude advised as Ariel began to jog energetically sideways.

Leya stifled a yelp as she felt her muscles in her back go into spasm.

"We aren't going to take off when we reach the top, are we? I'm sure that's what Ariel wants to do. Easy now." Leya slowed Ariel to a walk; the mare obeyed and began to enthusiastically chew on the bit, making a jangling sound on the metal. They left the road onto the bridleway that led up to the downs. It was a narrow path with high hedges either side.

Jude kept Nelson in check. He was a gentle, reliable piebald Irish cob. His owner was working abroad and so keeping him at livery at Littlebridge until she returned later in the year. Jude had taken a real liking to this coloured gelding and had realised, not long after his arrival at the yard ,that he had great potential as a show-jumper. She had schooled him over a low course of jumps and he seemed to be a natural. Not bad for a youngster of five. Jude would tell Nelson's owner of his ability and hoped she'd use him to his full potential upon her return.

She was suddenly alerted to Leya's cry.

"Jude. Which way are we going when we get to the top?"

"Malsham Monument direction, give them a little blow out along the ridge there, plenty of open space. I think Ariel needs to chill out a bit, doesn't she?"

"Just a bit!" came the tentative reply.

They reached the summit of the downs and turned towards Malsham Monument when Leya's mobile phone rang out shrilly. Ariel shied at the sudden high-pitched ring as the tone got progressively louder.

"Leya, shut that bloody mobile off! You need to be concentrating one hundred percent. Especially with the way Ariel is feeling today!" Jude was annoyed that Leya couldn't go anywhere without her beloved mobile phone.

It was too late. Leya couldn't reach the phone. It was jammed in her pocket. Ariel decided she was going to bolt away from the noise. Leya sat back, half-halted and tried to turn the mare's head. They fought against one another until Ariel began cantering sideways and then rushed off at a frantic uncontrollable gallop. Leya sat tight, pulling for all her might, leaning back into the saddle, half-halting the reins, but to no avail. The phone continued to ring, its irritating tone becoming louder the longer it rang. Ariel broke into a nervous sweat. Jude called from the distance on Nelson, who stood still in wonderment, watching Leya struggle to gain control.

"Turn her into a circle, Leya. Turn her! Turn her head!" Jude was incensed. Leya always seemed to be fiddling with her phone, either texting her friends or checking for missed calls or catching up on social media. She shook her head in annoyance. She didn't want to chase after them, as it would only make Ariel gallop on faster. It wouldn't be good for Nelson because, being a youngster, he would try to catch up and outrace the mare. It would give him the impression he could take off whenever he wanted to on future hacks.

Leya frantically half-halted Ariel, pulling on the outside rein in rapid double succession, trying to turn her in a circle to break her speed and get her back under control. She was concerned that the mare would do some serious damage to herself. She was also worried about the consequences of Manna's wrath if anything happened to her beloved event horse. She momentarily thought of the lorry accident.

"Whoa, Ariel! Whoa, steady now," she coaxed through a dry throat. "Easy girl, easy..."

Ariel finally slowed to a steady canter as Leya turned her in a large circle. Encouraging the mare to trot and eventually to walk, she patted Ariel's sweating neck with relief.

"Good girl... good girl... that's it! Oh my God! Urgh!"

Bang! A bird-scaring machine behind a hedge in the neighbouring field launched a deafening boom into the air, directly where Ariel and Leya were now standing. The noise sent the mare into a wild frenzy; her eyes bulged in pure panic as once again she bolted at an uncontrollable gallop, this time in the opposite direction, towards Jude and Nelson.

"Pull her up! Stop her!" Jude called out in alarm as she realised what had happened. Nelson had sensed the upset and started to jog on the spot. He fought against the reins and edged backwards, trying desperately to make his exit from danger. Jude patted his neck, which was becoming wet with sweat. She tried to calm him as Ariel and Leya careered past them out of control.

"Leya!" Jude screamed as Ariel thundered towards a ditch, which was fenced with taut barbed wire and a hedge on the other side. "Turn her, hold on and *turn* her! Don't let her jump *that*... oh... God... no!"

Just as the words left her mouth, she saw Ariel take the largest leap over the ditch Jude had ever seen a horse perform. She cleared it by at least two feet and landed in a ploughed field. Leya didn't make the jump. She was thrown high into the air and landed heavily in the ditch, head first. Her arm struck the barbed wire with a sickening rip and she narrowly missed being impaled on a fencing stake. An eerie silence descended.

"Shit! Come on, Nelson! Good lad." Jude encouraged Nelson into a steady trot towards Leya. Ariel was in the far corner of the field, reins trailing, spattered in copious amounts of mud. Her saddle had slipped underneath her and the stirrups dangled in twisted strips of scored leather. She was blowing hard with nostrils flared.

The sight of Leya sickened Jude.

"Leya! Leya! Can you hear me?" Jude called out as she dismounted Nelson in haste. She threw the reins over his head and led him towards the ditch. She didn't want to let go of him in case he bolted as well.

Leya didn't answer. She lay still. Her clothes were drenched in muddy water that was tainted with a blue-grey oily film on its surface. Jude grabbed hold of her shoulders and dragged her from the stinking, stagnant mess.

She noticed blood was oozing from a wound on Leya's shoulder. The barbed wire fence had ripped her jacket. She got Leya to safety and laid her carefully on the grass path. Quickly assessing the injuries, Jude decided she needed urgent back-up from the stables. She grabbed Leya's mobile and dialled Manna.

Manna and Natalie had just finished their lunch. Manna was keen to know about how Nat had got on speaking with her solicitor.

"So, what did he say when you phoned him?" she probed over another gin and tonic.

"He said I needed to make an appointment, so I have, for tomorrow. He will be able to tell me about this business partner. Do you know, I had no idea that Sam was so shrewd? He must have lived a double life. To keep all that quiet is way beyond me. I certainly wouldn't have been able to do that... For heaven's sake, talk about a mystery man." Natalie gulped her G and T until just ice and a segment of soggy lemon were left in her glass. She swirled the glass thoughtfully.

"You'll feel a lot better once you know all the details and once you've got a cheque in your hand," comforted Manna, as her mobile phone began to ring.

Manna answered immediately amidst the background din of chatter from the regulars at The Black Sheep. She could only just hear Jude on the other end of the phone and she listened in increasing horror before finally she prodded at her mobile to end the call. She looked very worried.

"I can't believe what I've just heard! This has to be some sort of sick joke!" Manna was very pale.

"What?" asked Natalie, biting into the lemon segment.

"It's Leya. She's taken a fall from Ariel, quite bad by the sounds of it." Manna concentrated on dialling 999.

Malsham Ambulance Control responded instantly. Manna relayed the message. There was a controlled urgency in her voice.

"How did it happen?" Natalie asked.

"She's fallen off and hurt herself. Ariel shied at something. Look Nat, sorry, I've got to get back to the yard. I'll phone Callum to pick me up and drop me back to Littlebridge. I'll need to take the horsebox to the downs to pick up Ariel. Sorry, must rush! I'll get Callum to take you home. What am I going to find *this* time?"

Manna looked really scared. Her face crumpled as the news sunk in. She made the call to Callum with shaking hands.

Jude removed her body warmer and draped it over Leya who remained unconscious. She was soaked in water and mud. Her breathing was very shallow. Jude glanced up and noticed Ariel had stopped galloping and was trotting across the field. Her head stooped periodically as she stumbled across the furrows. She stopped near the gate where Nelson stood. The youngster was still on edge with the drama that had unfolded in front of him. Jude reassured him by patting his neck and calming him with her voice as best she could. She secured the stirrups by running them up to the top of the saddle so he couldn't hurt himself with them. She held on to his reins as she stayed close to Leya. She stared at her watch.

After what seemed like hours, Jude heard faint sirens. She could just make out flashing blue lights at the road below. She saw a horsebox making its way up the narrow bridle path. Brambles and hedges caught the sides of the lorry as it forced its way through as far as it could to the accident site. Jude waved from the summit to where Manna and the ambulance were positioned lower down the hillside. Manna stopped the horsebox in a convenient gateway and hitched a lift with the paramedics to the top of the downs. Jude was so relieved to see them.

"Ariel went berserk. It was a bird scarer that made her bolt. She went crazy; Leya couldn't hold her! It wasn't Leya's fault."

Jude relived the incident as Manna looked down at the crumpled body on the grass. They left the paramedics to tend to her. They soon assessed her, placed her on a stretcher and slowly manoeuvred her to the ambulance. Jude looked down at the mobile phone. It showed a missed call.

"Bloody thing!" she muttered to herself and thrust it into her pocket.

Manna caught Ariel by her reins. She took a good look at the mare who was blowing very hard. Her entire body was caked in frothy white sweat streaked with mud and she had started to shiver.

"I'll get her back to the yard and get Mike Nicholls out immediately. She looks like she's cut her front legs. There's some blood but I can't see a wound because of the mud."

"Shall I walk Nelson back to the yard?" asked Jude quietly.

"No, we'll take him back in the box too; he'll be fine. There's some travel boots in the Luton that will fit him. Can you put a rug on Ariel and get Nelson rugged up as well? He's sweating a bit, isn't he?"

Jude nodded. She silently obeyed Manna and un-tacked Nelson. Manna made a call on her mobile to the vet's surgery and asked Mike to meet her at her yard.

"We're ready to be loaded," Jude announced as she led Nelson to the back of the horsebox. He continued to glance around, eyes on stalks and ears forward. His stride was short and bouncy.

"Okay, load him first so Ariel can see she'll be safe." Manna indicated towards the lorry.

Ariel had caught her breath and was not blowing so hard. Manna removed the saddle and noticed deep cuts across the leather. She looked towards the ambulance that had made its way back down to the lane and begun its journey to hospital.

"When we get back to Littlebridge, can you drive to the hospital to make sure Leya is okay, Jude. I'll get Callum to cancel the lessons booked for this afternoon. He's just dropping Nat back to her place at the moment. Hopefully Mike will have arrived at the yard by the time we get back."

Jude was impressed how Manna was able to methodically deal with problems when a crisis arose. She was, however, astonished that Manna's main concern was for Ariel and not for Leya. Manna could be very selfish. As long as her horses were alright, nothing else mattered. Manna was always the optimist. She believed humans were quite capable of looking after themselves, no matter how badly they were injured, but that horses were not. In this case, Leya was lying seriously injured and unconscious and helpless. Jude thought Manna was in denial and had not fully accepted what had happened. It was understandable, what with two accidents involving the yard occurring within days of each other, and both incredibly involving Leya.

They loaded Nelson into the lorry and Ariel painstakingly limped up the ramp after him. Blood had started to drip from her front leg and Manna grew increasingly worried. They arrived back at Littlebridge to find Mike Nicholls dragging his bag from the back of a black Range Rover. His yellow Labrador sat patiently on the rear passenger seat and gazed out of the window, sniffing the air.

"Hi Mike, thanks for coming so soon. I'll tie Ariel up out here so you can get a better look in the light. Jude, can you sort out Nelson, please?"

Jude nodded. She smiled reservedly at Mike who began to assess Ariel's wound.

"She's caught the top of her fetlock quite badly, probably on the barbed wire, when she jumped. Looks like a square cut. It's just a shallow flesh wound. She will be lame for a few days. Let's get the hosepipe and train some water onto her hoof. Get it cleaned up. Oh, and there's another couple of cuts below the knee area. They won't need stitching. Just warm salt water on them to clean the wound. I'll give her an injection to stop any further swelling and I'll leave some antibiotics and painkillers for you to give her twice a day in her feed. Give her box rest for a couple of days and I'll come back and check on her."

As Mike made his diagnosis, Manna was relieved it was only flesh wounds as opposed to anything more sinister. She felt a great weight lift off her shoulders.

"Thanks Mike. Okay, my girl, you'll be fine." Manna soothed Ariel and patted her neck as Mike hosed off her front legs and peered at the wound. He probed the skin around the wound with swabs and Ariel flinched.

"What about her rider?" Mike asked.

"She's gone to hospital; she's unconscious. Jude's going there shortly to see her."

"Oh, right, I see." Mike was surprised at how casual Manna was about her announcement. "Who was riding her?"

"Can you believe it was Leya?"

"Not again! That girl has had some bad luck, hasn't she? Have you told her parents yet?" Mike asked, administering the antibiotics. He collected spent clinical swabs from the concrete yard.

"No, I'll do that in a minute, when Ariel's sorted."

Jude finished rugging up Nelson and walked over to where Manna stood with Ariel and Mike.

"I'm off to the hospital, Manna. I don't know how long I'll be. I'll ring when I have some news," Jude said, and turned towards her car.

"Don't be too long, Jude. Don't forget there's the afternoon feeds that need to be done," Manna called after her.

Jude didn't acknowledge the last statement as she felt she could quite happily turn around and slap Manna across the face. How could she be so callous? She called out to Tag who rushed out of the hay barn and jumped straight into the car, without a second thought.

Jude was furious: furious at Ariel, furious at Leya and even more furious at Manna. She spun the wheels of her car in frustration out of the yard leaving a cloud of dust behind her. Manna didn't even notice as she was so ensconced with Ariel's injuries. She chatted aimlessly to Mike as he bandaged Ariel's fetlock. Manna had switched off any thoughts of Leya and focussed entirely on Ariel.

"This is all I need. I'm competing at Malsham Show on Sunday. I was going to take Ariel for the qualifier but that doesn't look like it will happen now. Why couldn't Leya have been more careful? She knows what Ariel's like. I'll have to make sure she doesn't ride her anymore; it's obvious she cannot cope! Come to think of it, can she cope with any of my horses?"

"I wouldn't make any rash decisions, Manna. Take one day at a time. You should be thinking about Leya and how she is. Your horse will make a full recovery." Mike looked on in amazement as Manna started to pace up and down in front of Ariel's stable.

"Oh, Leya! She'll be all right. She's a drama queen at the best of times," Manna announced and flicked a strand of hair from her face.

"But she's *unconscious*, Manna. That *is* serious, you know," Mike tried to reason.

"Oh well, I suppose I'd better go and see how she is." She stopped pacing about and thought for a moment. "Jude's there though. Oh, I'll go anyway. Jude needs to be back here for the afternoon feeds," she decided.

"It probably would be best if you went to the hospital, Manna. Ariel will be fine; she just needs to be rested. She won't be sound for Malsham Show though."

"I had realised, Mike, I'm not *that* thick!" she rudely returned and walked off. Without turning back she called, "Where's Callum? He can't still be with Natalie. He was only dropping her off. What the hell is he still doing there with her?"

Chapter Five

Jude sat in silence in the waiting area of A&E at Malsham General Hospital. She looked down at her clothes and noticed they were caked in mud and smelt strongly of horse pee and sweat. She didn't really care. Leya was lying unconscious in the next room. Nothing else seemed important. Jude glanced out of the window and saw Tag standing on her hind legs in the car, her paws moulding the passenger window. She looked over towards where Jude sat. She wagged her tail. Jude smiled and waved at her. At least Tag cared, she thought.

She waited in silence until a nurse came towards her. Jude stood up.

"Excuse me, are you Jude Armstrong?" the nurse asked, glancing at her notes.

"Yes, that's right. How is Leya?" Jude hardly dared ask the question.

"I'm afraid she's still unconscious. We are going to take her to have a scan shortly. She appears to have sustained a blow to the side of her head. Did you see what actually happened?"

"No, I didn't see her fall exactly… I mean, I was too far away. I just saw blood on her shoulder… when I reached her," Jude answered. She stared at the ground.

"If you can remain here, we'll let you know what's happening as soon as we can. Oh, we need to get hold of her next of kin. Do you have any contact telephone numbers?"

"Yes, they're on her mobile. I'll get them for you."

Jude fumbled in her pocket and retrieved Leya's phone. It had deep scratches across the front of the screen. She held the phone out for the nurse to jot down Leya's parents' number.

"Thank you. Go and get yourself a drink and I'll let you know directly I have any news," reassured the nurse. She smiled and went back towards the office.

"Thanks," Jude mumbled. She stuffed Leya's phone back into her pocket.

She turned to look out of the window again and noticed Tag had become tired of waiting and had decided to lie on the back parcel shelf in the car. Jude sat down and glanced at the various posters that adorned the waiting area, amongst which were a warning that attacks on members of staff would not be tolerated and an appeal for blood donors. Jude shivered. She hated hospitals.

She looked across the room and acknowledged a couple of people who were waiting to be seen and then looked towards the clock. It was late afternoon. She decided to tell Manna what was happening and, with an air of reluctance, fumbled for some change and made a call to the yard from the aged payphone in the waiting room. She didn't feel it appropriate to use Leya's mobile phone to make the call.

"Manna? It's Jude. No, nothing yet. They told me to wait here until they know something… No, she's still uncon… OK, I'll wait till you arrive. What? Sorry, my money's about to run out…"

Jude pressed the receiver sharply back on its rest. She shook her head. 'I can't believe that woman. She can't have a heart at all,' she thought to herself.

She wasn't going to go back to Littlebridge yet, even if the horses did need feeding. She was not going to leave without knowing what was happening with Leya. During the phone call Manna had instructed Jude to return to the yard, since she herself was coming to the hospital. Well tough, she wasn't budging. Jude grabbed a cup of black coffee and sat heavily back on the chair. She sighed and, as she did so, the couple across the room stared at her.

"Sorry! Bosses! Who'd *have* them?" she mumbled her apology for the distraction.

"Will your friend be all right, dear?" came a response from an elderly lady who was sitting on the other side of the room, fumbling with a string of yellowed pearls that hung around her neck.

"Don't know yet; she's still unconscious," Jude replied.

"Was it a riding accident, dear?" She pointed at Jude's jodhpurs.

"Fraid so," Jude bluntly replied. She didn't want to elaborate.

"Funny creatures, aren't they, horses? So unpredictable. I don't know why people ride them. It's much too dangerous, if you ask me," the elderly lady replied, twiddling her pearls in rapid fashion as though they were rosary beads. Jude interpreted her as a non-horsy person, trying to offer an opinion and right the wrongs of the equine world without any real knowledge of what she was actually talking about.

'Some people just talk for the sake of it,' she concluded to herself. She didn't bother to reply.

Jude got up and walked towards the window. She looked for Tag. She had fallen asleep on the parcel shelf and was curled up like a hairy white ball. The door of the side ward opened and a nurse called out to Jude.

"Jude? Can I have a word, please?"

Jude turned towards the nurse.

"Yeah, of course." Jude prepared herself for the news.

"Leya is still unconscious. We can't wait any longer for her parents. We are taking her for a CT scan now. If they arrive, can you let them know where we have taken her? Are you okay to stay for the time being? We don't know how long it will take. We can update them later on."

"I'll wait here, it's not a problem," Jude replied.

Jude decided that staying at the hospital was her only concern and that Manna, for once, could wait.

The nurse smiled at her and returned into the ward, the swing door closing quietly behind her. Jude sat back down on her chair and stared at the clock. She thought about Manna and the afternoon feeds. She felt that it was up to Manna to sort out arrangements for the horses that afternoon. It wouldn't hurt her to manage on her own. It wasn't as if she had to do it all the time. Perhaps Callum might be able to help. He wasn't keen on the practicalities of horses. He always seemed to be conveniently attending business meetings. He preferred to leave the animal husbandry to Manna and Jude.

Jude was thinking of the response she would give Manna when the doors of A&E suddenly burst open and Manna strode in. She had changed into riding clothes beneath a flowing, cream riding jacket. She briefly scanned the room until her eyes focussed on Jude.

"I'll take over now. Look, can you get back to the yard and feed the horses? Callum should be back. Where are Leya's parents?"

"They haven't arrived yet. That's why I'm still here. The nurse asked me to wait until they—"

Manna sighed and interrupted. "Okay. You go back and sort out the horses and I'll wait here," she announced and sat down near the coffee table of magazines. She avidly searched through a pile of well-thumbed magazines for a horsy one but wasn't successful. She opted for *Country Living* instead, even though it was over a year old. She clicked her tongue in disgust as some of the pages were stuck together. She shook back her hair and buried herself in the magazine with crossed legs. "I'll see you later!" She indicated for Jude to leave.

Jude begrudgingly left A&E. Manna's grand entrance and the sudden concern she was showing for Leya had been surprising and uncharacteristic.

'Perhaps she has a conscience after all,' Jude concluded.

She climbed into her car, which was crammed full of *Horse and Hound* magazines and various items of equine paraphernalia. Tag woke up and clambered swiftly to the front seat, shedding a mist of white hairs as she shook and stretched. The terrier spent the return journey gazing out of the window as they motored back to Littlebridge. Her nose glided against the window and left little streaks of moisture across it. Jude leaned across and opened the window and Tag immediately sniffed at the fresh air. It was full of wonderful odours that only a dog's sense of smell could fully appreciate.

Jude reached the stables to find Callum's car outside the house. She parked her car next to his and, with Tag running happily alongside, walked towards the stables. Callum was leading two horses in from a field. He looked extremely awkward as one horse was pulling him forward and the other was hardly moving at all. He waved a leading rein above his head in evident relief when he saw Jude.

"Oh! You're back! Thankfully! Can you grab this horse for me? Thought I could manage two. I think they sense I'm not much good at this lark, don't you?" He gratefully handed Jude the rope and the horse walked quietly alongside. Callum continued to chat. "How is Leya? Is she conscious yet?"

"No, not yet. She was due to have a CT scan when I left. Manna turned up and told me to come back to work and sort out the horses," Jude replied.

"Damn shame. Ariel must have been really spooked by that scarer," he concluded.

"It wasn't very nice. Ariel was on her toes anyway this morning. Must be the time of year. Well, either that or she's in season. She wasn't listening to Leya at all. The way she bolted off was like a maniac!"

"Don't let Manna hear you say that about her beloved mare!" Callum joshed and he guided Moonstone, a Palomino filly, into her stable, untied her rope and closed the door. "Can you deal with this horse when you're ready?" Callum called across the yard. He nodded towards Moonstone who was attempting to bite his hand as he tried to fasten the kick bolt. "I'll check on Ariel. She seems to have calmed down since Mike saw her earlier."

Jude nodded and carried on stabling the horses for the evening. Once they were all attended to, fed and rugged up for the night, she would be able to spend time with her own horse. She felt guilty that she had neglected Berkley. She usually spent time either schooling him or taking him out on a hack. But having one day off wouldn't hurt him. She would make it up to him tomorrow, when things had settled down and when, hopefully, there would be some news on Leya's condition.

She stopped at Nelson's stable. He was looking over the door. Jude patted his neck. She fed him a mint.

"You *were* a good boy today. Don't let Ariel give you any bad ideas," she softly warned him as he nuzzled his gentle velvety nose against her face. She smiled at Nelson. "See you later, boy."

Jude thought about Leya. She was still in grave danger and Manna was behaving like the accident was all Leya's fault and that she was pretending to be ill.

She bit her lip and strode across the yard. Callum was coming towards her. Jude shook her head and continued walking.

"Hey! What's wrong? You look really angry." He grabbed her arm and waited for a reply.

"Leya's still unconscious. It's not fair, is it?"

"I know. It's horrible, poor little Leya. I hope she wakes up soon," Callum genuinely looked upset. "She's certainly had a rough time of it lately."

"Yeah, she has." Jude shuddered as she thought of the accident. "I feel responsible for what happened. I should've ridden Ariel myself, not Leya."

"Don't blame yourself, Jude. Remember, it was an accident. You are not at fault, so get that out of your mind. These things do happen. Don't you worry yourself about it." He looked at her and tried to make her smile as he could see she was close to tears.

"Yeah, you're right. Sorry, I'll buck up." She drew her shoulders back and smiled at Callum. He looked at her and, for a moment more, held her arm.

Jude's mobile phone started to ring. She quickly answered and listened to the briefest of calls from Manna. Jude placed her phone into her pocket and relayed the message to Callum: Leya was still unconscious and Manna was going to stay at the hospital.

"Go home and forget about today. Tomorrow will be much better. I'll make sure it is!" Callum cheerfully prophesised.

"Ok, see you tomorrow." Jude managed a weak smile.

She walked through the field to her caravan. She had liked the way Callum had taken the time to reassure her. He was considerate and caring. He was so unlike Manna. Jude wondered why Callum put up with Manna's selfishness, but she felt she could never address the situation. It was so awkward as both he and Manna were her bosses and she couldn't speak to one without the fear of the other finding out. It was a difficult position to be in. On top of that, Leya would be off work indefinitely until she was fully recovered, which could be weeks or months. Jude would be expected to run the yard single-handedly. She'd have to speak to Manna to see if she would hire some temporary help until Leya was well enough to return.

Jude called out to Tag, who came bounding from the direction of Littlebridge House with Kier firmly running alongside her. She outran him easily and reached the confines of her own home. Kier gave up and sauntered back to the house with his tail aloft. Jude collapsed onto her sofa and threw her baseball cap on the floor and untied her hair. It cascaded out in all directions and she heaved a huge sigh.

"What a day!" she said aloud to Tag who was drinking enthusiastically from her water bowl by the table. Tag didn't respond but continued to quench her thirst. Jude unbuttoned her leather half-chaps and threw them in the same direction as her baseball cap. Tag decided to jump on to Jude's lap, just as her mobile phone bleeped. Jude dragged the phone from her pocket and read the message. It was from Callum.

'*I hope u r ok?*' it read. She was pleasantly surprised to receive his message. She smiled to herself and texted her reply, '*Yes, just knackered, thanks for asking.*' Another message swiftly returned, '*Good, glad to hear it. C u tomorrow.*'

Callum had never texted her before but deep down she felt glad that he had. She prepared her supper of a ready-meal lasagne in the microwave with renewed enthusiasm knowing that Callum was concerned about her. She felt a sudden warm feeling as she remembered him touching her arm. She left her mobile phone switched on for the rest of the evening, in case she received any more messages. She found herself disappointed when she went to bed that night without any further texts.

oOo

Leya was riding at a steady gallop towards a large brush fence, her face grim with determination to clear it. She held her breath as it loomed closer, closer, until her horse took off and sailed over it with ease. She patted the horse's neck, giving it a welcome confidence boost with encouragement and praise. They were now on to the next jump, the open ditch. It was five feet high and at least six feet wide. It was a huge jump, *the rider frightener...* Leya was determined to win. She was riding an incredible horse that could jump like a stag. She approached the jump. It was enclosed, like a tomb with sloping sides. She told herself it wouldn't be a problem… then she heard the screech of the lorry's tyres. Total blackness, then light…

Leya suddenly woke up to find she was lying on a hard bed. There were bright lights all around her with sounds of muffled voices. She could just make out someone saying, "Look, she's coming round, quickly, fetch the consultant."

Leya blinked a few times: her eyes still couldn't focus properly. She heard the voice again.

"It's okay, Leya, you're in hospital. You're safe," it reassured her in a sympathetic, soothing tone.

Leya opened her eyes fully. She looked around to visualise where the voice was coming from. She tried to lift her arm but it felt like a dead weight. She next tried to sit up but something was preventing her from doing so. Again she heard the voice.

"Leya? Can you hear me, sweetheart?"

Her eyes eventually managed to focus on a woman in a dark blue uniform that was in stark contrast to the room where she lay, which was bright white and smelt of antiseptic. The woman smiled cheerily at Leya and stroked her hand.

"It's all right, Leya. You had a riding accident, bumped your head and hurt your shoulder. You're in hospital now. Do you understand?" she carefully questioned, holding on to her hand.

Leya nodded and closed her eyes.

In the waiting area, Leya's parents were informed of the news and they all breathed a sigh of relief. Leya's mother burst into tears as her husband held her and told her that things would be fine and they would be able to see their daughter soon. Manna, who was sitting alongside them, got up from her chair, visibly relieved with the news. She reached into her pocket and pulled out her mobile phone.

"Just making a call, I'll be outside," she told Leya's parents. "Shan't be long."

She strode out into the car park and paged down her phone until she found Jude's name.

"Jude? Hi, it's me. Leya's just woken up! Can you tell Callum for me? I'm on my way back now, bye!"

Back in A&E, Leya's parents had left the waiting area. Manna thought it a positive thing if they were allowed to see her. She walked up to the reception desk and attracted the attention of a nurse.

"How is Leya Martin doing?"

The nurse looked up from her paperwork.

"Are you a relative?" she enquired.

"No, I am her *boss*, Manna Jacobs," Manna irritably answered.

"In that case, would you mind waiting? Leya's parents are currently being told about her condition."

Manna sighed heavily. "Okay. Can you give them a message? I *have* to get back to my stables. I do have very important matters to attend to! Can they ring me later tonight?"

"I'll make sure they get the message, Mrs Jacobs," the nurse replied, looking at Manna in some surprise. "Do they have your number?"

Manna, by this time, was hopping towards the door and slammed back without turning round, "They *do*."

The nurse shook her head in amazement. "Some people!" she muttered to herself and continued with her paperwork.

Leya was surrounded by her parents and the consultant, who was carefully explaining her situation and condition. Leya's father looked gravely at his daughter lying helplessly in front of him. He was in his early sixties, slightly built with silver-grey hair. His wife, petite and sporting permed grey hair, had a permanently fixed grin, which accompanied the erratic nod of her head from side to side whenever she spoke. Leya was their youngest daughter, whom they'd had later in life. Their first child, Jonathan, had died in early childhood. They looked more like her grandparents than her parents but the love they bestowed upon Leya, particularly her father, was immense. He doted on Leya without spoiling her and she was particularly close to him. Her mother was aware of this bond and felt that she was sometimes in the way of their relationship but, being a little thick-skinned, she played along and tried to ignore the fact. She loved them both dearly.

The consultant read through his notes.

"The scan and x-ray confirm Leya has fractured her collar bone, on the left side. She has a minor head injury, no brain bleed thankfully, but, more seriously, Leya told us that she can't move her arm. Can you try again please, Leya?" The consultant looked towards the slumped body in the bed.

"It's like a dead weight, like it's being pinned down," Leya replied. "Why is that?"

"I'm not sure, but once we have carried out further tests, we can establish the cause," the consultant concluded reassuringly.

"Do you remember anything about the accident?" Leya's mother asked.

Leya thought momentarily and replied, "I think I can remember Ariel shying at the bird scarer; it's a bit sketchy though. She was really wound up before that, she was pulling all the time, and she's not normally that bad. Then she bolted towards the fence and I can remember trying to stop her, pulling with all my strength, trying to turn her in a circle to slow her down. Then after that, it was… I can't remember… it all went black, then I woke up in here." Leya's eyes filled with tears as she relived the moments before the accident.

"It's all right, love, don't cry," her mother soothed and nodded her head. She stroked Leya's forehead and moved a strand of hair away from her eyes. "Don't cry… shush."

The consultant placed the clipboard back onto the end of Leya's bed. He looked at Leya's father and beckoned him to follow him out of the room. When they were outside, the consultant took him to one side.

"I cannot be one hundred percent sure at this stage, Mr Martin, but there is a possibility that Leya has suffered a paralysis in her right arm. Once I get the results back from the other tests, I can give a more accurate diagnosis. I need you to be aware that it could potentially be serious."

Leya's father looked stunned.

"But... she's only a young girl, she can't have done *that* much damage, not Leya. She's usually so careful, especially round horses. She isn't an amateur, you know. She does know how to ride a horse! What shall I tell the wife?" He took hold of the consultant's arm as the realisation began to sink in.

"You will *have* to prepare your wife for the consequences, Mr Martin. There is no point me saying to you that Leya isn't in danger, I can't do that."

"No, I understand, doctor. But it will break her heart. We lost a child, a long time ago, you know, and as for Leya, she won't be able to work, will she?" Mr Martin ran his hand across his forehead.

"We don't know that, not at this present time. But you need to prepare yourself, and your wife. I haven't mentioned this to Leya. She has only just regained consciousness and is still concussed and traumatised. It won't help her recovery. I don't want to cause her further alarm. Not at this stage. Once I know more, I will talk firstly to you and then to Leya. We can decide what happens from then onwards, okay?"

Mr Martin nodded. He smiled weakly and uttered his thanks to the consultant for the explanation and walked back into the ward, trying to put on a brave face for Leya and his wife.

"Everything all right, love?" he asked Leya. "How do you feel now?"

"Miserable and I ache all over. I just want to get better, Dad, and get the hell out of here and back to work."

"I know, love. But you need to get better first, once you know what's happening and all that."

"Dad, Mum. Look, why don't you go home now? I feel really sleepy. I'm sure the doctor will ring you once he has more news and then you can come back, say tomorrow or something? Don't stay for the sake of it, honest, I'll be okay," Leya announced to her concerned parents, who stood looking awkward.

"If you're sure, love. We'll keep in touch with the doctor." Mrs Martin drew the covers up closer to Leya's shoulders and patted them in a motherly fashion. "You take care, love, get some rest. Your father and I will come and see you tomorrow. Night, night love, sleep tight."

"Night, love," Mr Martin smiled at his daughter. "Take care. Oh and," he handed over Leya's mobile phone, "Jude left this with me; I thought you'd probably want it."

Leya managed a sleepy smile at her father. Her shoulder throbbed incessantly and now she wanted to be alone. She watched them quietly close the door behind them, the click of the catch only just audible, and once more she was on her own in the bright, white room. She felt tears welling up inside again as she tried to move her right arm. It still wouldn't move and it felt so heavy. She relived the accident in her mind once again. She remembered Ariel's outburst of uncontrollable energy and speed. She whispered to herself, 'I'll get her back, if it's the last thing I do…'

Chapter Six

Natalie Roberts parked her 4x4 in the bank's customer car park making sure she didn't hit any other vehicle. Her truck seemed to have a mind of its own and it was always when *she* was driving. She glanced at her watch and noticed it was a few minutes after three o'clock. She was late for her appointment with Neil Burrows, her bank manager.

She opened the branch door and stepped inside. She unzipped her fleece jacket revealing a low-cut tee-shirt. She patted down her hair.

"Hello, I have an appointment with Neil Burrows, I'm Mrs Roberts," she announced, placing her handbag firmly onto the counter.

She was invited to sit down to wait. Neil Burrows was aware that Natalie was always late for her appointments and today was no exception. When he received a phone call from reception to say that Natalie had arrived, he sighed to himself. He wondered how she would blag her way out of trouble this time. He'd heard most of her weak excuses over the years. Her overdraft was way above its limit and there were a number of returned cheques listed on her account status details. He steeled himself, straightened his tie and walked to reception to collect her.

"Hello Natalie. Would you like to come through?" he asked as he gazed at the figure perched on the edge of her seat. She held an unlit cigarette and he raised his eyebrows and looked towards the *No Smoking* sign.

"Hi, Neil. How are you?" she enquired, without bothering to listen to his response.

When they were safely in the interview room with the door firmly closed, Neil asked, "How are things, Natalie?"

"Well, as it happens, not too bad," Natalie responded, smiling at him and furtively crossing her legs. "I've come to ask for your advice." She smiled briefly and continued, "About this!"

She reached into her handbag and pulled out the diary. Flicking through the pages, she came across the letter from her solicitor but handed over just the accompanying slip of paper indicating the prospective figures to Neil, smiling as she did so.

"Can you give me a moment to read this?" Neil responded officially.

"I think this will explain all," Natalie replied. She sat back on the chair and uncrossed her legs.

"Well, I can certainly help you with any advice that you need, Natalie," he smiled back at her, a sense of encouraging new business filling his mind. Thoughts of overdrafts and debts on Natalie's account swiftly disappeared.

"I want to initially pay the cheque in, when I get it, and then clear the debts that are hanging over me," she announced. "After that, well… I'm *all* yours, so to speak," she added with a sly smile. She moved her skirt slightly above her knee as she spoke.

Neil felt his face colouring up.

"Right, okay Natalie. I'll make arrangements for the cheque to be credited to your account on a fast track basis when you bring it in and then I'll take you through your options, shall I?"

"Take me where you like, Neil," she replied, feeling a huge sense of relief. "The world is now my oyster, as I believe the phrase is!"

"Bear with me whilst I get one of the counter staff to take a copy of this letter and attachment." He got up from the desk and brushed past Natalie as she looked up at him. He smiled awkwardly. "I'll back in a minute."

Natalie looked around her and smiled. At last she had her bank manager where she wanted him. No longer would Neil be looking at her with his usual grave expression on his face, telling her that he would no longer honour any more of her cheques that would inevitably bounce all the way back to her. No more lectures on cash flows and cash projections and business plans. They were all issues that were now in the past and would no longer haunt her at night. She couldn't remember the last time that she was able to sleep without worrying about how she was going to pay her mounting debts. Sam was always watching their pennies and advising her that their finances could not afford her lifestyle. How naïve she had been in her lack of knowledge of his dealings. She had often wondered what he was doing with his business affairs but he had never invited her to be involved. He played down any talk about his business and let her know what he wanted her to know, nothing more.

"Not any more, Sam baby!" she muttered as Neil Burrows returned to the room.

"All done. I'll do some research on the best investments available. I'll also advise you on investing in some excellent ISAs we have and also get some information together on stocks and bonds that are currently performing really well, given the current financial climate." Neil Burrows handed back the original letter and slip.

"What about investing in property, Neil? What are your thoughts on that?" she quizzed him.

"Well, the market is pretty slow at present. It is only a case of riding out the storm. You can guarantee that things will start moving again. Prices will have levelled out a little more, making it a more attractive proposition."

"Would you like to call by the farm and we can perhaps discuss this over a glass of wine, or two? That is, if you're not *too* busy?" Natalie asked, running her hand through her hair as she did so.

Neil Burrows nervously adjusted his tie. His fingers found that it didn't need any alteration. He patted it instead to ensure he remained calm.

"Uh, yes, that won't be a problem," he confirmed.

"It's just that I don't want every Tom, *Dick* and Harry listening to my personal financial situation, you know: widow, money… you get the picture don't you, Neil?" She bent her head to one side and slowly closed her eyes, focusing them again as she blinked them open on him. Neil Burrows swallowed heavily and felt uneasy.

"Erm, yes. How about Friday? Would that be convenient to call then?" He cleared his throat and tried to concentrate on the job in hand.

"Friday will be great. I'll prepare us lunch as well." She got up from her chair and put her hand out to shake his. "It was great to see you again. Oh, and much love to your wife, Neil." Natalie diplomatically reminded him of his marital status.

"See you Friday, Natalie. Thanks for coming," he added, opening the door for her.

"I'll be saying to same to you on Friday!" She returned an innuendo which made Neil let go of her hand like it had burnt his fingers.

"Right!" He closed the door firmly behind her and let out a sigh of relief. He watched her walk across the reception area to the outer door and hastily looked at his desk as he saw her turn and wave him goodbye. A couple of the counter staff started to laugh as Natalie disappeared from the bank. A blast on the intercom system in Neil Burrows' room made him jump. He took the call hands free.

"Looks like you've scored, Neil mate! She's after you!" came the roaring response from the intercom.

Neil Burrows chose to ignore the gesture and cut the caller dead. "Who's the next appointment to see me?" he enquired, with a stifled laugh.

"Oh, it's a gentleman, Neil, don't panic!" was the hilarious reply amidst shrieks of laughter.

Neil Burrows composed himself with a deliberate shake of his head to waken his senses. He walked back into reception only to find, to his surprise, that Natalie had returned. She stood with her hands on her hips and smiled seductively at Neil as he looked for his next client.

"Oh Neil, I forgot to tell you. My treat, by the way, on Friday!" she cooed.

Neil felt his face redden once more and nodded his acknowledgement to Natalie and urged his next client towards the interview room amidst stifled hoots of laughter from behind the counter.

Natalie smiled, flicked her hair with enthusiasm and waved her goodbyes to the rest of the banking staff, like a diva in front of her adoring fans. She got into her 4x4 and drove off at speed without noticing the parking ticket that clung on desperately by its package to her windscreen. It had been there for over a fortnight. As she turned the corner it blew away into the road and then into the hedgerow. She rumbled on, none the wiser, through the twisting countryside lanes towards home.

oOo

Leya Martin stretched her arm above her head and momentarily flinched as her collar bone ached, reminding her of the riding accident. She had lain in hospital for days. The consultant had visited her that morning. He confirmed that there was little more that could be done about the paralysis in her arm and only time would tell. Leya was given the all clear over her head injury. It would be a slow recovery but there was no permanent damage. He also confirmed, to her delight, that she could go home. Leya was extremely grateful as she had been on the brink of discharging herself as the boredom and smell of the hospital were driving her mad.

She carefully dressed herself in a red tee-shirt and navy blue shorts with slip-on pumps. It was the easiest form of dress she could manage. Just dragging a hairbrush through her matted, lifeless hair was exhausting enough. She did have an opportunity to have her hair washed the previous afternoon but she couldn't bear the pain. She decided her hair would have to wait. She was going home. Not having to meet anyone else, just her parents, and they wouldn't worry about what condition her hair was in.

Leya sat on the edge of the crisp linen-clad bed and gazed out of the window. From her position in the ward she could watch the arrival of vehicles in the car park below. She was excited about the prospect of going home and sleeping in her own bed once more and being surrounded by familiarity. Her own bedroom and the horsy pictures that adorned the walls, with the smell of the air freshener on her windowsill and the organised chaos of belongings strewn all over the floor.

'I will have to tidy up,' she thought to herself.

Her paralysed arm hung pitifully by her side. She had no feeling in it at all. She had attended a physiotherapy session during her stay in hospital and the therapist had been pleased with her. It would be a slow process.

Leya closed her eyes and her thoughts meandered back to the accident. No matter how hard she tried to remember the events, she could only recall the last few minutes before the impact. She could remember seeing Jude waiting with Nelson as she bolted past them. She remembered the look of horror on Jude's face and her scream just before she fell. But after that, nothing at all.

She looked out towards the car park and noticed her parents' car had arrived. She took a deep breath as the door suddenly opened and her mother and father walked in with broad smiles. Mr Martin collected Leya's bag and kissed her gently on the forehead.

"All ready then, love? Won't be long now till we get you back home. You'll feel much better, when you're home." He appeared to be very positive and he warmed Leya with his optimism.

She smiled at him, "Thanks, Dad," and carefully moved off the bed.

"Can you manage all right, love?" fussed Leya's mother. Her husband glared at her as he took hold of Leya's good arm and guided her out of the room, leaving her mother looking helplessly on.

As they drove home, Leya gazed out of the window and was heartened to notice that life hadn't changed since she'd been hospitalised. She looked up to Malsham Downs as the car made its way through the narrow lanes. The trees were laden with their new foliage ready for the summer. Leya sat back into her seat, nursing her arm, eager to get home and back to sanity.

The car eventually drew up outside the family home. Leya breathed a sigh of relief as her collar bone had been shaken over every bump in the road imaginable and she felt quite queasy. She rubbed her shoulder and tried to look happy. She contemplated taking more painkillers; she had been discharged with a hearty supply of them.

Mrs Martin opened the front porch door and kicked off her shoes, leaving them near the wood basket. Mr Martin followed as he helped Leya edge her way out of the car. Leya, wide-eyed and tired, made her way into the lounge and carefully sat down in one of the armchairs positioned to either side of the fireplace.

"It's great to be home, Dad," she sighed and held her shoulder for a moment.

"Cup of tea, dear?" called Mrs Martin from the kitchen.

"Yes please, Mum. Can I have it in my room? I'm going to have a lay down. My shoulder is aching." She rose to her feet and winced.

"Let me help you." Mr Martin offered his hands out to his daughter, who gladly accepted and together they slowly made their upstairs, taking one step at a time.

Leya slowly leaned back on her bed; the pain was so intense that she cried out. She shook her head as her father looked on. He offered her a paper tissue, which Leya gratefully blew her nose with.

"When will I get better, Dad? This is driving me crazy!" she sobbed.

"It's going to take time, love. In a few weeks I guarantee you'll be much better, and who knows, after a few more physio sessions perhaps you'll get some feeling back in your arm and then life will become a bit more normal again. You'll be back at work, enjoying yourself and putting all this lot behind you. Here take these," he smiled reassuringly at her and offered her two painkillers.

"Do you really think so?" she questioned between sobs.

"It *will* happen, love! I'll go and find out what's happened to that cuppa." He shuffled out of the bedroom.

Leya blew her nose once more and looked around her room. She stared at the various pictures of horses and the array of rosettes pinned on her wardrobe door. Her mind wandered over possibilities of what would happen to her. She sighed again and gingerly turned over to face the wall. Tears filled her eyes once more. She heard the telephone ringing downstairs and her father answering. He chatted for a few minutes and then ended the conversation. He called up the stairs to Leya.

"That was Jude on the phone. She wants to come and see you tomorrow. I said that it would be okay. It is all right, isn't it?"

Leya smiled and called out, "Course it is."

She would look forward to seeing Jude and hearing all the gossip from the stables. She felt a surge of happiness and, feeling brighter, wiped away her tears.

oOo

Natalie had been thinking about Leya and the accident as she drove away from her meeting at the bank. She decided that she would drive past the house to see if there was any more news. As she pulled up outside the Martins' house, she was surprised to see their car parked in the driveway. Her curiosity overcame her as she climbed out of her 4x4 and knocked on their door. She clutched a bouquet of flowers she had bought from the farm shop at Culverton, which she had intended to display in her own kitchen, but decided it would make an ideal gift and would be a perfectly good excuse to visit.

Mr Martin opened the door.

"Hello, Natalie! You must be a mind reader! Have you come to see Leya?"

Natalie pushed a lock of blonde hair from her eyes.

"I was passing and I thought I would call in to ask how she is. I take it she's still in hospital?"

"No, Leya came home this afternoon, only a couple of hours ago. Come on in." He ushered her into the hall that was carpeted in a worn Axminster with a very hectic red and cream floral pattern. "Wait here a mo, I'll just check if she's up to seeing visitors."

He slowly began to climb the stairs. Natalie waited impatiently in the hall. She glanced around and noticed a set of three ornamental ducks flying up striped pink and white wallpaper and shuddered at their tackiness.

"Are you well enough for a visitor?" Mr Martin asked, peering around Leya's bedroom door.

Leya sighed. She had just spent the last half an hour speaking to LB on her mobile phone and felt drained by her incessant chatter. LB had recovered relatively quickly from the lorry accident. She was telling Leya how she had enrolled for a college course to study to be a beauty therapist.

"Yeah, 'spose so. Can you give me a minute?"

While Mr Martin called, "She'll see you," down the stairs, Leya carefully pulled the duvet over her shoulder, straightening it with her good arm and a deft flick of her foot. She nodded that she was ready and Mr Martin opened the door wider to reveal a large bouquet of flowers and Natalie smiling above it.

Leya was shocked to see her stood in the doorway.

"Natalie! Hi, how are you?" she stared in amazement. She hadn't expected to see her.

"More importantly, how are *you* feeling?" Nat asked sympathetically and bent down to kiss Leya on the cheek. She placed the flowers on the bed.

"It's going to take ages to get better, I've resigned myself to that." Leya looked at the flowers and smiled. "They are lovely, thanks. Dad, can you get a vase, please?"

"Course, love, back in a tick. Would you like a cup of tea, Natalie?"

"Ooh yes, ta lovey!" returned Natalie, sitting down on the bed and adjusting her skirt that had ridden up to her thighs. Mr Martin glanced momentarily at Nat's legs, cleared his throat and disappeared downstairs.

Once they were alone, Natalie looked directly at Leya.

"Right, down to business," she said and looked serious. "What are you going to do about *this*?" she demanded, pointing to Leya's paralysed arm.

"Not much, by all accounts. The consultant doesn't hold a lot of hope of regaining any feeling in it and being able to use it." Leya sadly looked at her arm.

"I think you can do better than that, Leya! What I mean is, how are you going to deal with the loss, financially?"

"I can't work, if that's what you mean. Not with horses. Whose gonna want a disabled groom?"

"You're missing the point, *dearie*!" Natalie had to spell out her definition. "I'm talking about compensation. You need to be thinking about suing the yard for your loss and disablement. Have you thought about it?"

"I can't say that I have. After all, it was my fault—"

Natalie stopped her dead.

"Don't!" she shrieked, making Leya jump and wince in pain. "Look, you *don't* admit to anything. It was the horse that caused the accident, wasn't it? You were working for Manna at the time. It happened during work time. Bloody thing wasn't fit to be ridden. It was clearly dangerous. Manna should've let you ride something else.

She knows what Ariel is like. How are they going to prove otherwise? Well, they can't! If you want security for your future, you *have* to blame the horse. Jude will back you up. She saw what happened, didn't she?"

"Yes, she did. But it was the bird scarer, and Jude knows that. You know how straight she is! She'll stand by the truth, she won't lie." Leya looked worried.

"*I'll* find a way to persuade her. You see, I've just had a letter about Sam's estate. I'll be inheriting some money. I can, if you get my drift... make her."

"You mean, *bribe* her?" Leya looked at Nat incredulously with wide eyes.

"If that's what it takes, then yes." Natalie looked defiant and pursed her lips. Her mind began to race as she realised what she had just said.

"Why on earth would you want to sue Manna? I thought she was your best mate?"

"She is, but let's say something happened a long time ago that I haven't mentioned before." Natalie looked reflective and bitter.

"Oh right, what? I have no idea what you mean. What happened?" Leya was intrigued by this revelation and she struggled to sit up. Her shoulder went into a spasm as she moved.

"A long time ago, before Sam died, Manna did something really bad to me. I vowed I would one day get her back. I've waited ages for this moment. Can't say anymore, Leya. You know, personal stuff!" Natalie shrugged off any further questions.

"But if this goes to court it's going to cost heaps of money, especially if I lose," Leya continued. "Look Natalie, thank you for the advice but I'm really not sure about this. I don't want to cause a scene and be the centre of your revenge. You know, problems between Manna, Jude, everyone. It will be horrible, just horrible! And

Manna is already on to me about the accident with Del and Fig. How is she going to react to *me* suing *her*! She will go ape! She might want to counter-sue me for the loss of Del! She won't even speak to the police about what happened."

"It's not really a police matter now, is it? Manna asked *you* to drive the lorry, but you weren't fit to drive after your fall. What about LB? She is surely in her own rights to sue Manna for negligence!" Natalie rose from the bed in anger. "You're going to give up even before you try, are you, Leya? I am really disappointed in you. Do you want to spend the rest of your life wallowing in self-pity and *what ifs*? Seems like it to me! You have got to start thinking about yourself in all of this!"

She got up and started to walk to the door.

"I'm sorry. My mind's all over the place," Leya apologised. "Let me think it over, get my head around it. Can I let you know my decision in a few days, *please*?"

Natalie sat back down on the bed. "Okay. But remember, you are the most important person in all this. Never, ever forget that, Leya. You don't deserve to live the rest of your life as an invalid and if Manna Jacobs had schooled that horse properly, the accident wouldn't have happened. Anyway, she's insured. She can cover the cost. Don't worry; I will help you all I can. And if you're that concerned over court costs, I will take care of that. Don't worry! I mean it! In a strange way, you'd be doing *me* a favour. Anyway, we're in a compensation culture these days. You must have heard of this no-win no-fee lark. It seems to be all the fashion."

Natalie stopped talking as Mr Martin appeared in the doorway carrying a tray with two china cups and a plate of biscuits. He placed them on Leya's bedside cabinet in silence and walked to the door.

"Don't mind me, ladies. I'll let you catch up on your gossip in peace!" He smiled and left the room, hands tightly clenched behind his back.

"Thanks, Dad," Leya called out after him.

Natalie placed a cup of tea in Leya's hand.

"Think about what I have said, Leya." She sipped her tea and selected a custard cream from the plate. She crammed it all in her mouth at once. "Biscuit?" Natalie grunted as she munched and hovered the plate near Leya's face. Leya shook her head.

"No thanks, I'm not feeling very hungry at the moment."

Natalie wiped the crumbs from her mouth and quickly drained her cup of tea. She noticed Leya was looking very tired.

"I must go. Call me at the end of the week and I'll come and see you again," she announced.

"Okay. Thanks anyway for coming in, Nat," Leya said a little uneasily.

Natalie kissed the top of her head. "Take care. Bye love," she softly whispered and turned on her heel and left the bedroom. "Thanks for the tea, Mr Martin. Bye!" Natalie called out as she breezed downstairs and slammed the door behind her.

Leya heard the sound of the 4x4 start up and wheel-spin out of the road. She lay back on her pillow and thought about their conversation. She glanced at a photograph on the wall beside her bed. It was of herself, Jude, Manna and Nat at The Black Sheep on one of their nights out.

There was a glisten of tears on her cheek. She sniffed loudly and cleared her throat. Natalie was forcing her to make the hardest decision of her life. She felt scared and very alone.

"Everything all right, dear?" Mr Martin stood in the doorway of Leya's bedroom.

"Yes, Dad," Leya whispered. "I'm tired. I think I'll get some sleep, if you don't mind."

"As you wish. Your mother and I are only downstairs in the lounge if you need us."

"Thanks." She smiled at her father and closed her eyes. She had a lot of serious thinking to do and she needed to be alone.

oOo

"Hiya! I've come to check up on you!" Jude announced as she stood at the bottom of Leya's bed the next morning.

"Hi! Are those for me?" Leya indicated the bunch of Michaelmas daisies that Jude clutched.

"Course not, I thought I'd bring them for a laugh! Silly thing! Course they are for you!" Jude joked and placed them on the bedside cabinet. She sat down on Leya's bed and produced a small box of chocolates from her pocket

"Thought you might need these as well." She placed them in front of Leya, balanced on her stomach.

"Thanks, I'll really enjoy scoffing them." Leya noticed it was her favourite brand of chocolates.

"So," Jude continued. "What's going to happen about your arm?"

"I'm going to have more physiotherapy. I've been getting some twinges in it. Dad seems to think I will be okay. But I don't know. I'm trying to stay upbeat. What if I never regain the use of it, ever? I've got to face up to the fact that it may never be any good, haven't I?"

"Life deals us really shitty blows and somehow we get over them. The thing is, Leya, you've got to stay positive. Believe that you are going to get better. If you think negatively about it all, nothing will happen. Life's what you make it. It is really promising that you're having twinges in it," Jude added.

"I know, but I'm also trying to be realistic at the same time. I must have been a bad person in a previous life with all that's happened to me lately," Leya answered and closed her eyes. "Anyway, cheer me up, that's what you're here for. Tell me about work. What's the gossip?"

"Nothing much. I'm there on my own with no sign of any help. Manna apparently has spoken to the police, at long last! Seems they aren't really interested in the accident now. Fig is doing well. He's coming back to the yard soon. Oh, and Callum has been a great help. He's got stuck in helping with the horses, mucking out and all that. He has been a star. Hopefully he'll carry on helping till you come back to work."

"If I come back, you mean. We know Manna, she won't wait around for me, not when her precious horses are concerned. I know she doesn't care about me. Even more so since the accident, or, should I say, accidents." Leya was angry and she felt her face redden.

"You said it," Jude spoke softly. She noticed Leya had begun to look tired. "I'd better get back to work, before I'm missed. You take care of yourself. Don't worry, you'll get better. Give it time, think positive and keep up the physio. Is he hunky, by the way?" Jude enquired, with her head on one side and her arms folded.

"*She* is hunky and butch at the same time but I don't intend becoming a lesbian!" Leya laughed.

"Oops!" Jude backed out of the room. "See ya!"

"Thanks for these," Leya pointed to her gifts.

Jude closed the door and sighed in dismay at Leya's progress, which wasn't happening as quickly as she had hoped it would. Mr Martin met her at the bottom of the stairs.

"Thanks for coming, Jude. I know Leya was looking forward to seeing you."

"That's okay, Mr Martin. I didn't stay too long; she looks pale. I'll call by next week to see her, stay a bit longer, if that's OK?" Jude smiled and buttoned up her jacket.

"Course it will be, my dear." Mr Martin closed the door behind her.

Leya spent the next few days upstairs in her room. Her parents were kept busy by periodically checking on her and providing meals.

One morning, there was a telephone call. It was from Leya's consultant. Mr Martin took the call and asked him to hold whilst he carried the phone to her bedroom.

"The consultant from the hospital is on the phone for you, Leya," he said as he placed the handset into her hand.

"Hello, Miss Martin. I've just been speaking to a legal friend of mine and after he heard about your accident, he has suggested you might be entitled to claim compensation for your injuries. He has asked for your phone number and I was wondering what your thoughts might be?"

Leya was slightly taken aback.

"Well, um, yes, he can have my number if he thinks I might be able to claim something."

"I'll tell him and then you can have a preliminary chat."

"Okay," Leya replied distantly. She thought of the implications of a claim and Natalie's visit, with her suggestion of suing Manna. She handed the phone back to her father.

"What did he want?" Mr Martin asked.

"Something about a legal person phoning me about claiming compensation," she shook her head as she spoke. "I don't know if I want to go down that route, not after what Natalie said—"

"What did Natalie say?" Mr Martin looked concerned.

"When she was here she talked about suing the yard. Suing Manna for my injuries, and that she was prepared to help me, you know, with the costs and all that."

"I thought she was—" Mr Martin began.

"Best friends with Manna, yes, so did I. Something has made Nat change her mind. I don't know what, but she seems keen to see Manna get a kicking from the claim. That's why she wants to see it through personally. I don't think she cares if I win, only that she somehow gets her own back on Manna."

"It seems a bit fishy to me. Do you want to get involved? I know the money will be of help, but think of the implications. You might end up in the middle of something nasty," her father warned.

"I don't get sick pay from Manna, nothing at all. This could be serious, Dad." Leya's mind raced.

"Yes, it could be, love. Still, have a chat to this solicitor chap. See what he has to say."

"I think I'll come downstairs for a while to get a change of scenery. I'll see you in a while." Leya slowly got up from the bed.

She walked to the window and looked first towards the downs and to the woods that blanketed the base of the hills. She took a deep breath and straightened her body. She began to wonder what had persuaded Natalie to suddenly want to take revenge against Manna. It must have been something terrible, especially as Natalie had kept it to herself and wouldn't divulge any more information. Leya felt a surge of anger as she looked down at her arm. She nodded confidently to herself.

"Let's see you squirm then, shall we, Manna!" she whispered and stared back out of the window.

Chapter Seven

An official-looking man, dressed in an expensive, light grey pinstripe suit, was walking from his silver Mercedes towards the Martins' house, laptop in one hand and a mobile phone jammed to his ear.

"Yes, okay, right… thanks." He ended the call and placed the phone into his breast pocket. He looked at the number of the house and pressed the doorbell twice.

Darius Cherry had an appointment with Leya to talk over her compensation claim. He waited impatiently for the door to be opened and tapped his fingers on his laptop case. He ran a tanned and carefully manicured hand through his thick, swept-back blond hair as Mrs Martin opened the door.

"Hello, Mr Cherry?" she asked.

"Hi, yes, that's me. I'm here to see Leya Martin," he announced without smiling. He held out his hand. She shook it and left self-raising flour in his palm. She swiftly apologised.

"Sorry, Mr Cherry. I'm baking cakes and scones. Come in, I'll take you to Leya," she fussed and closed the door behind him, leaving a streak of flour on the door handle. "Leya, the solicitor's here to see you," she informed Leya, who was sitting on an armchair watching a heated political debate on the television.

"Tea, Mr Cherry?" Mrs Martin wiped her floury hands onto her apron.

"Ya, two sugars please and milk," he responded and placed his laptop on the floor. "Pleased to meet you, Leya. How are you feeling?" He sat down on the armchair opposite and smiled falsely at her through brightly whitened teeth.

Leya turned the television off.

"My neck feels better but I still can't feel much in my arm," she replied and Darius Cherry nodded over-enthusiastically in a fake, sympathetic manner, slowly closing his eyes as he did so. She noticed he had a pained look on his face.

"Right, okay. Let's have a little chat about what I can do for you. What I need from you is as much information as you can give me about the accident. Anything at all, anything, no matter how small, no matter how trivial. And after we've gone through that, I'll see what you can claim for."

Mrs Martin carried in a tray of teacups and a plate of chocolate digestives and placed them on a glass coffee table in the middle of the room. She was followed by Mr Martin, who was keen to listen to what Darius Cherry had to say. He wanted to understand the procedure and was armed with a number of questions that he wanted to fire at him. Most importantly, he wanted to be there for Leya to help her understand what she was getting involved in.

"Okay, when you're ready. Can you recount exactly what happened and I'll ask you extra questions if I need them. Oh and by the way, I will be taping this interview. It's standard procedure. Are you happy with that?"

Leya looked taken aback. Still, if this was the way it had to be done, she had to adhere to it. She looked to her father and nodded her approval. Mr Martin made himself comfortable as the interview began, staring first at Darius Cherry and then back at Leya.

Darius Cherry took a digital recorder from his briefcase and switched it on. Leya took a deep breath as he gave her instructions.

"Before you speak, please make sure you give a clear account of what the weather was like, date, time, details of the horse, the equipment… or tack, as you horsy people refer to it as! And the stables, as much as you possibly can."

Leya felt uneasy but she began to recall the incident and events leading up to the accident. Mr Martin continued to sit observing Darius Cherry. He dunked a biscuit into his tea as Leya began her account.

"And when she galloped towards the hedge... I... I... can't remember anything else... not until I woke up in hospital." Leya wiped a tear from her eye. It had been very emotional for her to recall the accident again.

Darius Cherry pressed the stop button on the recorder.

"Thanks, Leya. Well done, that's great," he enthused and placed the machine back into his briefcase.

"Do you need any further information? About the medical side, I mean?" Mr Martin wanted to know.

"I've got a meeting with Leya's consultant tomorrow and he will be able to answer the medical questions for the proposed claim," Darius Cherry informed him and clicked his ballpoint pen.

"Then perhaps you will keep Leya fully informed on the progress," Mr Martin added.

"Yes, but it will take a while. I will need to write to Mr and Mrs Jacobs next to inform them of the claim. I'll get details of their insurers and solicitor. Whatever happens, you have a strong case for a claim against them. I believe you have a claim of negligence against the Jacobs for making you ride an unfit and dangerous animal," he announced as he rose up from the armchair. He collected all his belongings and tapped his pocket to ensure the mobile phone was still there.

"Thanks again, Leya. I'll be in touch." He offered his hand to Leya who shook it weakly.

"Thanks," Leya responded.

She wasn't very happy about what was about to happen. She knew it would rock Littlebridge to the core. She thought of Jude and anticipated her response. She thought about Natalie and her revenge against Manna.

"I'll see you to the door," Mr Martin offered and guided Darius Cherry out of the living room.

Leya decided that she should tell Natalie immediately. She got up from her chair and walked towards the telephone and dialled her number. She quickly updated her on Mr Cherry's visit and thanked her for advising her to start the compensation claim in the first place.

Natalie Roberts smiled as she put her phone down. She nodded to herself and sat down at the kitchen table. She rummaged amongst some paperwork she had been filing and found a phone number scribbled at the top of a letterhead. She dialled it.

"Hi Darius? It's Natalie, yes. Just had a phone call from Leya Martin. Well done! Sounds like you've convinced her! Pop in on your way through. Have a little drinkie with me? Okay, see you then, bye."

Natalie sat back on her chair with her arms behind her head and smiled smugly. At length she got up and opened the fridge door to reveal a number of chilled bottles of wine precariously balanced on one of the shelves. She selected an Australian chardonnay and proceeded to uncork it. Peeling the seal, she heard a car door slam outside in the yard. She smiled to herself and unbuttoned her blouse to her cleavage. The kitchen door opened and Darius Cherry stood smiling at her.

"Missed you, Nat." He strode over to where she was and slipped his hand inside her blouse and touched her breasts. "Missed you sooo much, and your lovely tits," he concluded, thrust his mouth over hers and kissed her vigorously.

Natalie, encouraged by his spontaneity, kissed him back, opening her mouth and drinking in his tongue. She still held onto the bottle of wine as he lifted her up on to the kitchen table and began to undo the remaining buttons on her blouse.

"Well, keen, aren't you?" she gasped as he began to unzip his trousers and loosen his tie.

She helped him disentangle himself from his suit and kissed his neck and ran her hands systematically through his hair. He pushed her gently onto the table amid the piles of paper that became crumpled beneath her body. He laid her arms outstretched above her head as he continued to kiss and suck on her breasts, making her tremble in anticipation. As he leant against her she could feel his erect penis probe insistently against her thighs. She sighed in delight.

"Oh Darius, I had no idea you were *so* randy!" she concluded, as he pushed her skirt up over her hips and pulled at her panties so that they were at knee height. She ripped open his shirt and ran her hands over his evenly tanned chest.

"And I had no idea you wanted me *so* badly!" he mimicked, and panted with anticipation as he proceeded to lie on top of her and grind his hips against hers.

Natalie held on to the side of the table as he pulsated in and out of her, kissing her neck, lips and breasts in succession. She wrapped her legs around his body and held his head into her breasts as they erratically changed position so that she was on top of him. She teased him by slowly lifting herself up and down on him. She kissed his stomach and held on to his arms, pinning them against the table. The papers that had creased beneath them scattered across the surface. The bottle of wine stood untouched at a safe distance; the glass still glinted with condensation.

Once more they changed positions and this time Darius laid Natalie over the table so she was facing the kitchen door. He stood behind her and continued to thrust in a vigorous fashion deep inside her. She groaned in delight. She loved his spontaneity as he held her hips and bent his head low against the side of her head.

"Like it, Nat? Now what's next?" he gasped.

Sweat built up over his body as he drove deeper inside her.

"I think we should finish on the floor, don't you?" she panted and slid off the table. She grabbed hold of the wine bottle and took a slug from it. She offered the bottle to Darius but he refused.

"Later, come on, let's finish it," he instructed and grabbed hold of her arms, forcing her on to the floor.

Natalie giggled and held on to the bottle. She swigged again from it before tipping a little over her breasts and indicating to Darius to lick them. He responded and she poured more over her breasts and then onto his head until they were both soaked in wine. They licked the wine from each other's bodies and continued to make love beneath the table. Darius was expert at positioning Natalie in whatever way he wanted and she responded because she loved the feeling of surprise and his masculine force. They climaxed amidst groans and giggles.

"Dar, may I say you were on top form today! I've never been shagged under a table before!" Nat exclaimed when she had got her breath back. Darius lay panting by her side.

"I'll call it a celebratory shag. We'll do it again, when the case is won!" he announced and kissed Natalie's head.

"Make sure you *do* win it! Think of it as *no win, no sex*," she warned, wagging her finger at his face.

"I need a shower. I stink of wine!" He got up from underneath the table and bent over to collect his clothes. Natalie slapped his bare backside.

"I'll have one with you as I stink as well!" she laughed and took off the remainder of her clothes that were drenched in wine.

She walked towards the bottom of the stairs and beckoned Darius to follow her.

"One more for the road?" he jested and pointed to her bedroom.

"If you're *up* for it!" Natalie returned and ran up the stairs laughing. Darius reached her bedroom and Natalie held his arm.

"No, let's get showered first. I don't want my boudoir stinking of chardonnay."

"The shower it is then!" Darius pushed her against the wall in the hallway and started to kiss her again. Natalie felt a surge of passion and started to kiss him back. They staggered, still kissing, into the bathroom where they clambered into the shower, turned on the water and started to passionately make love once more. The water cascaded over their bodies as Darius knelt down and started to kiss in circles around Natalie's thighs. His hands worked deftly all over her body, kneading and holding her, caressing her with his tongue, licking every inch of her skin until she started to moan in delight. She held onto his head and forced his face against her. Natalie gracefully lifted her arms above her head and savoured the second encounter in the space of a few minutes. This was the sex she craved and Darius certainly knew how to deliver.

They were in the shower for what seemed like ages and the water continued to pelt relentlessly over them but they didn't care. Sex was foremost in both their minds, so much so that they didn't hear the kitchen door slowly open and close.

"Natalie? Hello! Are you there?" called the voice from downstairs.

Natalie stopped kissing Darius and gestured at him to listen.

"Natalie!" called the voice again. "Where are you?"

"Oh shit! I forgot to lock the door! Wait here, I won't be long," She pushed Darius away and scrambled over him. He spluttered his disapproval in expletives about being interrupted.

Natalie grabbed her bathrobe and disappeared downstairs. She walked into the kitchen, drying her hair with a hand towel, and saw George Trippit by the Aga.

"I hope I haven't disturbed you," he smirked. "I've got a message from Manna, 'bout the weekend," he announced, gazing at Natalie and her state of undress. "We'll pick you up on the way tomorrow. She said she'd left a message on the phone for you. I expect you've got it already," he added.

Natalie felt annoyed at George's intrusion.

"Yes, I know! Is that *it*, George? Anything else?" she angrily replied.

"No, just wanted to make sure you got the message, that's all," George replied, continuing to stare.

"Well, I *have*, well and truly! Shut the door on your way out!" she curtly instructed and walked into the hallway, back to her abandoned lover upstairs in the shower. "Idiot! Coming over here just to tell me that! He could have bloody *phoned* me," she muttered and strode upstairs in annoyance. "Sorry, Dar, off the boil now, lovie, you might as well get dressed," she dictated from the landing and marched off to her bedroom to retrieve some clean clothes. "It was George Trippit. His excuse was something about the dressage at the weekend!" she called as she hopped into a clean bra and panties.

Darius appeared from the shower room with a thick white towel wrapped around his middle. He was fuming.

"So it was Trippit who interrupted my shag, was it?" he glared and folded his arms across his chest, peeved. "The wanker! I'll see he doesn't call here again without an invitation."

"Don't bother yourself with him, Dar. He's handy: I use him when I need him. He has nothing up top," she assured him, tapping the side of her temple. "I wouldn't waste your oxygen."

Darius seemed satisfied with Natalie's answer and made off downstairs to collect his clothes.

"Another drink?" Natalie called after him.

"No, I must leave. I have an appointment in town. Great shag all the same! It wasn't a completely wasted journey, was it?"

"I'll take that as a compliment," she replied, laughing quietly to herself as she thought of their passionate act under the kitchen table. "Good job the old bugger didn't call any earlier or he might have seen something he shouldn't have!"

"Yes, and I bet he would have got off on it!" returned Darius, picking up his wine-stained shirt and shaking the remnants of chardonnay from it. He glanced at himself in the mirror and repositioned his tousled hair.

"Have you got any spare shirts?" he shouted up from the kitchen.

"Yes, there are some of Sam's, they might fit you. I'll bring one down," Nat replied from the bedroom as she towelled her hair dry.

A quarter of an hour later Nat appeared in the kitchen with a clean shirt. She looked refreshed and alert. She handed the shirt to Darius who gratefully put it on. As he fastened the buttons and tucked the tails into his trousers, he looked over to Nat who was tidying the papers on the table.

"I'll let you know about the Martin claim. There shouldn't be any problems; it is a straightforward compensation claim for negligence."

"That's good. Let me know what your fees are for this and I'll settle up with you. Oh, and I'd better treat the consultant to a drink as well," she smiled at Darius seductively.

"As long as it's only a drink and not anything else," he retorted and took her in his arms.

"Darius, don't be silly. You know its only sex between us, nothing else. I don't want you getting all romantic on me now."

"Yeah, but I've got to look after my client's interests, haven't I?" he questioned.

"I'm fine. Just do your job and that's all you have to worry about, okay?" She squeezed him tightly around the middle and rested her head on his chest. "Go on, off to your appointment or you'll be late!" She urged him to the door.

"Speak soon," Darius returned with a kiss to Natalie's cheek.

"Get off my land! Be off!"

Natalie watched him climb into the Mercedes. He laughed and slammed the door of the car. Placing his mobile phone on its cradle on the dashboard, he reversed out of the yard like a whirlwind. He waved as he disappeared out of sight.

Natalie watched him drive away and felt proud of her achievements. She closed the door and began to tidy the kitchen. She glanced at her watch and remembered that her appointment with her solicitor was later that afternoon. She was very nervous about this meeting since it would reveal who the silent business partner was. She was a little worried about who it might be. Was it a complete stranger or would it be someone she knew?

She changed into a tweed skirt and green checked blouse unbuttoned to her cleavage. She tied a scarf around her neck, then, grabbing her handbag, she slammed the kitchen door closed and tottered in kitten heels to her 4x4.

As she drove to Malsham, she thought of Sam and his secret dealings. She wondered what sort of assets he had accrued and if it included any property. Her thoughts were soon allayed as she reached the solicitor's office. She waited nervously in reception, not daring to read any magazines. They looked incredibly boring. She watched various members of staff wandering through the reception area, whilst phone calls continued to pour in. It was a very busy office.

"Mrs Roberts? Mr Allworth will see you now," said the receptionist, and indicated with a wave of a hand for Natalie to get up and follow her.

Natalie was led into a dark, wood-panelled office, which was antiquated and smelt musty. There were massive volumes of legal publications on shelves throughout the office. There was a large oak table at the far end of the room. She was alarmed to see a figure sitting there, with his back to her, poring over some papers that were laid in front of him. Her observations were swiftly interrupted by Mr Allworth, who arose from behind a desk to her left.

"Good afternoon, Mrs Roberts. Please, sit down," Allworth gestured her to a leather-backed chair.

Natalie smiled, swallowed hard and sat down. She clutched her handbag to her cleavage. She could hardly breathe.

"Thank you for coming in this afternoon. I understand you have received my letter. I would like to go through a few items contained within it, if I may? Firstly, I think it would be a good idea to reveal who Mr Roberts's business partner is. Mrs Roberts, I would like to introduce you to him."

Natalie was taken aback. "Oh, right, if that is procedure, then okay, let's not waste any time." She adjusted her blouse and sat upright in the armchair, one hand on her handbag. She swiftly pushed a strand of hair away from her mouth. Her heart began to thump in anticipation.

Mr Allworth smugly smiled and walked over to the table. He touched the man's shoulder. The man slowly got up and turned to face Natalie, ready for the introduction.

Natalie blinked in amazement.

"Hello, Nat," he replied smiling and holding out his hand. "I hope I haven't given you too much of a shock!"

Mr Allworth continued to grin.

"I see you two are already acquainted. That is good news. Isn't it wonderful, Mrs Roberts, that you already know this gentleman? It will make life soooo much easier!"

Natalie choked back her surprise as she got up. Darius Cherry stood in front of her, smiling broadly.

"I had absolutely no idea it was.... *you* of all people!"

"Aren't you pleased, Nat? I hoped you would be!" Darius took her hand and kissed it gently.

"I don't know what to say, Dar, it's a bit of a shock." Natalie sat down on the chair, still clutching her handbag like an item of comfort.

"Would you care for a cup of tea, Mrs Roberts?" Allworth smarmily asked.

"Haven't you got anything stronger?" blurted out Natalie, trying to remain composed.

"Oh, well, yes. I can offer you a Scotch, if that is in order? I have a good single malt, dozen years or so old, I believe." Allworth opened a cupboard within his desk and drew out a bottle.

"Yeah, great." Natalie continued to stare in amazement at Darius. She felt her usual confident exterior begin to weaken and her face redden.

"Nat, we need to talk. Business things, you know, the will and all that." Darius dragged a chair and sat close to Natalie. "It won't be too taxing, I promise. Sam and I had a very good business relationship. Straight down the line; no problems, no hassles."

"How does this affect my inheritance?" Natalie snatched the glass of whisky from Allworth and drank it in one swig. She handed back the glass to him without acknowledgement.

"Well, Mrs Roberts. It means that Mr Cherry is entitled to a percentage of the assets that both he and your husband accrued over the years."

"What are the assets?" asked Natalie, still not able to take her eyes off Darius and the sickly grin that was fixed on his face.

"If you would like to take a look at this list, it shows what is owned within the partnership. Mr Roberts has indicated in his will that he wishes Mr Cherry to take over as Senior Partner in the partnership."

Allworth handed the list to Natalie who sat in silence, taking in the information laid before her.

"Oh my God! The partnership owns Heyrick Heights! But it can't! It was my parents' farm! It was always mine, never Sam's!"

"If you would care to read the paragraph from your mother's will, Mrs Roberts, it quite clearly indicates that, upon her death, Heyrick Heights was to be signed over to Mr Roberts and one other person. However, this person was not yourself. Were you not aware of this when your father died?" Allworth quizzed.

"No, because Sam dealt with the will. I was too upset to read it or take anything in. I trusted him when he said the farm had been left to us. What do you mean, another person?" Natalie felt tears in her eyes as the print became blurred in front of her.

"Ummm, it's Mrs Amanda Jacobs," Allworth continued.

"Manna Jacobs? What's she got to do with all this?" blurted out Natalie, enraged that Manna's name had been mentioned.

"Well, it states in your late husband's will that Heyrick Heights was to be left in equal share to the business partnership upon his demise. It states here that Mrs Amanda Jacobs is to take over as the second partner of the partnership. There is no reason given. There isn't a need for a reason: that was Mr Roberts's bequest."

Natalie was shattered. She steadied herself by holding on to the edge of Allworth's desk as she shakily got up from the chair. Darius Cherry rose at the same time to assist her.

"Leave me alone, Darius. I'm fine, just fine." Natalie made for the door.

"Just one more thing, Mrs Roberts. There's the question of your inheritance. And your settlement cheque."

Without turning around, Natalie froze. She closed her eyes and waited to hear her fate.

"Mrs Roberts, won't you sit down, please?" Allworth guided the bewildered Natalie back to the chair and sat her down.

"The figure in full and final settlement of your late husband's estate takes into account that the partnership invested a lot in property. It doesn't leave much in the way of actual cash. Here are the figures." He placed a document in front of Natalie for her to peruse.

Natalie hastily took a glance at the sheet of paper. She shook her head in disbelief.

"What happened to the £1.5 million? How come it only equates to this paltry sum?"

"As I previously mentioned, Mrs Roberts, the partnership tied much of the monies up in property, Heyrick Heights being the main investment, along with a few other houses and commercial properties. The sum of £135,000 is the cash amount Mr Roberts had in his private bank account and which he has left to you and your daughter, Calico. I have a cheque here for you to take today." Allworth flapped the cheque under Natalie's nose.

She glared in anger at Allworth. "That isn't the same as the £1.5 million, is it? For God's sake! What was he thinking?"

"It was your late husband's wish. Mr Cherry and Mrs Jacobs now comprise the partnership. Mrs Jacobs has yet to be informed of the situation. Unfortunately, I am not aware of your financial position, Mrs Roberts, but I suggest you speak to a financial advisor." He offered his hand to Nat to shake but she refused. "Well, if you have no further queries, Mrs Roberts, I wish you a very good afternoon."

Allworth got up from his chair and invited Natalie to follow him. Darius Cherry stood too.

"I'll catch up soon, Nat. You know, about the *other* business. See you!"

Natalie grabbed the cheque and stuffed it into her handbag. She marched out of the office and slammed the door behind her. Tears poured down her cheeks as she blindly made her way to her 4x4. She revved the engine and spun out of the car park like a demon. She had been wronged, well and truly wronged, and she had no way of escape. Her best friend and her lover were in a business partnership. The worse blow of all was Heyrick Heights wasn't hers. She began to worry about what Darius Cherry would do about her continuing to live there. The future wasn't clear to her at all.

She reached the farm and blindly ran from the 4x4 into the kitchen. She fell into the armchair by the Aga and sobbed her heart out. Her cat, Nell, came to sit on her lap, trying to console her distraught mistress. However, it would take more than a cat's love and affection to sort out the mess that Natalie was on the brink of being submerged in.

She spent the night in the kitchen with three bottles of wine, the letter from the solicitor and the pile of unopened letters scattered around the floor.

Chapter Eight

The following week, Leya opened the letter addressed to her with a horse-shaped letter opener. It was from Darius Cherry. She read it carefully and then passed it to her father, who was sat opposite her at the kitchen table.

"He's started the ball rolling then." Mr Martin gave the letter back to Leya who read it again for the second time. "Manna should have received a copy of this today. That will set the fireworks blazing at Littlebridge."

"Am I doing the right thing, Dad? This seems so surreal to me. Little old me, involved in a massive compensation claim." Leya still remained unsure about her decision.

"You had to do it, love. Face up to it. Like Natalie said, you don't want to spend your whole life wallowing in misery. When you win it will make things seem a lot better. You can plan your future then, can't you?"

"Yeah, suppose so. Oh well, I can't back out of it now. Let's hope Nat keeps her word or I'll be in deep trouble." Leya sipped her coffee and placed the letter on the table.

Her collar bone was healing well; the hospital was pleased with her progress following the latest x-ray. Leya had continued with her physio sessions and was encouraged by the therapist's report.

The telephone rang and it was Jude.

"Are you up for a visit today, Leya?" she asked. "I'll come up at lunchtime if that's okay?"

"Cool, see you then." Leya replaced the receiver and looked at her father. "Jude obviously doesn't know anything about my claim. I'm going to tell her when she comes here," Leya decided.

"No reason why not, and it's best if you tell her rather than she learns of it through hearsay."

Mr Martin got up from the table and tidied away the breakfast things. Leya got up as well and walked to the back door.

"I need to get some fresh air, Dad."

She strolled into the compact, well-kept garden and breathed in the morning air. The temperature was warm. It was a typical summer morning. The garden was adorned with dozens of colourful flowers. Seedlings had erupted within the vegetable patch, which was Mr Martin's pride and joy. He spent many happy hours tending and weeding there.

She walked around the perimeter of the garden and looked at the brightly coloured bedding plants. Their beauty gave Leya a lift and she again breathed in deeply. She looked at the bird feeders that had been freshly filled with peanuts and wild bird seed and noticed a couple of blackbirds standing quietly in the bushes, watching her progress across the lawn. They continued foraging for food when she had passed by.

Leya returned to the kitchen and sat heavily down at the table again. She sighed and glanced at the letter. It was amazing how one item of post could affect someone's entire life. One minute, life was normal, but the next it was full of dread and the unknown.

For Manna, her troubles were just beginning.

Manna opened her morning mail at the breakfast table. She immediately stopped eating. Callum had poured a black coffee and was watching the news on the television in the kitchen.

"I think you'd better take a look at this." Manna sounded cold.

Callum grabbed his cup and made his way to where Manna sat. She was holding a piece of toast in one hand, taking in what she had just read. Callum took the letter.

'Dear Mr and Mrs Jacobs,

Re: Claim for compensation – Miss Leya Martin vs. Mr C and Mrs A Jacobs

I am writing to inform you that the above-mentioned claimant has filed a claim for compensation following her riding accident whilst in your employment. Please find attached details of the claim and of the report received....'

Callum looked pale and gave the letter back to Manna.

"The little bitch! How can she claim compensation? It was an accident! How can she have the audacity to sue when she caused the death of my horse with her dangerous driving? I cannot believe that girl!" Manna got up from the table and drew a hand angrily through her hair. "What are we going to do, Callum?"

She began to pace the room, her mind blindly thinking of what action they would have to take.

"I think we need to sit down and talk this through before anything else. Who is acting for her? Oh, I might have guessed." Callum looked down at the signatory. "Darius *bloody* Cherry of all people. How the hell can she afford him?" Callum sat down and tapped the kitchen table with his fingers.

"What about the public liability insurance we've got on the yard? That'll cover it by loads, surely?" Manna was thinking aloud.

"Yes, it should do. But don't forget, I altered the policy earlier in the year—"

"You did *what*?" Manna blazed, turning to Callum in disbelief.

"The policy, I altered it. Reduced the premium and cover. It was costing too much, Manna. I had to make some sacrifices, don't you remember?" Callum replied, looking alarmed. "Why? How much does she want to claim?"

"She is intending to sue us for half a million quid!" Manna returned and slammed her fist on the table, making the cups jolt and spill their contents.

"Oh hell! Why *so* much? She's only a bloody groom!" He looked down at the floor in disbelief.

"Yes and a smart one, by all accounts! Got her head screwed on. Or rather, someone has encouraged her and told her what to do!"

Manna walked to the window and stared into the garden. A clutch of blue tits evacuated their feeder in alarm at her sudden appearance.

"Should we speak to her and come to an agreement, do you think?" Callum suggested.

"It's possible, I suppose. But we'll have to speak with our solicitor. I'll phone him in a while and get an appointment." Manna walked out of the kitchen and into the living room. "I've got this bloody show at the weekend and this will certainly put paid to that! It's the Blenheim qualifier too. How the hell can I concentrate with all this going on?" she roared to an empty room.

Callum heard Manna's outburst and shook his head in disbelief. He hoped that she might have refrained from even thinking about her beloved horse show but no, true to form, she had immediately thought of herself and nothing else.

"I give up!" Callum got up from the table and grabbed his coat.

"Where are you going?" Manna heard him in the hallway.

"Out! Just out!" He slammed the front door behind him.

Manna burst into tears and threw herself on to the settee. She was unaware that George Trippit had let himself into the kitchen.

"Everything all right, Mrs J?"

Manna sat up abruptly and wiped her face. Clearing her throat and composing herself, she called out, "Er, yes, George. Help yourself to a coffee. I'll be there in a minute."

She straightened her hair and walked to the mirror over the fireplace and checked to see if she was respectable.

"All set for tomorrow?" Manna breezed into kitchen and smiled convincingly. She collected the solicitor's letter that was prominently lying on the table and folded it in half, away from George's prying eyes.

"Yes, and I've called on Natalie and she's okay to come too," he said as he slurped greedily at his coffee.

"Good. Well, I've just got to make some phone calls and then we can start getting things sorted out for the show. Have you got much more to do outside?" she asked brightly.

"Only a few odd jobs. I should be done by lunchtime." George thoughtfully scratched his chin. "Yes, I should be done by then."

"Great. Well, I'll see you back here at lunchtime." Manna collected her mobile phone and went into the study and closed the door behind her. She heaved a sigh and threw the letter onto her desk.

"Right, Leya! You want a fight? You've got one!" she muttered to herself as she dialled her solicitor.

oOo

Jude arrived as promised at Leya's house at lunchtime. She was encouraged to find it was Leya who opened the door to her.

"Hi! You're looking much better this week!" Jude grinned and gave her a gentle hug.

"Come in. Would you like a coffee?" Leya asked and ushered her into the living room.

"Yes, I've brought my lunch with me. Hope you don't mind." Jude sat down on the armchair and started to unpeel the foil from her pack of sandwiches.

"No, I don't mind. Actually, I need to tell you something. But you must promise not to say *anything* to *anyone*, okay?"

Jude stopped unwrapping her sandwiches.

"Sounds ominous," she concluded and looked straight at Leya.

Leya took a deep breath.

"I'm suing the yard, for compensation," she announced and waited for Jude's reaction.

"What? Leya! That's seriously major, you know. Who put you up to it?"

Leya looked startled. "No-one! I mean, it *was* suggested by someone that I should, because of my arm and the paralysis and all that. I may not be able to work again, not in a yard at least, so I've got to think about my future."

Jude swallowed heavily and thought for a few moments.

"Someone's put you up to this, haven't they? You'd never have thought about that on your own initiative!"

"Maybe, but it makes sense, don't you think? Anyway, Manna's insurance will cover the costs."

"Oh, if *you* say so. So, how much are you claiming?" Jude reasoned.

"Half a million pounds," Leya uttered in a quiet voice.

"Bloody hell! Five hundred grand! Dream on, Leya! That's a huge sum of money. Who suggested that?"

"Well, Nat—" Leya began.

"Oh no, don't tell me, please! Not Natalie, surely? It gets worse! What the hell is she doing getting involved in this? If only Manna knew!"

"You *must* promise not to say anything!" Leya moved towards Jude and held her arm. "I had to tell someone, and I thought you would be the one to keep your mouth shut." She looked desperately at Jude.

"You have put me in a really terrible position, telling me all this. Why couldn't you have told someone else? I work for Manna! I could get the sack over this!"

Jude got up from the armchair and discarded her sandwiches. She no longer felt hungry. She paced around the room, cudgelling her brain for answers.

"Do Callum and Manna know about it?" she asked at length.

"The letter would have been delivered this morning. I got a copy of it through the post."

"No wonder I haven't seen either of them this morning. Manna's due to go away tomorrow to the Blenheim qualifier. Shit! It's going to be great fun, isn't it? What has Nat got to gain out of this anyway? She's Manna's best friend! Or was!"

"She wouldn't tell me," Leya answered and then kept quiet.

"She must be really pissed with Manna over something. This could finish Littlebridge!" Jude shook her head. "I'd better get back to work. Leya, I don't envy you at all. Please think seriously about what you're doing. Don't forget, Manna hasn't spoken to you about Del and the horsebox accident. This will add fuel to her fire! She could quite easily press charges against you for dangerous driving! Counter-sue you!" Jude warned. "I'll let myself out, see you," and she disappeared out of the house as fast as she could.

Leya drew back the net curtains and watched Jude march off to her car. She felt tears welling up inside and she headed up to her room. Her parents were out shopping so she would be able to compose herself before they returned.

Jude started her car, still reeling with amazement over what she'd just heard.

"Stupid cow! Stupid, stupid cow!" she muttered and revved the engine in anger. She sped out of the road, wheels squealing and spinning.

oOo

It was late morning when Manna put the phone down after speaking with her solicitor. After a lengthy discussion, he advised Manna to arrange a meeting with Leya to discuss her claim.

"I sense Ms Martin has been prompted by another to claim for such an excessive sum, Mrs Jacobs," he airily confirmed.

Manna reluctantly agreed and rang Leya. Leya answered swiftly.

"Leya? It's Manna Jacobs. I've received a letter this morning from your solicitor advising you want to sue us. I want to arrange a meeting with you to have a chat. When can we do this?" Manna was calm as she spoke but not so when she received Leya's response.

"Manna, I can't discuss this with you. You need to go through my solicitor. Make an appointment with your own brief and he'll advise you," Leya coolly announced.

"So you aren't prepared to meet to speak with me about this nonsense?" Manna stood firm but there was no response. "As you wish, Leya. Goodbye!"

Manna slammed down the phone and threw her hands over her face, unable to comprehend Leya's attitude. She screamed aloud.

"Erghhhh! *Who* has got to you?" she fumed.

She grabbed hold of the letter from Darius Cherry and phoned his office. His response was the same as Leya's.

"Mrs Jacobs, with respect, I have sent you this letter on the understanding that Ms Martin will be claiming compensation from you for the accident and injuries she has subsequently received which were caused by your horse. There will be no meeting between us. The matter is being referred to court. You will receive a court date in due course. With respect, please do not telephone my office again. Please let your solicitor liaise with me. That is the correct procedure. After all, this is a claim for negligence."

"Surely this is a conflict of interest!" Manna protested that Darius Cherry was acting in his official capacity as lawyer and not as her business partner. "And what about my dead horse?"

"I'm sorry Mrs Jacobs, but I am not prepared to discuss this any further. As for the loss of your horse, I am very sorry, but that doesn't involve me."

Manna slammed the phone down in disbelief. She drank in Darius Cherry's words... Court date. She shook her head with mixed emotions. She was seething with anger over the whole matter. She was upset that a situation like this had arisen and furious that Callum was making her deal with it alone. He had walked away to bury his head in the sand. All she could think of was the amendment Callum had made to their insurance policy, just a few months beforehand, to save money. Now this claim was going to cost them dearly. She phoned Callum's mobile. It rang for ages until he finally picked up.

"What do you want?" he angrily responded.

"Where are you?"

"I can't see that matters?" he rudely returned.

Manna could hear background chatter and knew he must be at The Black Sheep.

"Don't forget I'm going away this afternoon, staying overnight. Do you remember? It's my school reunion. I'll be back tomorrow morning. We'll talk then perhaps, before I leave for the show." Manna couldn't be bothered to speak with Callum any more.

"Bye!" He threw his mobile on to the bar. "Women! Or rather, wives!" he announced to the gathered crowd of locals and they all laughed with him, briefly acknowledged his plight and continued their drinks and gossiping.

Chapter Nine

After his visit to The Black Sheep, Callum ambled back to Littlebridge. He was immediately welcomed by Tag jumping up at his leg in her usual enthusiastic greeting. He patted the top of her head then gently pushed her away. Tag was puzzled. Callum always had time for her; he always played with her so she couldn't understand why things were so different today. He sighed and continued to walk down the line of stables, hands in pockets, scuffing stray pieces of straw with his shoes as he went.

Jude was in the tack room cleaning Ariel's tack. She looked up to see Callum in the doorway. He smiled but didn't speak.

"Hi Callum. Everything all right?" She wiped her hands with an old bath towel and threw it across the back of a chair. Tag arrived and stood with Callum, looking up at him with her bright, intelligent eyes and ears pricked.

"No, not really," he replied, looking straight into Jude's eyes.

Jude was surprised. He usually babbled on endlessly, making her laugh with his dry jokes. By the look on his face, she sensed he was troubled.

"Well, I've finished preparing Ariel's tack and was going to put the kettle on. Fancy a coffee?" She walked over to the shelf to retrieve the kettle.
Callum stopped her.

"Yes. I, er, mean no. Well, not here. Do you mind if we go back to your caravan?" He waited apprehensively for her approval.

"Oh well, okay, if that's what you prefer, okay." Jude was a little shocked. She placed the kettle back onto the shelf.

Callum walked out towards the sand school. Jude turned off the light in the tack room and shut the door behind her. She called to Tag, but she was already with Callum. She was puzzled by Callum's behaviour. She concluded that it must be because of Leya's compensation claim. Perhaps he wanted to get inside information. Jude decided she would have to think carefully before she spoke to him since she didn't want to cause any problems for Leya or, for that matter, for Callum. She felt a loyalty to them both.

She was still apprehensive when they reached the caravan. Callum stood aside as she opened the door. Tag ran straight inside and curled up on her tartan bed, underneath the table.

Jude went in, threw her keys on to the table and reached for the kettle.

"Coffee? Tea?" she asked, without turning around.

"Got anything stronger? A Scotch maybe?" Callum asked, looking down at the pieces of straw and dried grass that peppered the worn carpet.

Tag grunted as she settled down to sleep.

Jude frantically searched her cupboards and found a half empty bottle of Cognac. She attracted Callum's attention.

"How about brandy?"

"Yes, that'll be fine," was the lacklustre response.

She wiped the glass on her jodhpurs to hide any water stains from her poor attempt at washing up. She filled another glass with orange juice and took them over to the sofa where Callum sat expressionless. The brandy was liberally unmeasured, the glass brimming half full.

"So." Jude sat on the sofa and tucked her legs underneath herself and tried to get comfortable. "What's so bad that we have to talk here? It's not like you, is it?" she asked, sipping her orange juice.

Callum drained the brandy and took a deep breath.

"Have you, um, spoken to Leya lately?" he asked and looked directly at Jude.

"About a week ago, I suppose," Jude replied. She pensively awaited the next question.

"Did you know that she is planning to sue us?"

Jude looked genuinely shocked. Callum was her employer and he shouldn't be discussing this subject with staff. It was highly confidential. She felt uneasy.

"Um, I don't really think it's any of my business—" she began.
He swiftly interrupted her.

"Did you *know*?" he asked insistently.

"No… um, yes, I did… do. I know that she isn't happy about doing it, but she made me swear not to say anything!" Jude felt very uneasy and fidgeted in her chair.

Callum continued, "Well, she is doing it, and for half a million quid. She, or rather her brief, reckons it was the yard's fault that Ariel was unfit to be ridden and that she was made to ride the horse. And she has got a bloody good lawyer behind her who knows exactly what he's doing. Screwing us for as much as he can. We haven't got that sort of money. She'll ruin us and I'm worried. Really fucking worried."

Jude was slightly taken aback by Callum's outburst. She felt awkward speaking to him as an equal rather than as her boss.

"Have you talked this over with Manna?" Jude got up and poured Callum another glass of brandy.

"Yes, but you know what she's like. She appears not to give a shit! Buries her head in the proverbial, just waiting for it to go away or, rather, leaving me to deal with everything. It took her long enough to speak to the police about the horsebox accident." He swirled his glass in circular motions making the brandy edge towards the top of the glass. He looked across to Jude. He noticed the look of concern on her face.

"You're insured though, aren't you?" she questioned and sat back on the sofa.

"Yeah, but only for third party liability, usual stuff. I amended the policy to a lesser amount earlier this year, when it came up for renewal. It was only meant to be a temporary measure till we got a decent income. All, of course, depending on Manna getting enough new clients on board so we can fund her eventing. We haven't had this problem before — claims, I mean. Not on this sort of scale. This type of thing never happened years ago. It seems that everyone is trying to get on the compensation bandwagon these days. Must be the influence of the Americans and their compo culture. You know the sort of thing – fall over in the street so sue someone. Break a fingernail opening a packet of biscuits – sue the shop. Bloody hell! I never thought we'd get hit with this sort of claim." He gulped more brandy.

"So your policy won't cover the amount she wants to sue you for then?" Jude thought aloud.

"No. We're quarter of a million quid short!" He shrugged his shoulders in despair. "What am I going to do, Jude? I'm screwed, aren't I?"

He looked up at Jude. She could see tears welling up in his eyes and it made her feel compelled to comfort him as best she could. She put her hand on his shoulder. He gently placed his head against her body.

"Surely you have a good brief too, to get things sorted out? You're not alone with this. I had no idea that Leya was going to claim so much. I know she's got no use of her arm but surely you can fight this?"

"Good briefs cost a huge amount of cash, though," he replied and buried his face in her shoulder. He was leaning his whole weight against her.

"You shouldn't give up so easily," Jude soothed him. "You're strong. You'll get through this. I know you will!"

Callum looked up at Jude, his eyes wet with tears. "You're so sweet, Jude. I knew I could speak to you and rely on your support. It's more than I get from Manna. Even now she's away living it up at some sort of school reunion. She's left me here to sort this mess out."

He broke off whilst he composed himself. Jude ripped a piece of kitchen towel from its roll and thrust it into Callum's hand.

"Here, come on, don't let the bastards grind you down!" She held him close to her.

"Thanks, Jude," Callum got up from the sofa. "I'll get things underway. Get my lawyer on the case."

"There you are! Positive thoughts already!" Jude reassured him and patted his shoulder.

"I'd better go. I'm sorry I've depressed you with my problems," he smiled and, without thinking, drew her close to him and held her in his arms for a moment.

Jude was taken aback by his actions but didn't stop him. She returned the embrace and placed her arms around his shoulders. He drew back and, in doing so, gently kissed the top of her head.

"You mean a lot to me, Jude. More than you know," he whispered into her hair.

Jude felt a surge of emotion flow through her body like an electric current working its way from her head to her toes. They broke apart and, for a few seconds, gazed thoughtfully into each other's eyes. Callum leant forward and kissed her gently on the lips.

He spoke softly, "I shouldn't have done that."

"Why not?" she whispered back.

"I don't know. But, I want to do it again." He kissed her tenderly on the lips once more, with injected passion. Callum held her gently in his arms as the passion ignited into a frantic rush of enthusiastic lustful kisses.

"Jude. I need you," Callum gasped between kisses. "I really need you."

Jude was split between wild, lustful emotion and ecstasy, the unknown and the must have. She pushed Callum away. Her sensible mind was thinking of the dire consequences.

"This isn't right, Callum. What about Manna?" she tried to reason as Callum kissed her face and progressed to her neck.

"Who cares about Manna? She's not here and, when she is, she doesn't really care about me. She cares for herself and the horses," he insisted.

"I think you'd better leave, for all our sakes," Jude replied firmly.

"Is that what you really want, Jude?" Callum was playing mind games.

"No… yes, oh, I don't know. This is all happening too quickly," she blurted out.

"Okay, I'll put it another way. Do you *want* me to leave?" Callum continued.

Jude looked at Callum for a moment and then smiled. "No, I want you to stay." She ran her hand through his hair and he turned his face to kiss it.

They wrapped their arms around one another and Jude felt her inhibitions evaporate. She hadn't felt like this for years. It was a feeling that she loved and realised how much she had missed it. They stumbled into the bedroom in silence and lay on the bed.

"Jude, I really want to make love to you!" he breathed softly and kissed her neck.

"So, what's stopping you?" she whispered.

"Nothing," he replied and caressed her breasts with both hands, moving around her body and enveloping her closer to him.

Jude closed her eyes. She couldn't believe what was happening. It seemed like a dream, and one she hoped she would never wake up from. Callum was so gentle and affectionate. She drew him closer to her and, without speaking, they made love. Afterwards, Callum cradled Jude in his arms. He stared at the ceiling and noticed a gathering of spiders' webs in each of the corners.

"It's about time you cleared the cobwebs away," he commented.

Jude smiled ironically to herself. "I think perhaps I might have just done that!" Callum hugged her tightly and kissed the top of her head. They both dozed off.

oOo

Jude had already left the caravan when Callum reached across the empty bed. He rolled over and felt a warm, hairy body beside him. Tag had sneaked onto the bed, curled up and fallen asleep. Callum smiled and patted the dog. He couldn't believe his infidelity. He thought about what had happened. He realised bleakly that his feelings for Manna were very distant. He had taken a liking to Jude the day she arrived to work at Littlebridge. He was impressed by the way she threw herself completely into her work and he loved her commitment to every one of the horses within the yard.

He lay in bed and relived the previous night's passionate encounter. He hadn't felt so good in years. His sexual relationship with Manna was obligatory and there wasn't any spontaneity or excitement. Making love with Jude had re-awoken his own sexuality and he realised that he wanted her more than he wanted Manna.

He got up reluctantly and stretched his arms high above his head. Tag stirred in her sleep, her paws moved and she began to yap whilst still sleeping. Callum laughed and watched the Jack Russell as she chased imaginary rabbits in her dreams. He stroked her head and continued to dress.

He walked into kitchen to find a note propped up against a dirty coffee mug. He picked it up, rubbed his eyes and read.

'Dear C,

Sorry, I had to leave you. Didn't want to but if I stayed, the boss would have sacked me! Sorry, you sacked me last night, didn't you!

Miss you,

J. XX'

He shook his head and grinned at her wit. He screwed up the paper and lobbed it towards the waste bin. He missed his target and bent down to retrieve the paper. As he reached down, he heard footsteps outside the caravan. He sank to the floor and froze. Surely it wouldn't be his luck to be discovered after only one night of torrid sex with his wife's head groom? He held his breath and quickly glanced around him to make sure there was no evidence of him staying the night. He was, thankfully, dressed. He only needed to put on his coat. As he did so, he thought frantically. What excuse would he make? Maybe something to do with the plumbing? Oh shit! The door slowly opened and a voice floated across to him.

"Thought I'd find you here," the female voice announced.

He swallowed slowly, planning his excuse until the familiarity of the voice cut through his panic.

"Oh! It's you!" He looked up at Jude who stood in the doorway with her hands on her hips, holding a riding crop. She threw back her head and laughed.

"Did you think it was Manna coming to look for you?" she teased and walked over to where he was crouched.

"Come here! You nearly gave me a coronary!" He threw his arms about her and held her snugly in his grasp.

"I tell you what. You give me the day off, and I'll spend the time with you. How's about that then, boss?" she queried and teased the crop across Callum's shoulders, around his face and finally towards his trouser zip.

"How about I give you a good whipping for being so... so cheeky, young lady?"

He grabbed hold of the crop and spanked Jude playfully on her buttocks. She shrieked at each slap in mock agony.

Callum chased her up and down the caravan waving the crop high in the air and hooting with laughter. Tag woke up and started barking at the frenzied action and ran up and down behind Callum, trying to give him a nip on the leg. Callum and Jude collapsed with laughter into each other's arms and made their way into the bedroom. Jude let Tag out of the door and quickly closed it behind her so she couldn't get back inside. Tag ran straight up to the yard in search of an unsuspecting rat or other verminous victim.

There was a gorgeous bloke lying in her bed, waiting for her. It didn't seem real and Jude worried that she would suddenly wake up. She started to unzip her riding boots but Callum stopped her.

"Leave them on," he insisted and placed his arms behind his head. "I find it a bit of a turn on!"

"Do you?" Jude asked and knelt on the bed. She leaned across and kissed Callum's lips. "Well. Let's see what effect they have… shall we?"

He took hold of her shoulder and pulled her closer to him. Inspecting her face and body endlessly, Callum kissed Jude and they began another steamy session of sexual exploration.

oOo

Tag was in the livery yard when she noticed the car driving towards Littlebridge. She started to bark; her *warning bark*, as Jude called it. Tag stopped barking as she recognised the occupant who opened the driver's door and stepped casually out.

"Hello Tag!" Manna bent down to stroke Tag's head. "Where's your mummy?" she asked, as though she was expecting Tag to answer her question.

Manna stood up and called, "Jude, are you there?"

Silence. Manna found it odd that Jude wasn't in the yard. She walked along the line of stables and peered in each one. They were all mucked out, fresh bedding laid, water in buckets. All finished. The yard had been swept clean and everywhere was deserted. She shrugged her shoulders and took her mobile phone from her handbag and dialled Jude. It diverted straight to her voicemail. Perhaps Jude was out on a hack with Berkley, but she usually worked him later in the day.

Manna decided to walk down to the paddock to see if Jude was in her caravan. She reached the door and was about to lift her hand to knock when she heard Jude cackle with laughter. Manna decided to knock. The laughter instantly ceased and there was a loud bump against the side of the caravan. Eventually the door slowly opened.

"Hi… Manna! How are you?" breezed Jude. "Come in, I'm just having a quick breakfast. Do you want a coffee?"

She welcomed Manna inside and ushered her into the living area, slamming the bedroom door shut as she went past it.

"Hi. Yes thanks, I'd love a coffee." Manna made her way to the sofa and moved a couple of cushions and various magazine and wrappers. She perched on the edge of the seat. "I see you've had a tidy up. Are you feeling okay?"

Manna observed that the caravan was not as messy as it normally was. The CD collection was tidied away and there was an absence of spent coffee cups, dinner plates and cutlery that normally lived on the floor.

"Oh, yeah! Just a mad few minutes," Jude laughed nervously and kept an eye on the bedroom door. "Did you say coffee, Manna? Sorry, I'm a bit crazy today! Must be the time of the month, you know, hormones." Jude giggled like a naughty child.

"Hmm," Manna mused, staring around her.

Jude dropped a coffee mug on the floor and it smashed into pieces.

"Oh shit! That was my best one!" She angrily picked up the fragments of china and threw them into the waste bin.

"Life is a shit sometimes, though, isn't it, Jude?" Manna's voice had become slightly irritated. "Especially as I can't seem to find my husband. He's just never around when I want him."

"That's men for you, Manna." Jude poured boiling water into the two remaining clean coffee cups, her back turned to her boss.

"Yes, I suppose so. He's either gone to Culverton or he's shagging some unsuspecting trollop," Manna announced and flicked her hair in disgust.

Jude felt uneasy as she handed the coffee to Manna, who in turn smugly thanked her.

"Like I say, that's men for you. That's why I don't bother to get involved with them," she added and looked defiantly at Manna, her eyes boring into her.

"Don't you miss it, Jude?" Manna threw the question directly. Her blue eyes were searching for a chink of evidence. She made a face as she sipped at the coffee.

"Sex? No... not really. It's been ages, years for me in fact, and well, what I don't have, I don't miss. How about you?"

Jude bravely turned the question back to Manna, seeing as she was acting strangely.

"Well," said Manna, getting up off the sofa, "if you *do* see him, tell him I want to speak to him, will you? Oh, and thanks for the chat."

Jude followed Manna to the door keeping her eye on the bedroom door. As she opened the door Manna turned to Jude. "Just one more thing: what were you laughing at just now?"

"Me? Laughing? Must have been at the radio — there was a stupid sitcom on and it was hilarious!"

"Hmm," Manna replied, unconvinced. "I'll see you in the yard. Can you get Ariel tacked up for me?"

She closed the door before Jude had a chance to speak. Jude lunged towards the door and turned the key. Her heart was in her throat and she felt nauseous. She opened the bedroom door.

"Bloody hell! Was that close or what?" she exclaimed and bounced on to the bed, making the springs twist and groan. "Callum? Where are you?"

The room was deserted.

"That was way too close!" came a voice from the direction of the built-in wardrobe. Jude peered across the room and saw a forefinger holding the door closed. She laughed aloud.

"It's all right, you can come out now," she reassured him.

Callum reappeared in his boxer shorts and shirt.

"Shit! What the hell is she doing back so early?"

Jude went pale. "I don't know, but did you hear her going on? She was talking as though she *expected* you to be here. She was either pissed or she knows something!"

"She can't know anything, we only…" he broke off. "Do you think… it might be Randy?"

Jude looked at Callum and grinned.

"George, you mean? And how do *you* know we call him *Randy*?" she asked with keen interest.

"There's not much I don't know about this place!" he joshed.

"Well, he's always up her arse and you never know where he will appear next," Jude giggled. She thought for a moment. "Perhaps she's just calling my bluff. Anyway, you'd better go quickly cos she's looking for you."

Callum kissed Jude and she embraced him. Eventually and reluctantly unpeeling himself from her clutch, he finished dressing.

"I loved being with you and I want to see you again very soon!" Callum stroked Jude's cheek.

"You'd better behave yourself and don't keep disappearing!" Jude playfully slapped his backside. She turned and faced him with a deep, searching look. "So, I'm not a one night stand then?"

Callum looked alarmed at her statement. He didn't see her smirking at first then, when he did, his face broke into a lovely, warm smile.

"You wait!" He wagged his finger at her. She grasped it and drew him closer to her.

"I can't wait! When are you coming over again?" She held his face in her hands.

"I'll text you," he promised and kissed her cheek. "Keep an eye out for her ladyship. Don't rock the boat!" he added.

"Go away!" Jude pushed him gently towards the door. Callum turned and looked lustfully at her, "Thanks, Jude. For saving me from insanity."

Jude shook her head and smiled.

"You're very welcome," she murmured and closed the door.

Callum walked through the paddocks and breathed in the mid-morning air. There were swathes of gossamer strewn across the field like images of wispy clouds. He thrust his hands into his pockets and sloped his shoulders downwards. He caught sight of Tag running around in the other field and decided to walk around the back of the house, out of view. He rehearsed his excuse for when he eventually met up with Manna, who would inevitably quiz him, over and over. His mind returned to Jude and he sighed in contentment.

He reached for his mobile phone and dialled Manna's number. Regretfully, she answered and his heart sank.

"Hi, are you home? I'm in town, I'll be back in a while." He tried smiling as he spoke so as not to raise any suspicion.

"How are you, Callum?" Manna asked.

"Fine thanks. Did you have a good night?" he responded, walking through the fields towards the roadway, out of view.

"Not bad, caught up with a few old friends, you know, usual sort of thing at a school reunion. How about you?"

"Oh stayed in, messed about, you know…" He smiled when he thought of Jude.

"Okay, see you soon. Don't forget I'm off to the show after lunch today," Manna reminded him.

"Oh right, yeah, I'll see you before you go." Callum made a face as he thought of Manna and her beloved shows.

Manna nodded thoughtfully. She placed her mobile phone in her pocket. She stepped out from behind the line of stables where she had watched Callum leave Jude's caravan and walk briskly across the fields towards the road.

Chapter Ten

Manna packed up the last of her clothes into her bulging tan leather holdall. She fumbled with the zip and pushed vigorously with her knee on the top to ensure all her belongings didn't suddenly explode out of it. She glanced at her watch. It was 11:50. Her head ached with stress fatigue. She rubbed her temples with each hand and blinked a few times. She opened her bedroom cabinet and found a packet of aspirins and thrust two into her mouth without water. She shuddered as the pills left a bitter aftertaste. She hated taking any form of tablet as they always made her want to retch. She had a very busy weekend ahead of her and she needed to be fresh and focussed for the show.

She walked across to the window and gazed out onto the yard. She noticed the tack room door was open and heard Jude calling out to Tag. She saw Jude ferrying various cooling rugs and exercise sheets into the horsebox that stood in the middle of the yard, tailgate open, ready to receive its equine passengers.

Manna looked at her watch once more. It was noon and Callum was still not home. Despite everything that was whirling around in her head, she'd noticed he had become very distant. He didn't care to engage in any sort of conversation with her if he could avoid doing so, and when he did, she could tell he was obviously distracted. She sighed as she thought of the impending court appearance. Leya had made their life very difficult, particularly in light of her refusal to settle the matter out of court. Manna had broached the subject with Callum but each time he had insisted he was needed elsewhere and deliberately made himself scarce.

Manna pushed the court case to the back of her mind. It would be hopeless going to an event with this burden. Her concentration needed to be one hundred percent on the job of qualifying for the competition at Blenheim International Horse Trials.

Ariel was in peak fitness having fully recovered from the accident. She was on exceptionally good form. Manna had spent many weeks on her preparation. Jude had been a major contributor to the fitness regime as well. She had religiously hacked Ariel on trot rides twice a day for the past few weeks, ensuring that her muscles were continually toned and her stamina kept up to its maximum. Ariel would need to put in her best if she and Manna were to qualify. Manna knew that if she did qualify, it would ensure a constant flow of stabling and training fees from clients wanting to keep their horses at her yard. She had to rebuild her reputation and respect that had dwindled since the announcement of Leya's bid to claim compensation from her. The news had spread rapidly amongst the locals in Malsham and the surrounding villages.

Manna left from the window and collected her bags. She edged her holdall gingerly to the hallway. She dialled Callum's number on her mobile as she made her way downstairs and, to her amazement, he answered.

"Are you coming home soon?" Manna enquired, entering the kitchen as she spoke.

"Yeah, won't be long now," came the response.

"So, I'll see you later then? Will you'll be home before I leave?"

"Should be," Callum lied.

"Hope so," Manna returned.

She ended the call and tapped her phone against her hip in thoughtfulness. She wasn't convinced that Callum was being truthful. She sighed. She was leaving Littlebridge in less than two hours, just after lunch. She wanted to head off in plenty of time. She had reserved two stables at the showground to enable the horses to settle in before the competition the following day.

Manna was in a dilemma. She had initially wanted Jude to travel as groom but had since decided that she would be better staying at the yard as the horses could not be left unattended. On the other hand, now she wasn't keen on leaving Jude alone with Callum, not after what she'd seen the other day. She deliberated: what was more important, the horses or Callum? Manna walked into the yard and called for Jude.

"I'm really sorry. I can't seem to get any sense out of Callum and I can't rely on him being here over the weekend, therefore I need you to stay here to look after everything for me. I know it's rough. But, I've got no choice. I know I can rely on you. You know how important the horses are to me. Especially Fig."

Jude looked as convincingly disappointed as she could.

"That's a real bummer, Manna. I was so looking forward to going with you. But I know, you can't rely on blokes, can you? Don't worry, it's not a problem. I'll stay," she announced and managed a weak smile that looked more like a grin.

"Thanks, you're a star. Take the key to the house. I want you to stay there for the weekend, Tag as well. It will be good to have the house lived in. Deter the burglars, you know. Callum might turn up, but well, who knows," Manna added.

"Thanks Manna. It'll be nice to live in a house for a change," Jude smiled. "Who are you going to get to groom for you?" she asked.

"I've just asked George. He'll be able to drive the horsebox for me too. Oh, and I asked Natalie to come along as well. What do you think?" She looked at Jude for her approval.

"They'll be great fun and a help too, especially, Ran... eh... George," Jude replied.

"I thought you'd say that," Manna looked relieved. "I phoned Natalie earlier to confirm. I don't think she's doing anything this weekend. She won't let me down even though I haven't given her much notice."

Jude grinned and carried on loading the lorry. She thought of her meeting with Leya and the deceit from Manna's *best friend* Natalie. When Manna was out of sight, Jude punched the air in delight. She was going to have the weekend of her life and the icing on the cake was she would be spending it with *Callum!*

George was delighted when he put the phone down after talking with Manna. He never declined the opportunity to spend a whole weekend with his beloved boss and the chance of spending time with Natalie as well was a bonus. He broke the news to Beryl and she shrugged her shoulders.

"Who am I to stop you, dear?" she announced.

George put his arm around her shoulders.

"Thanks love. You know I couldn't let Manna down, don't you?"

"Of course not, George. Ring me when you get there, and please behave yourself!" Beryl smiled at her husband who had begun to collect some belongings together into a bedraggled rucksack he used for beating. He ushered her out of the way and made a beeline for the sideboard in the dining room where he loaded three bottles of wine and a handful of beer cans into his bag.

"Just in case," was his response as he saw Beryl in the kitchen doorway with her arms folded. She shook her head in silence and turned away. She realised that she would never defeat Manna Jacobs and the magical hold she possessed over her husband. She couldn't fight it. It was not in her good nature to retaliate. If George was happy, that was all that concerned her.

"I'll ring you tonight, love," George said as he kissed Beryl briefly on the forehead.

"Bye, George. Have a nice time and wish Manna good luck." Beryl waved him out of sight as George couldn't get to his car quick enough.

Closing the door behind her, Beryl stood and rested her head against the wall. There were tears brimming in her eyes. She wiped them away and stood in reflection. She hadn't envisaged spending the weekend alone. Her plan of cooking a special meal for their wedding anniversary was now a thing of the past. She walked into the living room and sat heavily down in an armchair and sobbed uncontrollably. George's loyalties clearly didn't lie with their marriage, but with Manna.

Jude had finished loading the horsebox when Manna arrived at the tack room door.

"All packed, Jude?" she enquired, scanning the room for saddles and bridles and tack that might be needed.

"Yep, it's all in there: sweat rugs, cooling rugs, grooming kits, first aid, everything."

"All the feed weighed out ready?" Manna mentally reckoned what amount to take.

"Yes, it's in two separate buckets: one for Ariel, one for Othello. That's for tonight's feed. The rest is bagged up separately and labelled so you know whose is what."

"You're a star, Jude. Thanks a million. Have you seen George?"

"Looks like he's just landed," returned Jude and smiled. "Ra... I mean, George is here!" she announced and looked away to stifle her laugh as she glanced at what George was wearing.

"Oh George! You look *fabulous!*" Manna cried as George appeared. He was wearing plus twos with thick green socks and brogues. On his head was a trilby and he wore a bright yellow waistcoat with a green checked shirt beneath.

"Wow! Watch out ladies!" hooted Jude in laughter as George walked with an air of importance towards them.

"Are we ready to go, Mrs J?" he queried in a serious tone whilst clutching his rucksack and repositioning his trilby after raising it in acknowledgement of the ladies' presence. Suddenly his phone buzzed to indicate a message. He glanced at the phone and his face fell. He looked deflated.

"Yes, all ready, George. Jude is going to load the horses and we're off. We're picking up Nat en route, aren't we?"

"Er, slight problem there, Mrs J. Natalie has just texted me to say that sadly she can't make it after all. Something has come up, but she didn't say what." George was clearly very disappointed.

"What? But she's given us no notice whatsoever! That's a real pain. Still, we have *got* to go now. I can't get anyone else at this late hour unless I make some calls on the way there." Manna was really annoyed at being let down by Natalie, but nothing would stop her competing.

George climbed in the driving seat and started the engine of the horsebox. As it thundered into life, the remaining horses in the yard stopped eating and thrust their heads over the stable doors to see who was going to be the lucky one to be loaded and taken out for a drive. It always amused Jude, but on the other hand she felt sorry for the horses left behind.

With Ariel and Othello safely loaded, Manna checked around for the last time and climbed into the passenger seat. She slammed the door shut and reached for her phone.

"I've got my mobile if you need me, Jude. I'll give it to George when I'm competing. It'll be on most of the time. See you on Monday. Oh… and if you see Callum, can you say goodbye to him for me?"

"Yeah, okay, I will if I see him. Good luck!" Jude called as the horsebox groaned and grunted and puffed out a cloud of smoke as the party set off for the show. George was wearing the largest grin Jude had ever seen. He was in his element.

Jude watched the lorry disappear out of the yard to the top of the lane and she thought of Manna and George spending a whole weekend in each other's company. She ambled back to the tack room and paged through the names on her mobile. She stopped when she reached Callum's name and dialled his number.

"Hi! She's gone, yep, just this minute. See you at the caravan, yeh? In half an hour, great… ooh yeah, so do I!" She giggled and ended the call. She held the mobile close to her chest and sighed aloud. "Ooh, you're gorgeous, Mr Jacobs. If only you knew that!"

She placed her phone into her pocket and walked out into the yard.

"Tag! Come on pups!"

Tag obediently arrived at Jude's side and they made their way to the caravan in the paddock. Jude had only just arrived when she heard the sound of someone walking behind her. She turned around in surprise.

"That was a *quick* half hour!" she exclaimed.

"My half hours are always quicker than everyone else's!" Callum laughed and took Jude into his arms. "I've really missed you," he whispered as he kissed Jude urgently on the lips.

She prised him away so she could take a long, lingering look at him.

"Not as much as I've missed you, Mr Jacobs!"

"I love it when you're so formal," he whispered again, nibbling her cheek and stroking back her hair so he could nuzzle the nape of her neck.

"Come on, let's go inside. I've got a bottle of wine somewhere." Jude released herself from his grasp as he stood spellbound and helpless. He followed her into the caravan.

"Your wish is my command!" he joked and nearly tripped over Tag as she dived headfirst into the caravan between his legs. "For God's sake, Tag! Get out of the way! One day I'll squash you!" Callum was slightly shaken as the terrier made her way to the sofa and promptly bagged the best seat. "I'm sure Tag knows what's going on," Callum said as he climbed carefully into the caravan and took off his jacket and draped it over a chair.

"Course she knows: she knows everything because I tell her everything!" Jude filled two glasses with wine and offered one to Callum. They sat down together and gazed at each other. "Did you know Manna wanted to see you before she left?" Jude asked.

"Yes, I spoke to her a couple of hours ago. I couldn't be bothered to see her. Why should I? She's only thinking about that bloody Blenheim qualifier and the horses. Nothing else matters to her, does it? Just the horses."

"You're right. She's number one, don't you know?"

"Not in my books. She's slipped out of the top ten now. Oh, and guess who's number one?"

"Do I really want to know?" Jude coyly looked into her glass.

"I think you know already. It's you!"

"You daft bugger!" Jude blushed. "Come here and kiss me, you gorgeous bloke!"

"Who? Me?" Callum stood up and lifted his hands high above his head in submission. He held a huge grin on his face.

"Yep, you!" Jude announced and shaped her hands into an imaginary fanfare trumpet. "Why did I just do that?" she looked confused. "There is definitely something about you that makes me go a bit mental!"

"Why thank you, good lady! I would like to thank my mother, my wife for being such a confounded selfish bitch, and finally my lover… that sounds strange," he mused for a few seconds, then continued, "for being, no, I mean for keeping me sane!"

Callum broke off his banter and pulled Jude into his arms. He kissed her tenderly on the lips for a few moments until passion erupted between them and progressed to a lustful endeavour of embracing that led them towards the bedroom. Jude closed the door firmly shut with her foot. They continued to meaningfully kiss each other and fell on to the bed.

Later, Callum awoke to the sound of his mobile phone ringing persistently in his trouser pocket. The sky had darkened into early evening. He leaned over and fumbled with his trousers that lay strewn on the floor.

"Hello?" he murmured, trying not to wake Jude.

"Are you home?" Manna's voice woke him up immediately and he sat up to attention in bed.

"Um, yeah, only just," he replied, rubbing his eyes.

"Have you seen Jude?"

"Yes, I have," he smiled as he turned to look at Jude curled up asleep next to him. The sheets slowly rose and fell as she breathed.

"Everything okay? You sound weird? Just wanted to let you know we've arrived safely. The horses are fine." Manna sounded content.

"Great. Good luck for tomorrow," he returned.

"I told Jude to stay in the house, if you weren't about. You don't mind, do you?"

"No, I don't mind at all," Callum smiled. "See you later, bye."

Callum threw the phone back onto the floor. Jude stirred as she felt him move in the bed.

"Well? How is she?"

"Who gives a shit?" Callum muttered. "Her horses are okay, so bloody what?"

"Ooh, don't get so wound up. You're with me now, for all the weekend, so you'd better get used to it!"

Jude wrapped her legs across Callum's body and they began to kiss.

"I've got horses to feed, boss!" Jude said at length. "Let me get up, there's a love."

"Okay, if you insist. Do you want me to help?"

"No, it won't take me long and then I'll be back in your arms again," Jude replied and threw the bedclothes to one side. She stretched her arms above her head and glanced at the clock radio. "Shit! It's nearly seven o'clock!" she gasped in horror and frantically searched for her clothes.

"So you *do* require help then?" Callum didn't appear too bothered about the horses.

"*Would* you be a darling? I'll make it up to you." Jude enticed Callum by playing with her breasts against his face.

"You better had," he replied and kissed each breast in turn. "As long as you dress up for me!"

"You *are* incorrigible!" Jude threw on a baggy tee shirt, shorts and her Hunter boots and called to Tag who was waiting just outside the bedroom door.

All three walked back to the yard and began to administer feeds to the equine residents who looked peeved at having had to wait so long for attention this evening. Callum called across the yard to Jude to remind her.

"Fancy staying in luxury tonight?"

"The house, you mean?" She had her back turned to Callum as she fastened the door to Berkley's stable.

"What you do think? Takeaway or my special homemade dish?"

"Which is less likely to give me food poisoning?" Jude questioned as she collected the spent feed buckets.

"I reckon… a takeaway, because I haven't cooked for ages and I might make an utter and complete mess of it!" Callum joshed and ran across to where Jude was. He hugged her. "I wish it was always like this: you, me and no one else."

"Well, you never know what the future holds. I am a great believer in fate, you know," Jude rubbed her nose against Callum's chin.

He smiled gratefully at Jude and kissed the top of her head.

"I'll phone the order through. What do you fancy?"

"I'll leave it to you to decide: that'll make it a surprise and special, cos you will have personally chosen it!" she diplomatically replied.

Callum walked into the kitchen and shuffled through a pile of takeaway menus that were balanced next to the telephone. He decided on Chinese, made his selection and phoned the order through. He returned to the yard where Jude had just finished her duties.

"The takeaway will be ready in about half an hour. I'll go and collect it if you want to change into something more suitable and open a bottle," Callum suggested.

Jude looked up and smiled at Callum, who was making his way back into the house. She had to pinch herself to believe that she was having an affair with her boss, and a married one at that. This was a secret she couldn't share. She intended to keep it that way. She did, however, long to have a girly chat with someone but she decided to put it off for the time being.

Jude wandered back to her caravan with Tag at her heels. She spent the next half hour trying to decide what to wear. It was going to be a romantic meal and she wanted to show Callum that she was able to look feminine. She decided on a crimson dress that had thin shoulder straps. It was figure-hugging and it would accentuate her curvy body. She also draped a thin, see-through black cardigan across her shoulders. She decided to carry her shoes and wear her wellingtons as the dew on the grass would drench her feet. She tied her hair back into a bun and slapped a small amount of make-up on her face. Spraying her favourite perfume on her wrists and behind her ears, she felt ready to meet her dinner partner. She took a deep breath, called to Tag and set off to the house.

Jude had just reached the porch of the house and was trying to change into her shoes when Callum opened the door. The first glimpse of Jude made him laugh aloud.

"I wish I had a camera at this moment!" he laughed as Jude struggled to push off her Wellingtons and desperately tried to look glamorous. She dropped her shoes onto the paved step and leapt on the spot as she tried to keep her feet off the cold stone. She glared up at Callum.

"You look absolutely stunning!" Callum announced after he had stopped laughing. "Come here."

He helped Jude steady her balance as she stepped into her shoes and abandoned the boots at the doorstep. She straightened her cardigan and tried to look sophisticated and plumped up her hair. He bent forward and kissed her on both cheeks.

"Thank you for helping me," Jude mumbled as she made her way into the house. Tag had already pushed her way into the drawing room and made herself comfortable in front of the fire.

"Dinner is served, madam." Callum ushered Jude into the kitchen where he had lit two candles and laid the table. The two wineglasses glinted in the flicker of the candles.

"This looks really lovely!" Jude smiled as she appreciated the effort that Callum had made. A tablecloth adorned the table, with cotton napkins and matching placemats. "You have been busy!" she added as Callum seated her and placed a napkin on her lap. As he stood behind her, he bent down and kissed her neck.

"It's my pleasure, madam," he whispered and began to pour the wine. Then he sat at opposite her and arranged his napkin on his lap.

"Dig in!" he pointed to the varying foil dishes of rice, noodles and a large selection of meats. "I didn't know what you liked best, so I order most of the menu!"

"So I can see." Jude raised her eyebrows and took a slug of wine.

"This is the ideal opportunity of getting to know you. A one-to-one without disturbance or fear of someone gate-crashing our soiree!" Callum smiled at Jude as he beckoned for her to pass her plate to him to fill with food.

'Well, I think we know each other pretty well. I've been here for a few years, so this isn't exactly a blind date, is it!" Jude passed her plate. Their fingers touched as she did so. Callum smiled again. "You seem to be happier now," Jude surmised.

"Who wouldn't be happy in your company?" he returned. "So, you haven't answered my question," he reminded her.

"What?" Jude talked with her mouth full.

"Who are you, exactly?"

"Stupid question!" Jude smirked. "We have slept together, twice now, so you should know a bit about me and what I am like."

"I mean, your background, your upbringing, the usual stuff. God, I am rubbish at chatting up women!" he concluded. "I think I'll shut up now!"

"Okay, so, what makes you tick?" Jude continued the conversation.

"Well, I'm unhappily married to the most selfish woman I could ever care to meet. She loves her horses more than me and expects me to pay for the privilege. There you go. In a nutshell, I am a sucker for punishment I suppose." Callum gazed into his wineglass.

"Not to me, you aren't." Jude reached out and brushed Callum's hand with her fingers. "I like you just the way you are. That's what is so appealing about you. You have an air of innocence about you. You are classy, and not bad in bed either!" she joked.

"Good answer! Very good answer!" Callum laughed, and as they continued to eat and chat, Tag sat beneath the table in hope of the odd titbit or two.

Jude was feeling very bloated and decided she would take a walk around the gardens and check on the horses in the yard to let her meal digest. Callum tidied away the remnants of the takeaway packaging and threw them into the dustbin in the back yard. There was a chill in the air and Jude hurried back into the warmth of the kitchen. She rubbed her shoulders, as her cardigan didn't provide much warmth.

"Are you feeling less full?" Callum asked as he placed their dirty plates into the dishwasher.

"Much better, thanks. It is such a beautiful evening, but getting a bit chilly. Am I right in thinking it's your birthday soon? What am I going to get you for a present?" she asked.

"Just give me your body, that's all I desire," he replied and looked at her with a boyish grin.

"So you don't want me to buy you a tacky sweater or boring socks then?" she teased.

"You can, if you so wish. Because, if you bought it, I would wear it," he kindly returned.

"Ooh, you liar!" Jude grabbed a tea towel and playfully slapped him on the backside.

"Ow! That hurt! You wait! I need to be armed, and then we can have a duel!" Callum rose to the challenge with great enthusiasm. "I couldn't do this with Manna.

She'd tell me I was childish and to leave her alone. But you certainly are different!" He smiled approvingly.

"Yeah, and about ten years younger!" Jude shrieked as Callum chased her with his tea towel slapping close to her bottom.

"We're just a pair of kids really, that's the difference. Manna is too square!" Callum decided as his tea towel reached its target.

"Argh! Just you wait!" Jude anxiously rubbed her backside which Callum's tea towel had made contact with. "I'll be covered in bruises and welts!"

"Shall we call a truce?" Callum offered as he held out his tea towel and waved in surrender.

"I think we should or we'll both end up crying or fighting or something." Jude threw her towel on to the kitchen table.

"I quite like the sound of the 'something'. Do you think we ought to give it a try?" he asked and came close, kissing her gently on the cheek.

"I think so, come on, I'll race you upstairs!" Jude broke free from his embrace and ran to the stairs. "Which room?" she called back to Callum.

"Any one you fancy," he called back and turned the key in the kitchen door. He made his way to the landing where Jude was waiting.

"Come on," he said softly. "I'll lead the way."

"Wait!" Jude stopped in her tracks. "How about we spend some time downstairs?"

"We could, I suppose," agreed Callum. "Perhaps we should relax in the drawing room. Might not be a bad idea seeing as you are still full of Chinese. There is a fire lit so it'll be cosy and warm," Callum contemplated and then carefully turned Jude around so she faced the stairs.

They went back downstairs and Callum steered Jude into the drawing room.

"I'll get another bottle of wine; go in and relax. Light a few candles, if you want to. There are some matches on the mantelshelf." Callum headed into the kitchen and retrieved another bottle of wine, along with the corkscrew.

Jude made her way to the drawing room and was welcomed by flames flickering within the inglenook fireplace. The embers glowed as the fire devoured three hefty apple wood logs. She carefully arranged some candles around the room, which created a relaxing, romantic aura. She sighed happily to herself and felt a warm glow inside her. She smiled as she noticed Tag lying outstretched on the rust-coloured fluffy hearthrug. Tag growled and sighed contentedly and settled in for a well-deserved snooze.

Jude sat down on the rug and became mesmerised by the dancing flames. She was so engrossed that she didn't hear Callum enter the room and turn on the CD player, which proceeded to play a soft ballad. It was one of his favourite compilation love songs albums.

"Manna doesn't like candles; she's always worried about the fire risk," he commented, with a hint of disapproval in his voice as he looked around the room.

"I'm very careful though," Jude replied and continued to gaze into the fire. Callum walked over and smiled at Tag.

"Spoilt, isn't she?"

"You bet! I haven't got anyone else to spoil." Jude leaned over and stroked Tag's hairy body. Tag growled softly as her sleep was interrupted.

"Poor old Kier isn't allowed in this room cos of his muddy paws," said Callum as he placed the bottle of wine on a nearby occasional table and balanced two glasses in his hand. He made himself comfortable on the sofa directly in front of the fire and began to uncork the bottle.

"You could always towel dry his feet until they're clean," Jude suggested.

"Yes, but he only gets dirty again," Callum reasoned. "So what's the point?"

"Oh, you're just being lazy. You ought to clean him up and then he could come in here. Don't you want to lie on the rug with me?" She glanced round at Callum on the sofa.

"Don't you want to lie here with me?" he returned and looked beseechingly at her.

"Okay, you win." Jude got up from the rug and sat beside Callum on the sofa. "I can't lie down, not just yet, cos if I do, I'll get indigestion!"

"Don't worry, I have a king's supply of indigestion tablets," Callum offered with a smile.

He sat up on the sofa and placed his arm around Jude's shoulders. He kissed her cheek and stroked the top of her head. As he did so he softly whispered close to her ear, "This is *so* romantic. I can't tell you how much I love being with you." Jude felt a shiver run over her spine. She turned to face Callum.

"And I love being with you. I didn't realise how much I cared about you. My feelings seem to have been hidden away for so long, that is, until now."

She nestled happily into Callum's shoulder and placed her head against his neck. They both stared at the fire. The room, with the aromatic scented candles, was very peaceful. A thought-provoking and relaxing ambience filled the room and it wasn't long before Callum and Jude, in turn, drifted off into a restful sleep. Their breathing was rhythmical and contented.

Their slumber was shortly disturbed by Tag jumping on to Jude's lap.

"Tag! What are you doing?" Jude's voice was lethargic as she woke and realised where she was. She blinked at the fire. The embers were almost out. She glanced at her watch and noticed it was after eleven. She decided to top up the fire with more wood and loaded it with the two remaining logs from the wicker basket by the side of the hearth. Callum hadn't stirred. He snored quietly; he still managed to look refined even in his sleep.

Jude thought that it would be nice to spend a little more time in the drawing room, mainly because she didn't want the evening to end. She grabbed her cardigan and made her way to the log store outside in the back yard and collected some more logs. Tag decided to go with her to see if she could catch any rabbits that might be lurking in the garden. Jude hadn't noticed Kier in the shadows outside in the yard. She didn't see him make his bid to get into the house. Kier ran straight into the drawing room and, in his excitement, knocked against the table by the sofa causing the bottle of wine to fall onto the hearth. The candle, also on the table, toppled on to the hearthrug. Immediately flames ignited on the dry, fluffy rug and smoke began to billow around the room. Callum remained sleeping and unaware of the danger he was in.

Jude was in the garden. She called Tag back towards the house. Tag had found a couple of rabbits in the garden and had given chase into the lower paddock. She was not going to come back until she had completed her pest control. Jude continued to call but the little Jack Russell was in no mood to return. Jude hurried to the porch and pulled on her boots to go after her. She began to get angry. Tag was normally very obedient, except where rabbits were concerned.

"Tag! Here! Come back here now!" she called out into the darkness.

She stumbled across the lawn as the security light decided to bathe her in its halogen glory. It dazzled Jude and she blinked to accustom her eyes to the brightness. She could hear Tag yapping in earnest in the field.

"Just you wait!" she snarled and stomped off in her boots across the field. "I must be mad!" she murmured.

The wind blew a chilling breeze. Jude eventually caught up with Tag in the bramble-encrusted hedgerow near the caravan.

"Come here!" She lunged at Tag and grabbed her by her collar. "No more rabbits. Are you trying to deliberately ruin my entire evening?"

Jude turned to make her way back to the house and froze in horror as she saw smoke and flames billowing from the drawing room window.

Chapter Eleven

Jude dropped Tag on to the ground and ran as fast as she could back to the house. Tag ran with her.

"Callum! Callum! Where are you?" she screamed in horror. She raced through the garden, stumbling over molehills and stray branches of trees that George hadn't tidied away. She reached the house and was horrified to find the whole downstairs ablaze. She frantically searched through the windows, trying to catch sight of Callum.

"*Callum!*"

She ran to the outside of the house, to the drawing room window, and anxiously peered inside. Callum was still asleep. He was enveloped within a veil of acrid, grey smoke. Kier was lying on the hearth next to him, not moving.

"I've got to get you out of there, now!" Jude cried and ran back to the porch. She took a deep breath and plunged through the smoke, choking as she fought her way into the drawing room. The whole room was ablaze. She hurried towards the sofa and tried to wake Callum. He wasn't conscious. She slapped Kier on the side and grabbed his collar and moved him to the doorway. She turned and slapped Callum on the face, trying to get a response but to no avail. Somehow, and with superhuman strength, Jude grabbed hold of Callum and dragged him out of the room. The adrenalin surged in her body as she knew this was her only chance save him, no matter how heavy he was.

She heaved his lifeless body out into the back yard and laid him gently on the ground. She reached into his pocket and found his mobile phone. Dialling 999 she got through to the operator and screamed for the fire service and an ambulance.

"Hurry please! We're at Littlebridge Stables, Malsham. The downstairs is ablaze. I can't do anything! Please hurry!" she cried into the phone.

She tore off her cardigan and laid it under Callum's head to try to make him more comfortable. She glanced at Kier and noticed he was still motionless. She slapped his ribs a couple of times and tried to prise open his mouth for resuscitation. As she did so, Kier took a gulp of fresh air and opened his eyes. He looked distant, but he was alive. She patted his head and laid him on to the ground beside Callum.

"Now, if only I can do the same for you, baby," she sighed and began to massage Callum's heart.

She had laid him in the recovery position. Luckily she had been trained in first aid when she had begun to work at Littlebridge. Manna was a stickler for regulations and Jude momentarily thanked her for her diligence. It was certainly time to put what she had learned into action to try to save Callum.

"Come on, Callum. Wake up! Come on!" she encouraged and continued to massage his heart. "Don't leave me. Not when I've only just found you!" She continued her labour, only stopping intermittently to listen for his breathing.

She could hear sirens in the distance and Jude sighed in relief. The blue flashing lights of the fire engines were followed closely by an ambulance. Jude carried on trying to resuscitate Callum.

"Don't you dare give up on me!" she screamed at his motionless form and shook him angrily, trying to wake him.

Jude felt a hand on her shoulder. She looked up to see a paramedic at her side.

"It's okay, love. We'll take over now. What's his name?"

Jude blinked away her tears. "It's... it's... Callum..." She could hardly speak.

All around her firefighters were unreeling hosepipes and connecting up to the fire hydrant in the front garden at Littlebridge. She was ushered to one side by a paramedic.

"We need to get Callum to hospital straightaway. Is there anyone you should call?"

Jude was in a daze as she spoke. "Uh, yeah… I'll… um… go with him. I'll ring his wife. She's away at the moment. I need someone to stay at the stables, to look after the horses whilst I'm not here. Give me a minute, please."

She looked on helplessly at the house as the fire continued to blaze out of control. Tag was by her side. Jude dialled Natalie's number on her mobile and waited for a reply.

"Natalie? It's Jude. Littlebridge is on fire! Callum is unconscious! I need to go to the hospital with him. Can you come down and take care of things… the horses and the dogs? Perhaps you can call Mike the vet to check on Kier? He had stopped breathing, because of the smoke… yeah. Thanks, Nat. I really appreciate your help." Jude closed the call and began to shake. The reality of the fire and the shock of seeing Callum unconscious hit her hard and she sank to the floor. She was lifted up by a firefighter.

"I think you need to be checked at the hospital as well, love. You're in shock," he advised.

Jude brushed him away. "No, I'm fine, really I'm fine. I need to be with Callum but I have to wait for Natalie to get here."

She paced up and down the driveway, closely followed by Tag, who looked scared. Jude looked at the house and the array of flashing lights and heard echoes of explosions within the burning walls. She thought of Manna and her reaction and shivered at the thoughts of how she would cope with *this* tragedy.

The paramedics carefully lifted Callum on to a waiting trolley and wheeled him towards the ambulance. The lights on its roof flashed blue, but were hauntingly silent. The flashing lit up the outline of the trees amidst the burnt sienna skyline of Littlebridge. Jude paced anxiously around the front garden, peering into the darkness, waiting to see car lights appear at the top of the lane.

She didn't have to wait too long before Natalie screamed into the yard. Natalie got out of the 4x4 and stared at dismay at the house that billowed smoke from every orifice. Natalie rushed over to comfort Jude. She placed her arms around Jude's shoulders.

"Are you all right? What happened?"

"Look at the house! Sorry Nat. I need to go with Callum to the hospital. Can you look after Tag and Kier for me?"

"Sure, what about Manna? She'll need to be told. How did it start, Jude… the fire?"

"I wasn't there when it started." Tears started to fall down Jude's cheek. "I don't know," she sobbed.

"Poor Callum, he will be all right, won't he?" Natalie gently tried to get information.

"I don't know," Jude rubbed the tears from her face, "but I need to go with him, in case he wakes up. Natalie, can you *please* phone Manna? Let her know what's happened to Callum. Poor Kier needs checking, he suffered smoke inhalation." Jude shook as she spoke.

"Don't worry, I'll tell her. Where's Tag?"

Jude pointed to the corner of the yard. "Over there, I think she's okay. You can stay in the caravan tonight if you want. Sorry, it's a bit of a mess, but someone needs to be here for the horses. I think the fire brigade will be here for a long while yet, judging by the state of the house."

Natalie hugged Jude.

"Go with Callum in the ambulance. And if you need to get a lift back, ring me and I'll pick you up. I'll get Manna to come back straight away. Sod the competition. This is serious. I'll stay overnight and keep an eye on the horses for you. Don't worry! Just get going! The paramedics are ready to go. Oh, and give my love to Callum, won't you?"

Jude nodded and hugged Natalie tightly. "Thanks so much, Nat," she whispered.

Jude climbed into the back of the ambulance next to Callum's still body and the paramedics beat a quick retreat up the lane. As they passed the house, the drawing room windowpanes cracked and exploded from the heat. Jude crossed her arms over her body and shivered.

Natalie headed off to the caravan with Tag and Kier on leads, checking the horses down the stable lines on her way.

Jude looked down at Callum. His face was covered in smuts of soot and smoke. He had an oxygen mask placed over his nose and mouth and was snugly tucked beneath a thick red blanket, strapped tightly with two support bands. She leant across and grabbed hold of his hand beneath the blanket.

"Callum, please don't die, I couldn't cope without you," she whispered and bent her head until it touched the top of the blanket.

The paramedic travelling in the back of the ambulance reassured her.

"He'll be fine, love. Don't worry, we'll be at A&E soon. They'll take great care of him."

Jude smiled nervously. "I hope so."

The paramedic smiled at her. "You really care about him don't you?"

"Yes, yes, I do," Jude tightened her grip on Callum's blanketed hand. "He means everything to me."

"He's a lucky man to have you. Have you known him long?"

"Yes," Jude's reply was barely a whisper, "a while. We're very close."

"Let's get him sorted out and then you can soon be together again."

Jude nodded in a childlike fashion.

The ambulance arrived in rapid fashion at Malsham General Hospital. Callum was rushed into a waiting cubicle and Jude was asked to wait in the relatives' room until a member of staff was able to take details and update her.

Waiting in the small, stuffy room, Jude tried to imagine how the fire had started. She wished she had been with Callum to wake him up so he could have escaped the smoke. She shivered as she relived the ferocity of the flames and how helpless she had felt.

She glanced nervously about her and noticed a pile of magazines on a coffee table in the corner of the room. She turned to see two pictures that adorned the walls at either end of the room. They were abstract subjects which, when viewed, could conjure up any form of mood the viewer felt necessary. To Jude, everything was empty. The coffee table was dated and badly stained and a rather cloudy, dark fish tank sat on another table. A few goldfish swam in the gloom looking expectantly at Jude for food. She felt sorry for them and turned away.

She knew there would be many questions to answer: questions that she couldn't answer, questions that she wouldn't answer. Her thoughts were interrupted by the appearance of a nurse in the doorway. She cleared her throat.

"Hello, I'm Carrie," the nurse cheerfully announced. "I wonder if I could get some details about Callum Jacobs from you. It won't take long. Would you like a cup of tea or coffee?"

"Tea, please." Jude straightened her dress and pushed a strand of hair behind her ear.

"Is he your husband?"

"Uh no, I'm his girlfriend. That is unofficial, by the way."

The nurse looked up. "Whatever you say is confidential anyway. So, is there a Mrs Jacobs? Callum has a wedding ring on his finger. That's the only reason I'm asking you."

Jude sighed, "Unfortunately, yes, there is a Mrs Jacobs. She is away at the moment – I think she has been told."

"Okay. Can you give me his date of birth?"

Jude looked embarrassed, "Sorry, I don't know. We haven't been seeing each other for very long. I do know his birthday is coming up soon though." She broke off as she remembered Callum making love to her.

The nurse was very understanding.

"Don't worry. Do you know if he's on any medication at the moment?"

Jude shook her head, "I don't think he is, but I can't be completely sure. You really need to speak to his wife. I'm so sorry, I am no help at all. Can you just tell me how he is?" Jude was desperate for news.

"I'll go and find out. Give me a few minutes."

The nurse left Jude pacing the room. She bit her lip in anticipation as she thought of Callum lying nearby. She felt sick with worry and the consequences of their liaison. The nurse returned after what seemed like eternity. She smiled at Jude as she closed the door quietly behind her.

"He's still unconscious but his condition has stabilised. He's been placed on a life support machine for the time being to assist his breathing."

Jude shook. "That's terrible, a life support machine…"

The nurse spoke in a reassuring tone, "Don't worry, it's procedure in this type of case. It will help Callum towards his recovery."

Jude was still shocked. "How long will he be on the machine for?"

"However long it takes. It's up to him and how soon he regains consciousness."

"Poor Callum." Jude sat down heavily on one of the chairs. She stared in front of her, trying to take everything in. "Do you think he knows where he is?"

"Probably not," the nurse replied and sat down beside Jude. "But that isn't such a bad thing. You know what men are like: they don't like doctors or hospitals, do they?"

Jude managed a wry smile. "I know what you mean. Silly really. You are here for them, to help them; except they never want to help themselves. They always wait for someone else to do it for them" she babbled.

"I should imagine that you'd like to see him, would you?" The nurse got up and opened the waiting room door.

"I'd love to… thanks."

"Follow me to the unit, but don't stay too long. Anyway, I imagine you need some sleep. You look exhausted. When you see him, talk to him, think positive thoughts for him. That's great medicine in itself. "

Together they walked to ICU where Callum was lying beneath crisp white linen sheets within an oxygen tent that was neatly arranged over his bed. The life support machine bleeped rhythmically by his side. He looked peaceful, warm and clean. The room smelt of disinfectant and a nurse sat quietly writing notes at a desk, only a short distance away from Callum. She looked up, smiled and spoke in a lowered tone.

"Don't stay too long, just a few minutes. Oh, and I think I should warn you that Mrs Jacobs is on her way."

Jude nodded and pursed her lips in defiance. She was visibly moved as she walked towards the bed and took in the sight of her new-found love struck down so lifeless, so helpless. He lay still and silent as though he were dead. She took hold of his hand beneath the tent. She felt a tear spill down her cheek. She blinked it away and tried to smile as she spoke.

"Hi babe. You look cosy, are you having a good sleep? I could do with some shut-eye as well. It's been a long night. So much has happened. When I leave here, I'll find out how Kier is. Oh, and Tag sends her love too. Wake up soon, babe. I need you so much. Just wake up soon. I know you will... I... I love you..." Jude's voice faltered as she spoke.

There was no response from Callum. The life support machine continued to bleep in time with his chest that rose and fell. He looked as though he was in a restful sleep. Jude squeezed his hand tightly and kissed it gently before placing it back on top of the sheets. As she got up to leave, she heard a familiar voice in the reception area.

"Yes, Callum Jacobs, my husband."

Jude steeled herself for her reunion with Manna. She wiped her eyes, took a deep breath and walked towards reception.

"Hello Manna," she croaked.

"What on earth happened? How is he?"

Jude looked to the floor. "I don't know. All I can remember is seeing the house on fire. Tag was in the field chasing a rabbit. I was with her when I saw the flames. And when I got to the house, I looked through the drawing room window and saw him. Callum was asleep on the couch. Kier was lying on the floor and the smoke was… was everywhere. I couldn't see very well when I dragged him out. Oh Manna, it was terrible, bloody awful, and now he's fighting for his life!" Jude burst into tears.

"But from all accounts you saved him! You risked your life to save him!" Manna blinked a few times in disbelief and suddenly grabbed Jude and enveloped her in a bear hug. "I can't thank you enough for what you have done!" she blurted out in genuine gratification. "He could have died in there!"

"He's unconscious, Manna. He's on a life support machine. I wish I could have got there before. If it hadn't been for Tag… I couldn't find her; she just ran off when I went to check on the horses."

"I won't forget what you've done." Manna kissed Jude on the cheek. "Look, here's twenty quid. Get a taxi back to the yard. Try and get some sleep. I'll stay here with Callum. I'll let you know directly there is any news, okay?"

Jude took the note and nodded, "Okay. Ring me won't you?" she confirmed.

"Course I will," Manna said reassuringly.

"What about the house?" Jude hesitated.

"Natalie rang a few moments ago to say that the blaze is out now. The fire crew are damping down. It's not the end of the world; houses can be re-built."

"You're taking all of this so well," Jude remarked.

"Expect it will sink in soon. Probably the shock or something." Manna smiled bravely and walked towards the ICU. She froze as she saw Callum. She clasped her hand to her mouth, "Oh my God! What happened to you?"

She bent closer towards the plastic tent in suspended animation. She reached for his hand and held it firmly, pressing her lips against his skin. The life support machine broke the silence — *bleep, bleep, bleep,* monotonous but insistent.

Tear welled up in Manna's eyes and the realisation of her love for her husband made her cry out, "I'm sorry I wasn't there… really, I am." She held his hand to her face and her tears trickled softly on to his skin. As they did so, Callum's eyes flickered open. Manna, however, had closed her own eyes, her mind racing through everything that had happened. Then she opened her eyes and stared at Callum. She blinked and stared at him again.

"Callum?" she whispered and held his hand tightly. "Callum?"

Callum's eyes flickered again. He opened his mouth to speak but all that came out was an exhalation of air. He coughed and tried to clear his throat. He spoke again and Manna was able to hear what he said.

"Juu… de."

Manna wiped her face and felt anxious. Had she heard him correctly? Perhaps he was suffering from shock or delusion.

"It's Manna," she whispered.

Callum spoke but this time there was no mistaking what he uttered, "Juu…dde."

"No, it's Manna, can you hear me?" She let go of his hand and looked around for the nurse. "Nurse, come quickly, I think he is coming round," she urged.

There was a sudden flurry of activity as three nurses appeared and stood around the bed. They removed the oxygen tent and began to study the read outs from the computer. By this time Callum was fully conscious.

"Where... where is Jude?" he croaked as an oxygen mask was rapidly placed over his nose and mouth.

"Callum, I'm here, it's Manna. I'm here, it's *me*." She pushed her way past the blue uniforms and leant over the bed. "How are you?"

Callum didn't respond. Instead he chose to stay silent as he drifted off into sleep.

"Callum? Is he all right, nurse?"

"Don't worry, Mrs Jacobs. We don't want to tire him out; he needs to sleep now he is able to breathe on his own."

Manna was startled.

"But he needs to know I'm here for him! Can't you wake him up?"

"I don't think that is a good idea, Mrs Jacobs."

"But why does he keep asking for Jude? She's gone home now." Manna remained puzzled and concerned.

"Perhaps it was because she was the last person he remembers before the fire," suggested one of the nurses. "He's still traumatised."

"It doesn't matter." Manna appeared disappointed.

"The mind does play tricks on people who have lost consciousness, Mrs Jacobs. People do say odd things. Don't you worry, he'll be fine. He needs to sleep now, though. Why don't you get some rest? You can't do anymore. We'll make a bed up for you so you can stay the night if you would like?"

"No, no. I need to go. But please keep me informed if there are any changes in his condition, won't you?"

"Of course," said the staff nurse. "If you would like to leave a phone number at reception, we'll call you to update you."

Manna looked dazed. "I'll have to leave my mobile number, because the home number… well, won't be working because of the…"

"Are you sure you're all right, Mrs Jacobs?" The nurse showed concern as Manna seemed to be incoherent.

"Yes. I'll be fine. I'll get a cab. To see what's happened to my house." She looked distant; her eyes had glazed over.

Manna had received the telephone call from Natalie around midnight. She had been asleep for an hour and it was a phone call she couldn't ever have imagined, turning her life upside down as it had. She'd had a brilliant practice session with Othello earlier that day. She was in a good position to get a top placing in the dressage.

Manna glanced at her watch. It was 3am. She walked to the car park and dialled George's number on her mobile phone.

George was pacing up and down outside the horsebox when his phone rang.

"Hi, it's Manna. Callum has regained consciousness," George heard Manna announce.

"I'm so glad. The horses are fine; I've been out to check on them. They seem happy enough." George spoke with relief.

"Great, now, do you think you can hang on there?" Manna questioned.

George was puzzled. "Does that mean you aren't scratching from the show?"

Manna smiled triumphantly. "Come on George, you know me by now. I don't give in to anything, do I? Not now I have got this far. I'll get a cab back. I should be at the guesthouse about five. My dressage is timed for early afternoon. There will be heaps of time for me to get some sleep and prepare in the morning."

George was shocked. "Are you really sure, Mrs J? What about Mr J?"

Manna replied, "He'll be fine. I'll get Jude to take care of him for me. And Natalie. She's at the house too."

"If that's what you want, Mrs J."

"Yes it is, George. It *is* what I want," she snapped and placed her phone into her handbag, just as the taxi arrived at the car park.

"Littlebridge Stables, please," she breezed and jumped into the back seat of the taxi, sat back and sighed as she thought of what would await her upon her arrival home.

Natalie saw the lights of a car at the top of the drive. The fire was out and the house smouldered against the late night sky. The fire crew were damping down. She met the taxi and hugged Manna before she had a chance to steady herself after getting out of the car.

"How's Callum?" she gushed with sympathy.

"He's conscious, Nat. I've left him sleeping like a baby. He'll be fine. How are the horses? Where's Jude?"

"Trying to get some sleep. The horses are all okay, especially Fig. Kier has been checked over by that gorgeous vet of yours and he's keeping him in the surgery overnight."

Manna looked towards her home. "Look at the state of it!" she gasped walking towards the smoking house. "It's bad, isn't it?"

Natalie placed a hand on Manna's shoulder. "Well, put it this way, you won't be sleeping there tonight, lovie."

"No, I'm going back to the guesthouse. I just need to speak with Jude, then I will..."

Natalie looked in amazement. "You cannot be serious, Manna! For crying out loud! Look around you! You can't leave all this!"

"Just watch me, Nat. I've got this far. The horses are sound, I had a great practice session today: I just can't scratch from it now!"

Natalie was disgusted. "You're mad, Manna. How can you do it to Callum? To yourself?" she spat in fury, glaring at Manna.

"I know what I'm doing Nat. I can't do any more for Callum. He's being looked after," Manna replied crossly.

"Do you? Do you *really* know what you're doing, Manna? Isn't it just a case of burying your head in the sand, hoping it will go away? This won't go away! You do know that, don't you?"

"Leave it, Nat. Just leave it! I'll speak to Jude: she can look after things, it's only another couple of days."

"But she's in shock, Manna. She isn't in any fit state to work. She has had a terrible night; you can't expect her to cope!"

"Well, that is where you come in, Nat. Come on, don't let me down, not now!" Manna pleaded.

"I'm sorry, I don't agree with what you're going to do. Aren't you forgetting about your husband? He's seriously ill!"

"I'll make sure Jude visits him, and it's only for a couple of days. Please Nat, this may be my only chance of getting somewhere. I've worked so hard to get this far!"

"You are truly selfish, Manna Jacobs. I cannot believe you sometimes. I'm not happy to do this, but I will. Not for you, though, I am doing it for Callum's and Jude's sakes."

Manna was a little startled by Nat's outburst. She felt deflated as she didn't want to hear what Nat was trying to make her comprehend.

"I really do appreciate it, I'll make it up to you, I promise." She reached for her mobile phone.

"I don't want to hear it." Nat stormed away from Manna towards the stables. "We'd better wake poor Jude and tell her what you are planning to do."

They walked in silence to Jude's caravan and knocked on the door. It was a while before Jude answered. Tag was barking from inside.

"Jude! Manna's here. She wants to ask you something," Nat bellowed outside the door. She pushed Manna to the door.

Jude slowly opened it.

"How's Callum?" she asked. She was still in her clothes. She looked completely exhausted and still covered in remnants of the fire.

"He's awake, Jude. Still groggy but awake," replied Manna softly. "Look, I need you to keep an eye on things, until I get back."

Jude squinted at her, puzzled. "Why, where are you going?"

Manna took a deep breath. "Back to the guesthouse. It's the dressage tomorrow. Nat is looking after things here. She'll help you with the horses."

Jude slammed the door shut without answering. She was unable to take in what she had just heard.

"I'll be back next week, Jude. Can you visit Callum for me? Tell him where I am? He mentioned your name when he woke up, so I imagine he'll be pleased to see you." Manna continued to talk through the door as Jude collapsed to the floor of the caravan and wept. She could barely contain her anger but somehow her voice was calm.

"Whatever you say, Manna. You go on. Do your own thing!" Jude muttered in disgust.

"Thank you, Jude." Manna started to walk back to the stables.

Natalie shook her head and whispered to herself, "Where have I heard that before? Yet again you've got your own way."

They walked in silence to the waiting taxi. Manna turned towards Nat.

"I'll see you next week."

Natalie grimaced without speaking and watched Manna climb into the cab and speed away back to her beloved horses and the trials. Dawn was beginning to break and the birds had started their early morning verses.

"Don't think you've got away with this, Manna. Don't you think that you have!"

Natalie walked back towards Jude's caravan to spend what remained of the night there.

Chapter Twelve

"Hey! You're looking better this morning!" Jude peered around the door of Callum's ward, clutching a bunch of grapes.

Callum smiled weakly beneath an oxygen mask. He attempted to lift himself up in the bed. He had managed to sleep on and off. He reached across for a glass of water on the bedside cabinet. Jude came over to the bed and plonked the grapes on the cabinet. She leant across and kissed his cheek. She took hold of the glass and offered it to Callum who, having pushed his mask up onto his forehead, gladly sipped a small amount of water. The coolness of it made his eyes close momentarily. He blinked and spoke.

"How are you doing?" He reached out and gently touched her hair.

"Better now that I have seen you," she replied. "I thought I'd lost you last night. What happened in there?"

"I have absolutely no idea. The candles must have started the fire. Perhaps I knocked them over in my sleep or something, I just don't know."

"All I remember is seeing the house on fire and trying to get you out of there." Jude took hold of Callum's hand tightly and held it to her face.

"You saved my life last night," he whispered. "I will never be able to thank you enough."

"You don't have to, I'd do it again and again."

"I don't intend to risk it again. So I won't have to call on you too often!" He managed a laugh, which developed into a coughing fit. Callum composed himself. "Sorry, my lungs are still a bit ropey. Hopefully it won't be long before I'm up and about again. Watch out then, Miss Armstrong, because I will be looking to make mad, passionate love to you again."

He broke off amidst bouts of laboured coughing. He lay back on the pillow exhausted and replaced the oxygen mask over his nose and mouth.

"Here, have these when you feel like it. I'd better go. I was told not to stay too long and tire you out," Jude offered Callum the grapes.

"Don't go yet, stay with me. I want you here with me for a while longer. Promise you won't go?" His voice was muffled beneath the mask. He looked concerned.

"Okay, they'll have to throw me out of here then. I'll stay as long as you want me to," Jude reassured him. She leant across and kissed him tenderly on the forehead. "Just get well, do you hear me?"

Callum smiled. Jude stayed at his bedside until the staff nurse asked her to leave. Not once did he mention Manna's name and not once did he show any interest in her. Jude didn't make a point of talking about Manna and her disgraceful behaviour; she didn't want Callum to become stressed over her selfishness. As she got up to leave, Callum took hold of her hand and made her bend towards him. He whispered close to her ear.

"I love you, Jude. I really love you."

Jude smiled at him, gathered his face in her hands and announced, "I love you too, Callum... a lot! See you tomorrow, same time."

"See you, can't wait," he added and closed his eyes in complete satisfaction.

Jude felt her heart almost bursting with passion as she replayed Callum's words. She walked to the car park where Tag was waiting for her in the car. She got in and sat down in ecstasy.

"Tag, he said he loves me! Can you believe it? He said he loves me and I told him I loved him too. Bloody hell! I think I am actually in love and someone is in love with little old me! Shit!"

Jude arrived back at Littlebridge to find a car parked in the driveway. Natalie was talking to a man dressed in a suit and carrying a briefcase. She saw Jude arrive and flagged her to stop.

"How's the patient?" she called out.

"He looks a lot better this morning, Nat. I think he is on the mend."

"Great. This is the insurance assessor, Mr Billings. Manna phoned him this morning. He's taking some notes, about the fire and all that. Can you make a coffee for us, please? Meet you in the tack room shortly. Is that okay?"

Jude nodded and parked the car. She let Tag out and the dog immediately ran off in search of rabbits in the corner of the paddock. Jude soon returned from the tack room with a tray and three mugs and a grubby jar of sugar.

"Milk and sugar, Mr Billings?" Natalie asked. She smiled sweetly as she spoke.

"Just milk, please. Right, have you any more questions you need to ask?" He looked at Nat as he sipped from his cup.

"No, I don't think so. Mrs Jacobs has given you all the details, I'm sure," Natalie replied.

"Okay, so we don't know how the fire started. It will need to be investigated by the fire brigade and they will have to submit a report. After that we can get things in motion and submit the claim." Mr Billings was reiterating what he had previously said to Natalie. In fact, he was starting to annoy her as he continually repeated himself in a patronising manner.

"Well, I've got to get back to my own home." Natalie placed her cup in Jude's hand. "Thank you, Mr Billings. Mrs Jacobs will be home next week so if you have any queries please give her a call and arrange to meet with her if you need to."

"Thank you, you have been most helpful," returned Mr Billings, draining his cup and in turn passing it to Jude.

"Well, good day to you ladies." He strode off back to his car.

"Thank Christ for that! He nearly drove me to open a bottle of wine!" Natalie heaved a sigh of relief as Billings drove away. "What a tosser! Talk about Mr Thorough!"

"They have to be, Nat. You should know that with how long it took to sort out Sam's stuff. Anything legal or insurance related seems to be a nightmare. Anyway, he was certainly here quickly enough." Jude tried to sound intelligent.

"Yes, you know Manna, once she gets the bit between her teeth! Good news about Callum, by the way. Did you tell him about Manna?" Natalie asked.

"No, I didn't want to upset him. I didn't see the point."

"Good move. I wouldn't have said anything either. He doesn't deserve to be hurt anymore."

"I couldn't do it to him." Jude returned the cups to the tray.

Natalie looked at her. "You really care about him, don't you?"

"What do you mean?" Jude continued to busy herself with the cups.

"Callum. You seem to care about him... quite a bit, don't you?" Natalie continued to fish for information.

"Wouldn't you, in the circumstances?"

"Of course, but I mean I think there is more to it than just last night, isn't there, Jude?"

"Like what?"

"Feminine intuition, I think you call it. Come off it, Jude, I can see a mile off that you really like him. Go on, admit it!" she taunted Jude in a friendly fashion.

"Okay Nat, I do care about him, is that what you want to hear?" Jude retorted.

"I knew it! Does he know?"

"Know what?"

"Oh, for God's sake! Does he know you care about him?" Natalie was getting impatient.

"As a matter of fact…" Jude hesitated before she continued. "As a matter of fact, no he doesn't. So our conversation is purely between us and no one else, okay?"

"Sure thing, don't worry, mum's the word and all that. You sly old thing, Jude. You know what they say about the quiet ones?"

"Yes, that they are the ones to watch," Jude finished off Nat's proverb. "Come on, we've got horses to feed."

Between them, Natalie and Jude fed and watered the horses at Littlebridge. In less than two hours they were in Jude's caravan mulling over the previous night's events with a bottle of wine and two half-filled glasses on the table.

"They were covered all right with their insurance," replied Nat as she swigged from her glass. "Luckily, or it could have been a bit of a bummer."

"Yes," replied Jude, staring at the table. "What with Leya suing them as well."

"Oh, so you know about that, then?" Natalie gazed at Jude.

"Leya told me the other week… and she also said that you suggested she do it."

"Yes, you're right."

"Why? That's a bit off, is it? Especially as Manna is your best mate? I don't get it." Jude frowned at Natalie and awaited her response.

"Because, Jude... just because — it's a very long story," Natalie began.

"I'm not going anywhere. So, what happened?" Jude quizzed and took a slug of her wine.

Natalie sighed and sat back in her chair.

"Well, if you're sitting comfortably, then I'll begin! About fifteen years ago, although it might be more — I can't and don't really want to remember the exact year — Manna had an affair with Sam. She doesn't know that I know about it. They were pretty cute, kept it very low key. Callum doesn't know either, by the way. The only reason I know is because of George."

"Don't tell me, Randy knows everything that goes on, doesn't he!" remarked Jude with a smile.

"Anyway, George told me about the affair. He'd caught them near the woods at Rillder, parked up in Sam's 4x4 and at it like rabbits apparently. Okay, so I know I'm no saint, but it really hurt me. Cut me to the bone. I vowed that one day I would wreak revenge on her for all the upset she caused me. My sex life was non-existent: Sam was getting his fill from her and not me. Can you imagine it? Prim and proper Manna Jacobs shagging in the woods? I couldn't and still can't get my head round it."

"Did you retaliate in anyway? You know, play them at their own game?" asked Jude enthralled, her eyes wide with anticipation.

"Well, yes, I suppose I had a couple of flings, nothing serious though," replied Natalie. She gazed into the air as she reminisced. "What I am getting now is much more fun."

"So you're not living like a nun then?"

"No way! There are too many lovely men out there!" Natalie smiled as she thought of Darius Cherry under her kitchen table and the smell of wine on their bodies.

"This is how you're taking your revenge on Manna?" Jude surmised.

"It's taken a while and a lot of white lies, getting her to think I was still her best friend. I feel a bit of a cheat really, but I need revenge. I have to get back at her."

"Sounds like it," said Jude. "What about Callum?"

"Callum? It's unfortunate that he's involved with her. I hate the fact that he's getting hurt through her infidelity. He's such a lovely bloke."

"Yes, he is." Jude thought wistfully of Callum in her bed, his tender kisses and passion.

"I am right then. You do have a thing for him?"

"Okay, I give in," sighed Jude. "Yes, I *do* have a thing for Callum, as I told you."

"And he really doesn't know?"

Jude hesitated but couldn't help herself. "Ummm… yes! Yes, he does know about it."

Natalie's eyes shone with excitement.

"Oh. My. God! You and Callum? You are joking, right? This is brilliant. Have you… you know?"

"And yes, Natalie, we have shagged, several times, and it was absolutely wonderful!" Jude felt relieved to offload her secret. She smiled as she took in Natalie's reaction.

"This is ace! Brilliant! Fantastic!" Natalie clapped her hands enthusiastically.

"Why are you so happy, Nat? You should be lecturing me about fidelity and taking another woman's husband and all that."

"No way. This is the best news I've had for years, Jude. This could really work to my advantage!"

"Advantage? What advantage?" Jude was puzzled. She took a sip from her glass.

"I can finally get back at her big time and not hurt Callum. Cos he will be with you, won't he?"

"That's what I would like to think, but it's early days."

"So she will be on her own, with no one to love her!" Natalie was ecstatic. She jumped up and down in the caravan, making the whole area shake. "This is priceless, Jude. Don't worry, your secret is safe with me. I will make sure neither of you suffers. Just give me time and I will get my own back." Natalie got up to leave. "It's past my lunchtime, lovey. Must dash."

"Have you got a nice man to meet?"

"What do you mean? You make me out to be some kind of floozy!" Natalie leant forward and kissed Jude on the cheek. "See you soon. Give my love to your man." With that she disappeared through the door into the midday sunshine.

Chapter Thirteen

That night, Jude lay wide awake. She couldn't sleep. Tag was on the bed gently snoring and periodically kicking her paws as though she was running in her sleep. Jude placed a hand on Tag's flank and patted it gently. She was thinking of Callum lying in hospital. She thought about her conversation with Natalie earlier that evening and how she had shared her secret. Jude was worried now that Natalie might let her down by gossiping about her affair with Callum but, on the other hand, she surmised, Natalie would need to remain silent to enable her to carry out her revenge on Manna. Jude decided that she should try to trust Natalie. But she couldn't help thinking about Manna and how Natalie had deceived her. It was similar to her situation with Callum and deep down she felt guilty about their affair.

A burst of tone from her mobile phone made her jump and Tag woke up with a start. She glared at Jude, the perpetrator, who had disturbed her from her sleep.

Jude picked up her phone and found a message. It was from Manna. It read, *'Hope all is well, give my love to Callum when you see him, am doing well at show. George has been gr8t help. C u soon. M x'*

Jude disappointedly placed the phone back on her bedside table. She'd hoped it had been from Callum. She sighed and turned over. Suddenly the phone rang out again.

"Oh for God's sake!" she muttered, and reached out for her mobile. As if by coincidence, there was a message from Callum.

'Love u lots, come c me!' it read.

Jude smiled in satisfaction and returned a message.

'Love u 2. C u 2moz. Sleep tight! X J'

She was delighted Callum had been able to text her. He must be recovering from his ordeal. She couldn't wait to see him in the morning and she made sure her alarm clock was set for six so she could get her work done and then go to the hospital to see him as soon as possible. She turned over and drifted off into a contented sleep.

oOo

Next morning the alarm rang out its shrill reminder but Jude was already awake and dressed. She sipped coffee and finished her breakfast. Tag was, until the alarm went off, in a deep sleep. She stretched and yawned, rose to her feet, ready for another exciting day chasing vermin at the yard.

Jude was happy. She was so excited about seeing Callum again and hoped that he would soon be allowed home so she could take care of him, albeit in the caravan, until Manna returned from the show.

At ten Jude arrived at the hospital with a bag of chocolate raisins for Callum. They were her favourite and she hoped that he wouldn't be too keen on eating them so she could eat them for him! She walked with joy in her footsteps towards his ward only to find one of the nursing staff standing at the door with someone very familiar. Callum was out of bed and talking to the consultant. He smiled broadly when he saw Jude.

"Hey! Guess what? I can come home," he announced in a croaky voice.

Jude smiled at him.

"That's fantastic! Are you ready to go now?"

"Yes. I've just had a chat with the consultant and he has agreed I'm fit to go, so, let's do it!"

Callum was a little shaky when they reached Littlebridge. It had been three days since the fire and the lower part of the house was completely destroyed. Callum looked in dismay at the wreckage.

"It looks terrible. I had no idea what was happening. If only I hadn't lit the candles, this would never have happened." He choked as he spoke.

"Don't upset yourself. The main thing is that you are alive and able to stand here and look at the house. You survived! I don't know what I would have done without you," Jude squeezed his arm. "Come on, let's get to the caravan. I've had a tidy up, so you can stay with me until Manna comes home. Then you will have to decide what you want to do. Whether you want to move to another house whilst Littlebridge is renovated… or whether you will tell Manna to get lost and live with me in this lovely little abode. Perhaps you might want to buy a mobile home and we could set up a hippy commune! What do you think?" Jude was trying to cheer Callum up.

"You are full of such wonderful ideas, aren't you?" He pulled Jude close to him as he spoke. He kissed the top of her head. "I couldn't be away from you, not now. I realised whilst lying in that hospital bed that I don't want to let you go. Not ever! So I'm afraid you could be stuck with me, for a while."

"What are you going to do about Manna?" Jude questioned.

"Well, I'm afraid you may have to sit tight for a while. We need to get this lawsuit sorted out first and come to some sort of agreement with Leya, which I'm sure we can, and then I'll tell her. I can't go on the way we are together. It isn't the best for either of us. She is so wrapped up in her horses, she can't think of anything else. At least we haven't got children to worry about." Callum's thoughts turned to Manna and her selfishness.

"Have you ever wanted kids?" asked Jude out of curiosity. As soon as she said it, she wished she hadn't. It wasn't her place to pry.

Callum was silent for a moment.

"I don't know. Part of me does and part of me doesn't. But, given the choice, and," he paused, "if the chance was with someone like you, then I'd probably say yes."

Jude didn't say anything but just smiled. She felt a warm feeling envelope her body and she hugged him closer to her.

"Come on, let's go to the caravan. I'll make you comfortable. There are a few bits of mail for you."

"Have you heard from Manna?" Callum asked as they slowly walked to the caravan.

"Yes, she texted me last night to ask how you were. But I didn't bother to reply. I suppose I ought to tell her you're home." Jude felt angry as she thought of Manna's neglect to be with her husband.

"Don't bother yet. She won't miss me, so let's have some quality time together before the shit hits the fan," Callum responded. "I feel really knackered, like I've been in the ring with Tyson Fury."

"You're safe with me," Jude soothed him as he sat down in the living area. "Do you want to sit here or go to bed?"

"I've only been home for a few minutes, woman!" laughed Callum. "And you want my body already!"

"I didn't mean that! Oh, you're incorrigible!" Jude gently tapped Callum on the knee. "I can't tell you how happy I am that you are here *and* with me," she continued and kissed the top of his head.

Callum held on to her waist and hugged her as she stood.

"Jude, I want to tell you that I love you. I really love you," he said quietly. "Don't ever leave me, will you?"

"Don't worry, I'll be here with you through hell and high water! Whatever it takes, Callum."

They kissed and Jude sat down beside him and rested her head against his shoulder. Callum laid back and closed his eyes, thankful to be alive and to be with Jude.

oOo

Jude carried out her afternoon duties in the yard. She had left Callum sleeping in the bedroom. He was so exhausted from his ordeal. Jude was closing the tack room door when her mobile phone rang. It was Natalie.

"Hi, how's everything going at Littlebridge?"

"Great and guess what? Callum's home!"

"Really? That's brilliant news. Where's he staying?"

"With me in the caravan until Manna gets back. Then I don't how what he is going to do."

"Well, if it's any help, he can stay here with me. I've got loads of space and it's not that far away from Littlebridge. Oh, and before you ask, don't worry, I won't steal him from you, I promise!" Natalie joked.

"It would solve a lot of awkward questions when Manna gets back if he stays with you." Jude felt relieved that Natalie was prepared to help her.

"Do you think he ought to come over sooner rather than later, just in case anyone sees or gets to hear that he's out of hospital? You know what this place is like for gossip. Christ, the locals at the Sheep know most things before they've happened. No doubt they will be queuing up to look at the house. And this would be a scandal for them to mull over for ages to come."

"You're right, Nat. I'll have a word with him when he wakes up and try to get him over to you this afternoon."

"And you can come over and stay the night as well, if you like," offered Natalie.

"I would love to but I can't leave the horses on their own. Just in case anything happens. We've had enough dramas here to last us for a lifetime!" Jude was trying to be sensible in her decision.

"Well, at least come and have supper and spend the evening here. That would be great for the two of you."

"The only trouble is, I haven't told Callum that you know about us. I don't quite know how he will take the news." She spoke without thinking.

"You'll find a way. Even if it means jumping into bed with him to reassure him," hinted Natalie with a laugh.

"Don't worry, I'll tell him," said Jude. "I'll see you later on."

Jude ended the call and placed her phone back in her coat pocket. She was determined to tell Callum about confiding in Natalie but she wasn't sure how he would react to the news. When she reached the caravan she could see he was awake and pottering around inside.

"Hey, how are you feeling, baby?" she asked, giving him a hug.

"A lot better now I've had a sleep. I think it must be the drugs making me sleepy. But I feel like I could eat a… I was going to say 'horse' but that isn't quite appropriate, is it?"

"Well, I have some news about supper. Natalie phoned a short time ago to see how you were and has invited us both to dinner. Also, she is happy for you to stay at Heyrick Heights until Manna gets back. What do you say?"

"Bloody hell!" Callum exclaimed. "Talk about being caught in the boudoir with Madame Nat! Am I safe with her? You know what she's like. She'd seduce the milkman, if she had one!" he joked.

"And there is one other thing." Jude was building up to her big announcement. "Natalie knows about you and me…" She waited for Callum's response.

He was silent for a time, nodded and then spoke.

"Right. Did you, um… tell her? Or did she work it out, or was she informed by someone else?"

"I told her," admitted Jude. "I had to tell someone and it happened to be her. Are you okay with that?"

Callum thought for a while. "Yes, I suppose so. As long as she can keep her mouth shut, we'll be okay. You do know that until Manna is told, things will have to be secret and kept under wraps, don't you? It isn't going to be easy and when she does find out, she will be difficult. You will probably lose your job so you've got to be prepared for all those things, Jude."

"I don't care. If it means I get to be with you, then I will wait. I don't have a problem with that," Jude replied and gazed at Callum with sincerity. "I'd do anything for you; you know that, don't you?"

"That, Jude, is why I love you so much. For your loyalty and sincerity." He bent his head towards her and kissed her cheek very tenderly. "Now, would you do something for me?" he whispered.

"Course. Just name it," said Jude.

Callum moved closer to her ear and whispered again. "Get your clothes off, put your sexy boots on and make love to me!" he laughed.

"I thought you'd never ask!" replied Jude, immediately starting to take off her clothes in a seductive fashion.

They made very slow, tender love in the living room area and afterwards cuddled closely together under Jude's duvet, eating chocolate biscuits and watching the television, before driving off to Heyrick Heights, to Callum's temporary home and supper with Natalie.

oOo

Natalie was cooking in the kitchen when she heard the car arrive. She looked out of the window into the yard and smiled. She put down the salad she was tossing and met Callum and Jude at the door.

"Hey, big guy! Nice to see you," she greeted Callum, with a firm kiss on his cheek. "How are you feeling? You've made such a great recovery!"

"Yes, it's good to be home, or at least here. And thanks for your offer of a roof over my head. I will be glad to stay with you as long as I don't get in your way, Nat."

"Oh, don't you worry about that, I'd soon sweep you off your feet! Oops, sorry, better reword that. Callum, you won't be in the way. Just concentrate on getting better. Hey by the way, great news about you two," she added and waited for the response.

"Oh, yes, thank you." Callum was a little uneasy about his situation. "We would appreciate it if you didn't say anything to anyone. You know what this place is like," Callum laughed nervously and looked towards Jude, who was struggling up the path with two bags of belongings.

Natalie looked at the bags.

"Do you want to put them straight in the wash? I expect they stink of smoke, don't they?" She turned her nose up.

"Yes, that, and the smell of the hospital," agreed Callum. "Jude managed to get these from the house before we came over. She said the upstairs seems to be intact. It's mainly the downstairs that's destroyed."

"Do you know when the building work might get started?" Natalie continued to vigorously toss the salad.

"I don't know. I'll have to phone the insurance company next week," he replied. "Do you mind if I sit down. I'm shattered!"

"Sorry, how rude of me. Go on, have a seat in the lounge. I'll bring in some drinks. Is beer okay?"

"I think I'll stick to water," announced Callum as he perched on a comfy chair. "Don't think I could face alcohol just yet."

Natalie followed him into the lounge carrying a tray with iced water and a bottle of wine and two glasses.

"I know Jude will have a glass of wine, won't you, dear?" She offered Jude a glass.

"Thanks, Nat. Just the one as I'm driving," Jude replied, watching Natalie generously pour the chardonnay into her glass.

"Well," said Natalie. "I propose a toast. To Callum for his survival and to Jude for saving him! Cheers!"

They raised their respective glasses and drank Callum's health.

Jude and Callum spent an enjoyable evening with Natalie.

Jude glanced at her watch. "Sorry guys, I have to go. It's half past ten." She went to get up.

"Do you really have to go?" asked Natalie, who was relaxing next to the fireplace with a glass of wine in her grasp.

"Yes, I really do. Some of us have to work, you know!" Jude joked.

"I'll see you out," Callum said and staggered to his feet. He was very tired and in need of sleep.

They walked to the front door. Jude paused and looked at Callum.

"I hate leaving you. I want to spend the night with you, but you know I can't." She nestled against his chest. "Life's a bitch sometimes. But I can't be responsible for anything that might happen if I'm not at Littlebridge. Besides, Tag is all alone in the caravan."

Callum kissed the tip of her nose.

"Don't worry, I'll be quite safe here with Nat. We have known each other for a long time and she hasn't tried anything yet."

"I'll know if you get up to anything. Just remember, I know everything!" Jude warned Callum with a smile. "I love you lots, take care and I'll see you in the morning." She kissed him firmly on the lips.

He returned her kiss.

"I love you, gorgeous. Hurry back in the morning."

After Jude had gone, Callum returned to the lounge.

"You're a sly old dog, Jacobs. How did you manage it?" Natalie was keen to know the details of his relationship with Jude.

"Do you want a night cap?" offered Natalie.

"No, better not thanks. The drugs are still in my system. I think I'll go to bed."

Natalie looked after him as he headed to the doorway. "You care about her, don't you?"

Callum stopped and turned to face her.

"Yes, Nat. I really do," he replied with a smile on his face.

Chapter Fourteen

It was Monday morning. Jude was mucking out Nelson when she heard the sound of a lorry trundling down the driveway. She stopped what she was doing and stepped out into the yard. The bright summer sunlight glinted on the lorry's windscreen and made her squint. Manna and George had arrived back at Littlebridge. Jude hurried over to greet them.

"Hey, you two! How are you? How did you do?" she called out.

Manna jumped down from the lorry and slammed the door shut.

"Good, thanks Jude. Guess what? We qualified! What do you think about that? Both horses! They were real stars!"

"Brilliant! Oh, and by the way, Callum is out of hospital," Jude announced.

"Oh, is he! That's great news. Where is he?"

"He's staying at Natalie's. The house isn't fit to live in yet and well, there isn't any room in my caravan. So Nat came up with the suggestion for him to stay with her. And you as well, when you came back."

Manna was silent. She looked disgruntled.

"Oh, right. But I've already arranged with George to spend a few nights at his place, until the house is sorted out. Has anyone heard anything from the insurance company?"

"Not since the assessor's visit. I think Callum said he was hoping to hear something this week," shrugged Jude.

George in the meantime had climbed down from the cab and was stretching his legs.

"George, can you unload the horses for me and put them in their stables, there's a dear. I need to see Callum. I'll drive up to Natalie's. I won't be long."

With that she strode off towards her car and departed in a cloud of dust up the lane. George and Jude stood in amazement, their mouths gaping.

"I can't believe her," began Jude.

"Can't you?" asked George. "Well, I certainly have seen another side to Mrs J over these last few days. I think I know her a little better now, and what she is like." He shook his head as he spoke.

"Give me the horses, George, I'll get them sorted out in their stables. Do you know if they've had a feed this morning?"

"Yes, about three hours ago," George replied, rubbing his shoulder which was stiff from the driving.

"Right, I'll give them some hay then," decided Jude. "Their stables are ready for them."

George didn't answer. He was staring at the house and the burnt-out state of the ground floor.

"Do they know how it happened?" he asked.

Jude responded with, "They don't know. Callum was unconscious when I got to him, and so was Kier. It was terrible. They both nearly died."

"Thank God you were here then, Jude."

Jude smiled ruefully.

"What raised you to find them? After all, the caravan is way out of sight from the house, isn't it?" quizzed George with interest as he continued to stare at the house.

"Tag was out in the fields chasing rabbits. I couldn't get her to come in, so I went out looking for her and that's when I saw the house on fire." Jude felt her face redden, as she was being a little economic with the truth.

"Good for Tag, then. Catch any rabbits, did she?"

"I'm not sure, but as usual she didn't come back when I called her," said Jude, busying herself with filling hay nets.

"Log falling off the fire, do you reckon?" George still continued his barrage of questions. Jude was tiring of his inquisition. She knew he was building up evidence so he could report back to all the gossips at the pub.

"Don't know, George. Perhaps you ought to ring up the insurance company and get a full breakdown of what actually happened as I really can't tell you anything more!" she hissed.

"Okay, don't get your knickers in a twist, Jude. I was only asking. Seems to me that you're a little tense over everything."

"I think I have a right to be tense, don't you?" she reacted. "Having seen my boss nearly die in front of me, the house burning down, here on my own with all these horses and you two swanning about at the Blenheim qualifier. I think I'm perfectly entitled to be tense!" she retorted angrily and stormed off, hoping her reaction would send him off the scent of what really happened.

George took the hint and walked towards the house. As he did so, his phone rang. It was Manna. She was speaking hands free on her mobile as she drove to Natalie's house.

"George, I've just spoken to the insurance company and they're happy for us to start work on the house. The assessor has given his go-ahead, after a little encouragement by moi. The fire brigade are coming back to do a final check. When they've done that, please will you order a skip or two and start getting the house cleared for me, there's a darling."

"Will do, Mrs J. I'll unpack the horsebox and I'll get onto it straight away," he assured Manna.

In truth, he couldn't wait to get inside the house to search for clues as to the cause of the fire. He was annoyed that he would have to wait for the fire brigade to carry out their investigations. He wanted to be the first person to evaluate the cause himself so he could relay his findings to the locals at The Black Sheep. After all, it was great to be the provider of fresh information for the village to digest.

Manna reached Heyrick Heights and parked in the front yard. Callum watched her arrival from his bedroom window. He had received a text from Jude to warn him that Manna was on her way. He braced himself and prepared to act as naturally as he could.

Natalie was doing a good job as she rushed out to greet Manna.

"Hi, darling. Callum's fine. He had a good night and is just getting dressed. Do you fancy a coffee?" she gushed and ushered a speechless Manna into the kitchen and sat her down at the table.

"Great, thanks Nat. Look, thanks for looking after Callum, but I've arranged for us to stay with George until we can move back in. I hope that won't put you out."

"Oh no. That's fine, do whatever you think best. I hope you have enough room at George's. After all, they only have a small cottage. You're more than welcome to stay here and Callum has settled in well. It would be a shame to move him while he's convalescing."

Manna thought for a moment. "Well, I suppose it does seem a little silly to keep moving him about. But I would hate to say no to George, seeing as he has been so kind over the last few days, you know, helping me. Oh, we qualified by the way. So we're off to Blenheim. Isn't that great, Nat?"

"Yes, wonderful news. Now, I'll call Callum downstairs," she announced. Natalie ran up the stairs and knocked on Callum's door.

"She's here, Cal," she hissed in a loud whisper.

"Yes, I know. I saw her arrive. I'll be down in a moment," Callum replied in a low tone.

"Are you all right?" asked Natalie from behind the door.

"No, I want Jude. I want her with me. I don't want to be in the same room as Manna!

"Don't overdo it, Cal. Get your arse downstairs. You know the score; you must remember our arrangement? I get the impression there is a little more to your liaison with Jude than we planned. Like not getting romantically involved, for one!" Nat prompted Callum.

Callum sighed deeply behind the door. He felt sick and wished the floor would swallow him up so that he didn't have to face Manna, or Jude. He thought about his secret meeting a few weeks ago when Natalie had contacted him after receiving the solicitor's letter and the shock revelation that first Darius Cherry, and now Manna, were the two business partners in Sam's enterprise that owned Heyrick Heights. During their meeting they discussed how they could devise a scheme to persuade Jude to be on their side: to turn her against Manna. They swore their allegiance and Callum agreed to help in any way he could, even if that meant seducing Jude and feigning love interest in her. He hated himself for his betrayal. He hadn't wanted to hurt Jude, not ever. But he'd found that instead of playing along with the hatched plan, his feelings for Jude were genuine ones of real love. But it hadn't meant to be that way.

The agreement was that he would bed Jude, sweet-talk her against Manna so that she would deny all knowledge of the bird scarer that had spooked Ariel. Callum hoped he could coax Jude, now that she was involved with him, to state that Ariel had been unsuitable to ride and had not been adequately schooled, pushing the blame onto

Manna and thus making Leya's bid for compensation much more likely to succeed. His motivation for these actions was down to the fact that Manna had betrayed him with her affair with Sam Roberts. Manna had no idea he knew about it as, Callum being the gentleman that he was, had hadn't wanted to confront Manna. He preferred instead a stealth attack, fuelled by Nat's determination for revenge and to secure the farm into her own name. He thought this was the only way he could deal with the whole sorry situation. It would likely break Manna and himself financially, but although this was a huge risk he was prepared to take it. He would worry about the consequences afterwards.

There was so much at stake. But Callum didn't want to hurt Jude. He felt like he was in the middle of a nightmare. Callum somehow had to tell Natalie the truth, and soon.

He swallowed hard and began his descent to meet Manna. He braved a smile as he walked into the kitchen. Manna took one look at him and flung her arms around him.

"Thank God you are all right! How are you feeling?" she gushed.

"Not so bad, thanks. Do you mind if I sit down, I still feel weak." He broke off from her grasp and slid into the armchair next to the Aga.

"I think he'll live, Manna. He can stay here for as long as he likes," added Natalie, handing Manna a cup of coffee.

Manna sat down at the table opposite Callum and sipped from the cup.

"How did it happen, Cal?" she quietly quizzed. Natalie hastily looked at Callum for his reaction. He remained calm as he spoke.

"I don't know: one minute I was awake, the next I woke up in hospital. I have no idea. I lit a fire, so it must have been a log falling out onto the rug. There's no other explanation."

"So you didn't have company then?" Manna sipped at her coffee, her suspicious eyes not leaving Callum.

"No, I was on my own. K'ier was outside as usual — it was just me indoors." He kept his eyes on the floor.

"The fire brigade are carrying out a search later today so we'll know for sure." Manna drained her cup.

"Fancy another?" quipped Natalie.

"No, I must get back to the farm and do some schooling. I'll give you a ring later, Cal. To let you know the outcome from the fire brigade. I'll see you later. Thanks once again, Nat."

Manna rose from the table, grabbed her handbag and rushed off. Natalie was concerned over Manna's suspicion.

"Do you think she suspects something?" she asked.

Callum sighed heavily. "To be honest, Nat, I don't really care what she thinks. All I know is that I need to be away from her, for good. I can't stand to be in her company, she really irritates me."

"You've got to hold it together, mate. Remember what we planned? We need to get Jude to swear it was Ariel and not the bird scarer that caused the accident. We need her on side. That's why you're having this fling with her."

"So what happens if I tell you that I'm serious about Jude?" Callum announced.

"No way, you can't be!" Natalie paced around the kitchen. "Callum! I should have guessed. Why can't you be level-headed and get over it? You just cannot get involved with her. You'll blow everything. All this will be for nothing." Natalie was furious. "She'll cave in whilst being cross-examined in court; it could all go terribly wrong!"

"You'll be telling me next that the riding accident wasn't an accident!" Callum interjected.

Natalie remained silent. Callum looked her in the eye.

"It was an accident, wasn't it?" Worry overcame his face.

"Course it was. Leya couldn't have arranged for that much of a spectacular fall, could she!" Natalie smirked.

"I'm beginning to doubt everything now." Callum sat back in his chair and cleared his throat. He knew Natalie's capabilities and how manipulative she could be to get her own way.

"Don't worry, it *was* an accident. Even I couldn't magic that up. And it happened at the right time. We need a result on this: I need money to clear my debts, and I need this place to be signed back to me. And to get all of this, we need to sue Manna."

"And what do I get out of this?" asked Callum.

It was starting to sound like he was having second thoughts about the whole thing. That simple revenge against his cheating wife was no longer enough. Natalie paused and thought for a while.

"Well, now you'll get Jude. When all this is over, but not before. You need to play it cool with her, Cal."

"I need assurance that I *will* get something out of this, Nat. I am the one taking the biggest risk here. I stand to lose it all. Manna's a survivor, as long as she has her horses, she'll always be fine."

"Don't worry, I'll see to it that you'll be all right." Natalie rubbed his back. "I'll make sure of that. I'll get Darius Cherry on our side. He owes me, after all the favours I've given him in the past."

"Sexual or non-sexual?" Callum smiled wryly.

"Sexual, of course. I had no idea of his intentions," Natalie joshed. "Now that I *do* know what he's up to, I'll have to be very careful around him and not upset him."

"Does he know about your connections with Manna?"

"Course he does. I will really have to play my cards closely to my chest to get out of this mess. It will probably get nasty. Very nasty," she added and stared into space.

They remained in the kitchen in silence, each running over in their minds the dilemmas that would face them in the coming weeks.

Chapter Fifteen

Manna had finished her rigorous schooling with Othello for the afternoon. Blenheim International Horse Trials were looming ever closer and perfection and winning were foremost on Manna's mind.

Jude had cleaned all the tack and was heading back to the tack room. She carried a dressage saddle but her principle aim was to put the kettle on. She was gasping for a cup of tea.

"How did he go, Manna?" She stepped out of view into the tack room.

"He went well, thanks. Won't be long now till Blenheim. He's at peak fitness and feeling really well in himself."

Jude smiled in return. "Clever boy!"

Work on the house had begun and the builders were getting to grips with the reconstruction of the downstairs rooms. The first floor of the house was smoke damaged and a few roof tiles needed to be replaced, but otherwise it had been deemed fit by the fire officer. His report had revealed that 'the fire had been caused by a candle located in the drawing room'. Manna had instantly challenged Callum over this. He had held his hands up in defence stating that he had indeed lit the candle but he couldn't remember what happened after that. Manna needlessly reprimanded his carelessness by lecturing him over the dangers of candles and fires. Callum apologised emphatically, although Manna naturally took her time to forgive him. There were many repetitions of '*I told you so*' for him to endure.

George Trippit was in his element of project managing the rebuilding programme. He remained vigilant in overseeing each of the builders to ensure they were able to carry out their specific task. He watched their every move. He pulled them up if he felt that the work hadn't been done to his satisfaction. Manna gave the impression she was grateful for his assistance, but felt the builders were competent enough without George's input.

Manna led Othello back to his stable. She ran the stirrups up each side of the saddle, loosened his girth and untacked him. She patted his neck and placed a cooling rug over his back and fastened the straps. She walked to the tack room and put the saddle and bridle on to their allotted rack. Jude had made tea and handed her a cup.

"Heard anything more from Leya lately, Manna?" she enquired, blowing at the steaming cup.

"No, we're just waiting on a date for the hearing. I wish she would see sense and settle out of court. The amount she's asking for is preposterous. She wouldn't earn that if she worked here for several lifetimes. I don't know where she got those figures from."

"She must have a good solicitor," concluded Jude.

"Yes, Darius Cherry, no less. He's a *big* fish in the sea of lawyers. The best. I still don't know who put her up to this."

"I'm due to go and visit her this afternoon. I can see if I can find out some more information if you like." Jude offered an olive branch to Manna.

"Well, she probably won't say much, but you could try. See what you can do, Jude," replied Manna, staring into space. Her mind was focussed on Blenheim and not on Leya and her compensation claim.

She finished her tea and placed the cup on the desk.

"I'd better go and check on George and those builders. See who is upsetting whom the most!"

Jude smiled and took the cups to wash them under the outside tap. Manna strode away just as Jude's mobile phone rang. It was Natalie.

"Hi! How are things?"

"Not too bad, thanks. Manna is focussing on Blenheim and Ariel and Othello's schooling programme. At least the house is beginning to resemble some form of home, albeit slowly."

"Glad to hear it. Look, have you got time to pop past this afternoon? I need to have a chat about something. I can't talk over the phone."

"I'm supposed to be seeing Leya and, of course, Callum later, but I could drop by on the way. I'll be over in about an hour, okay?"

"No problem, lovey. Callum is upstairs resting but I am sure you can coax him downstairs when you arrive!" Nat replied.

Jude finished her chores and arrived at Heyrick Heights within the hour. Natalie poured two glasses of homemade lemonade and waited for Jude in the kitchen.

"Hi, come on in Jude, have some lemonade." She offered a glass to Jude who took it in gratitude.

"As long as there isn't any vodka lurking in it! Oh, and is Callum awake?" Jude laughed.

"You act as though you don't trust me! And, no I haven't heard anything from Callum. Let sleeping dogs lie!" Natalie smiled and indicated for Jude to sit down. "Right, I'll get to the point, Jude. I want to talk about Leya. Seems to me to be an ideal time to have this chat before you go and see her. As you know, I am secretly helping her in the background to sue Manna. I'm prepared to pay her legal costs when it gets to court. Do you remember our chat a while back?"

Jude listened to Natalie in silence and nodded.

"When it gets to court, Manna will get a kicking from my lawyer, Darius Cherry, and hopefully, when we win, she will get her just desserts, so to speak. I'm going to meet with Darius later on this afternoon to discuss matters. I hope it won't drag on forever, like some cases do."

"But what about Callum?" Jude was concerned over what effect this would have on him. "Surely if Leya wins the case, it will ruin him and Manna and push them in their separate ways. That would mean he and I can be together."

"He'll be fine. I will make sure he doesn't lose out. Let's say I will be arranging to pay him a lump sum. I need his help to get me through all this."

"What's he doing to help you?" Jude was sensing something wasn't quite right.

Natalie hesitated and smiled.

"Nothing for you to worry about, Jude."

"No, come on Nat. What sort of help? You're starting to worry me... tell me now!" Jude insisted.

Natalie bit her lip and swallowed.

"You won't like what I'm about to say, and I don't want to say it cos I don't want to hurt you."

"What the hell are you talking about?" Jude rose out of her chair. Her heart was pounding. "Tell me!"

"Okay. When I got the letter through from the solicitors, it said that Sam had a partnership arrangement. I confided in Callum when I found out who it was. Like me, he couldn't believe that it turned out to be Manna. He was desperate to get back at her for hiding such a massive secret, so we hatched a plan. But, well, for it to work we needed to have *you* on side, so to speak. To testify that Ariel wasn't spooked by a bird scarer but that she just bolted as she hadn't been schooled properly and that it was dangerous; to shove the blame on to Manna."

"So where did I come into it then?" Jude stood with her arms folded. Natalie remained silent. "Come on, out with it!"

"Callum and I thought that, to get you on side, he would… show an interest in you. In order to persuade you to see our way of thinking."

Jude strode up to Natalie and slapped her across the face.

"You bitch! You absolute bitch! How can you sit there calmly telling me that it was a set-up? For God's sake! How do you sleep at night? And Callum, well, he's no better! The bastard, setting me up! A free lay! Taking advantage of my feelings. I can't believe you two!"

"Jude! Please listen to what I have to say…" Natalie pleaded and grabbed Jude's sleeve to pull her back to the table.

"Hands off! You are nothing but scum, Natalie! I hope you rot in hell, and that bastard Callum too! You won't get away with this, not now. You've blown your chances! I'll definitely make sure Manna wins the case!"

"And if I tell her you're bedding her husband?" asked Natalie, holding on to the table. "That won't go down well, will it? After all, it's the truth, isn't it, Jude? You'll lose your job and your reputation. You'll gain a new one as a husband stealer. Think carefully before you act, that's all I say. Think about it long and hard, then come back to me and we'll talk."

Jude stood in the doorway of the kitchen fuming. Her face was scarlet in anger and humiliation but she resisted the urge to cry. She was too proud for that to happen. She was confused over her feelings. She loved Callum but now she hated him too.

She didn't know what to do. She breathed heavily as she took in what Natalie had said. After a time she spoke.

"I can't win, can I? You've got me over a barrel! You and your accomplice. You certainly are sly, Natalie. God help anyone who tries to cross you. Just let me take all this in for a while, and anyway, I need to see Leya. What a complete mess this is, and I'm tangled up right in the middle of it!"

"Call me later Jude. We'll talk more," concluded Natalie and showed Jude to the door.

"When you see Callum next, thank him, won't you, for messing up my life, unless I see him first then I will tell him myself! I almost wish I hadn't saved him now!" Jude slammed the door behind her and marched towards her car.

She sat in front of the steering wheel for a few moments. Her whole body was shaking. She drove off at speed. Natalie watched from the house. She reached for her mobile phone and dialled a number. It was answered almost immediately.

"Dar? It's me. Get over here… now!" She snapped the phone shut and threw it on to the work surface.

Darius Cherry arrived at the farm within the hour. He had hardly got into the house when Natalie threw herself on him and hugged his neck.

"Oh Dar! I think I've messed up, big time! I need you to get me out of this shit."

Darius looked perplexed. "What have you done?" He roughly pushed Natalie away so he could look her square in the face. His eyes were piercing.

"I told Jude about our plan. She wheedled the information out of me somehow. I don't know why I told her but I think I've blown it."

"You stupid cow! It was only a matter of time! Why couldn't you keep you big mouth shut? Right, so we need to work out a way to deal with this. How have you left things with Jude?"

"I tried to double bluff her. I told her that I would tell Manna about her affair with Callum. Told her she would be labelled a slut, that she'd lose her reputation."

"Okay. We'll keep to our plan then, but we need to add to it."

"Add to it? What do you mean?" Natalie was worried.

"You are obviously aware Manna is the other partner in the business. We need to get her out of the partnership, by any means. It needs to be something more than the accident to affect her capacity to be a partner. It would then free me up to be managing partner. I could bring someone else into partnership with me, someone I could control."

"That sounds like bribery to me," Natalie pondered. She poured herself a Scotch and offered a glass to Darius.

"Thanks," he replied, his mind racing. "Right, I think I have it. She needs to lose Leya's case, no matter what, so she is sued for the full half a million, plus costs. I will arrange an appointment with her and put her on the spot. She can't take money from the property investments as they are tied up indefinitely until one of us dies." Natalie looked at him as alarm flickered across her face. "Don't worry, I don't plan on killing her. She's going to need money to cover the rest of the claim. That's where we get Heyrick Heights involved. Manna's share is half the value of this place, which I reckon to be about two hundred and fifty thousand. Bingo! She sells her share of Heyrick Heights to me and I get it lock, stock and barrel. She is out of the equation." His eyes widened, seemingly with greed as he spoke, and his jaw became set. He paced the room.

"But what if she wins?" Natalie brought Darius back to reality.

"She won't have a chance in hell. Not with what I intend to hit her with. I'll do some digging, make her look like a tart, you know, the affair with Sam. I'll make her out to be a selfish slapper. Nobody likes a slapper. She won't stand an earthly. We'll destroy her character."

"What shall I say to Jude?" Natalie gulped at her Scotch.

"Offer her money, anything, to get her back on our side."

"Callum is really smitten with her. I feel terrible that she is going to give him hell over this. It wasn't his fault. I need to speak with him."

"Let her do it. Let her have a go at him; they'll sort things out. Don't worry, it isn't the end of the world. We just need to get this case done and dusted and Manna out of our hair."

"And after all this is over, what will happen to me?" Natalie needed to ask the question. Her whole future depended on Cherry.

"You won't go without. As long as we have our arrangement and I get my leg over frequently, then you won't have to worry. Talking about getting my leg over, I'm in need of sex... now!"

He leaned across and placed his hand between Natalie's thighs and rubbed her leg. She obliged by placing her empty glass on the table and sat astride his lap.

"This is getting to be a habit in this room," he smiled as he ran his hands over her breasts and over her shoulders. He grabbed a handful of her hair and drew her head roughly towards his. He slyly licked her face, leaving a trail of saliva across her cheek.

"You'll be my sex slave. How would you like that, Nat?"

Natalie was alarmed but decided it was in her best interest to play along.

"I could think of nothing better, Dar, I was born to please," she added and placed her hands on his face and kissed him on the lips.

Darius got up and carried Natalie to the sofa. He dropped her onto it and roughly parted her legs, then hitched up her skirt.

"Haven't done it on here yet, have we? I want to explore all of you, all over this house. I want no stone unturned, do you get what I am saying?" he hissed in her ear and kissed her neck.

"I hear you, Dar. Don't worry, we'll do it. We'll do it."

Natalie closed her eyes and swallowed hard. She didn't like it when Darius was in this mood. She felt he was punishing her sexually. She was relieved when he climbed off her. He zipped his fly, straightened his shirt and walked to the door. He checked his reflection in the mirror. Running a hand through his hardly tousled hair, he didn't bother to face Nat.

"I'll be in touch. See you!"

He closed the door and drove off. Natalie remained on the sofa with her skirt still lifted up. She began to sob. For the first time, she felt cheap, dirty and wretched. She got up from the sofa and reached for the whisky. Trembling, she poured a four-finger measure into a tumbler and gulped it down; she made a face as she did so. She was scared that Darius was taking control of her. He could undoubtedly manipulate the situation to take everything she owned away from her, including her dignity.

"What have I let myself in for?" she sobbed out loud.

Chapter Sixteen

Jude drove to Leya's house. Tears poured down her face as she tried to take in what Natalie had told her. She experienced all possible emotions at once. She was furious with Natalie, distraught over Callum and his deceit, and bitter with Leya because of all the mess she had caused. The whole mess that was affecting so many people's lives.

She reached her destination. She tried to compose herself as Leya's father opened the door. She failed.

"Hello, Jude. Are you—" he began.

"Can I see Leya please, Mr Martin? I can't explain at the moment," she sobbed.

Leya was standing behind her father in the hallway. She pushed past him.

"Jude, come on, up to my room." Leya bundled Jude up the stairs. She looked back at her father and nodded in reassurance. Mr Martin knew the look was for him to keep a low profile.

They reached Leya's bedroom and Jude broke down completely.

"Oh Leya, I don't know where to start with all this. I can't believe what Natalie has just told me. I feel so let down, such an idiot!"

Leya sat on the bed. She had guessed the reason for this outburst.

"Natalie told you about the case, I take it. What else has she told you, Jude?"

Jude shook her head, still in shock. "What I am about to tell you has to stay within this room. If it doesn't then we're all in the shit, understand me, Leya?"

Leya was alarmed and confused. "Yeah, course."

Jude swallowed hard and explained. "Callum and I are having an affair. Well, that is what I thought it was until Natalie kindly informed me that he was simply using me to get at Manna over this bloody court case of yours. It seems like they are out to revenge Manna themselves. Manna apparently had an affair with Sam Roberts years ago and Natalie has been waiting to get even ever since."

Leya glared. "So that's the reason why she wants to *help* me then. Not for my benefit at all but for her own gain. What a selfish bitch!"

"Yeah," Jude sniffled. "So, part of the plan was for Callum to have a fling with me so that I wouldn't stick up for Manna; they could get back at her that way. And now Natalie is bribing me because she says if I don't help her, she will tell Manna about Callum and me. So muggins here is stuck in the middle of this whole thing."

"Jude, I am so sorry. I had no idea things would get out so of hand. It's all over money, isn't it? I cannot believe that Natalie can be so cruel. I am so disappointed in how she has acted!"

"Well, our so-called *friend* is only out for herself. And she has Darius Cherry representing you, which is bad news. He never loses a case, so, whatever happens, Manna is going to lose, big time. Her place, her home, her husband, the list goes on."

"All for the sake of a torrid affair," surmised Leya, looking towards the ceiling.

"And the ideal opportunity arose for Natalie when you had your accident. She could then persuade you to sue Manna. She wants me to testify that it wasn't the bird scarer that made Ariel bolt but that it was Manna's negligence by not schooling the horse correctly, thus putting you at risk."

"And if you say that it *was* the bird scarer, then Natalie will tell Manna about you and Callum?"

"You've got it, so I lose out either way. Talk about a sitting duck. How could Callum be so cruel? He seemed so genuine about us too. Seems like he's just as bad as Natalie."

Leya thought for a moment. "Unless you have the guts to tell Manna exactly what is going on."

"Oh yeah, can you imagine that? I'll lose my job and my reputation. The only way out of this, Leya, and I know it's hard, is for you to drop the case. To not take it any further. How do you feel about that?" Jude looked desperately at Leya.

Leya was silent for a while. She closed her eyes and thought. "I can't do it, Jude! If I were to drop the case, I'd be in the same situation as you, wouldn't I? In fact, I think we're both for the chop." She closed her eyes once more and thought. "I think you need to talk this through with Callum. Let him know exactly what's going on and what our problem is. Do you think you can do that?"

Jude sighed. "Yeah, you're right. I need to do something, and fast. Before it all goes wrong and we lose everything." She got up. "Thanks for the chat. Don't forget, not a word to Natalie or anyone. We need to sort this mess out ourselves."

Leya got up and held out her good arm to Jude for a hug. Jude briefly held her. "I'll do it for both of us, Leya. We'll be okay. Remember, if you talk to Natalie, pretend I haven't spoken about this to you."

And Jude was gone.

Leya was furious. The whole situation was spiralling totally out of control. She prayed that Jude would somehow find a solution. She sat in her room staring at the wall. Her mobile phone rang. Natalie's number came up on the screen. Leya decided to take the call.

"Hi Leya, how are you?" Natalie breezed.

"Hello Natalie, fine thank you," Leya curtly returned.

"Oh, right, um, has Jude been over to see you today?" Natalie tried to sound cool.

"Yeah, why?"

"Has she said anything to you about the court case?" Natalie sounded anxious.

"No, she was just talking about the horses, the yard and Blenheim. It isn't long now. Manna must be getting really nervous." Leya purposely chattered on.

"Yes! Yes! So she must. But Jude hasn't said anything to you… anything about the case?" Natalie repeated, this time with more urgency in her voice.

"No. Why? Should she have?" Leya was stalling extremely well.

"I just thought… Look, it doesn't matter, Leya. I have to go, bye!" Natalie rang off.

Leya smiled to herself and hugged the phone. She felt a little less angry but was determined to support Jude as best she could.

oOo

Jude drove back to Littlebridge, mulling over the afternoon's events. She still couldn't believe Callum could be so cruel and calculating. She had to speak with him. It was going to be hard but she somehow needed to clear her name from the mess that was unravelling in front of her.

She reached the yard, parked her car at the entrance to the field and called Tag. The little Jack Russell immediately ran to her side and they walked to Jude's caravan. Jude fumbled in her pocket for her phone to text Callum. She reached the mobile home and opened the door. Sitting inside was Callum. As she was about to speak to him, his mobile phone rang to indicate he'd just received a message.

"Don't worry, it's only me texting you. I need to talk to you." Jude sounded cold.

Callum got up to kiss her but she pushed him away.

"How could you? How could you use me like that? You really had me going, Callum. If they gave out Oscars for your performance you would rank as the number one bastard of all times. How do you feel? Does it make you feel like a *man* to know you bedded a dozy groom? Jesus, how could you be so cruel?"

Callum sat down in silence. He looked at the floor. Jude was on a roll.

"What has Natalie *fucking* Roberts got over you? Are you *that* weak that you need her to bail you out of your marriage? I want you to tell me exactly what is going on?"

She stood over Callum. Her face was inches from the top of his head. She was seething.

"I... I don't know what to say. I—" Callum began.

"If you say you're sorry, I will throttle you on the spot!" Jude spat and pushed against Callum's shoulder with the palm of her hand.

"If it makes you feel better, hit me. I deserve it." Callum didn't look up.

"Just talk!" hissed Jude.

She folded her arms waiting for the answer. Callum swallowed hard.

"I really didn't mean to hurt you. I really *don't* want to hurt you. I just wish I could make things better."

"All words, Callum, just words." Jude still stood over him like a hawk watching its prey. "Go on, not good enough!"

"Manna had an affair with Sam. But I expect you know that bit. Natalie found out and wanted to someday get even with her. Leya's accident was the ideal time to start things moving. Problem was that Natalie didn't know Manna was the silent partner in Sam's affairs. Nor that she has a share in Heyrick Heights and that Darius Cherry is the other partner. Cherry has got it in for Natalie, although the stupid cow can't see it. He wants to get his hands on the money. The trouble is, Natalie is in the way. If they manage to sue Manna successfully, then Cherry will make sure Natalie is paid off and out of his hair. All he wants is Heyrick Heights. He doesn't give a shit about anything else. But I'm worried about what is going to happen to Natalie. She is in the middle of all of this and Cherry is a very dangerous man, legally and physically. But Nat can't see that. All she sees is the sex and nothing else."

Jude listened intently. Her eyes were wide and ready for a fight.

"What gave you the right to hurt me in the process?" she snapped.

"Natalie needed us to get you on our side."

"So, what do you get out of this? Surely you cannot be so stupid as to think that you aren't going to be affected?" Jude fired her question with venom.

"I get to be free of Manna. Our marriage hit the rocks a long time ago and, well, it hasn't been right for a while. She keeps running up debts; I try to keep the books afloat by cutting back on expenses, or trying to. The biggest mistake I made was to reduce the cover on the insurance for the yard. Proved to be my downfall. I was at a low ebb; Natalie was my shoulder to cry on. She suggested—"

"That you get into my knickers. Get me to declare my undying love for you and use me for yours and her gain!" Jude finished Callum's sentence.

"That was the plan yes, but it didn't happen like that—"

"You mean you got that wrong as well? I don't believe it! How did you mess up on that?" Jude shook her head in disbelief.

"The mistake I made was I fell in love with you."

"Oh my—"

"Please, let me finish, Jude. I know at this moment you will probably think I'm lying, but I'm not. I've fallen in love with you. That's where I messed up; so, there you have it." Callum looked up at Jude's face. There were tears in his eyes. He bowed his head and gulped. "Sorry, I don't mean to be weak but believe me, that *is* the honest truth."

Jude pursed her lips and thought for a while.

"So you aren't having it off with Natalie then?"

Callum shook his head.

"No! She does nothing for me at all!" he choked.

There was an awkward silence then Jude eventually spoke.

"At least that's something. I would hate to think that I had competition with that tart!"

"You're much better than that, Jude. Better than all of us. But you know that. God, what a mess this is!" Callum closed his eyes.

"So how are we going to get out of it, especially now that Natalie has made the biggest blunder on earth by getting involved with Darius Cherry? She needs to get her brains back in her head and not in her underwear."

"As far as I'm concerned, all I want is you, and as long as you feel the same way, then I swear to you I will never hurt you again, Jude. You have my word."

"What about Manna? What's going to happen with her?" Jude needed to know exactly where she stood.

"Manna and I are definitely history. I think, deep down, we both know that. As far as the hearing is concerned, we still have to go through with it: that is, as long as Leya still wants to pursue the claim."

"What if she drops the claim?"

Callum pondered for a while.

"Then we win. We survive. But surely Leya will want to go ahead, won't she? If, for instance, she does drop the case, then Natalie will be the one in the shit. Not only will she have Darius Cherry to contend with, but she will have lost the chance to get her own back on Manna. I think she will be in serious trouble if Cherry doesn't get his way. In fact, I don't think he would let her get away. I can't imagine what he would do to her. I'd be genuinely worried about her safety."

"So much so that she may need to *disappear* for a while, do you think?" Jude was trying to make sense of the situation.

"Yes, but Cherry would do his utmost to find her. He'd be like Tag with a rabbit: he wouldn't let go until he found her. He'd probably kill her. I know it's a terrible thing to say, but, as I said before, he appears like he could be a very dangerous man legally. He has so many connections and who knows what else."

"With the law on his side?"

"Yeah, that's the danger. He is a very clever lawyer who could bend any situation to suit himself. That's why he is good at what he does. He is the Goliath to Natalie's David."

"So do we risk Leya dropping the case? What we have to think about is whether our own lives and future are more important than Natalie's? At this present time, I couldn't care less if Cherry did murder her. She is an evil, conniving cow who deserves all she gets."

Callum shook his head.

"All for the sake of bloody horses, isn't it? The root of all this evil is bloody horses! I ask you!"

"And hunt, and women, and weak blokes wanting to bed everything they see," finished Jude. "Let's face it Callum, we're all involved now, even the bloody horses. Cos if Manna goes down, they go too. Everything goes!"

Callum got up and grabbed Jude.

"What are you doing?" she exclaimed.

His eyes were wide with excitement. He was bursting to speak and shook her gently as he did so.

"I've got it! I've got it!" he exclaimed and planted a kiss on Jude's lips, taking her by surprise.

"Hang on! I haven't forgiven you… yet." She pushed him back so she could look him in the face.

"I know the solution! It is pretty far-fetched, but it might just work. We need to get Darius Cherry out of the picture somehow, don't we? So that he isn't a threat to Natalie and Leya?"

"Got it in one, Sherlock. So how do you propose we do this, by public hanging? A vicious murder at midnight on Malsham Downs? Alien abduction?" Jude cynically suggested.

"Give me a bit more credit, Jude. What's the best way we could hurt Cherry?" He awaited Jude's response, but she decided to keep quiet. Callum answered his own question. "Through his wallet!"

"How through his wallet?"

Callum leapt about in excitement. He was still holding Jude's shoulders, making her sway.

"By hitting him where it hurts, in his pocket. Turning the tables on him. We sue him. It's going to take a lot of groundwork and planning, but we could just about do it. Expose him to the public, so they know how much of a bastard he really is. And how do we do that, you may ask? Well, in one short word... LEYA! Get her to lead him on without him actually realising it and then get him charged for sexual harassment. It will be his downfall as he has such a squeaky clean public image. Member of the Masons, Rotary Club, you name it. It will be sweet revenge. So sweet that he will never bother us again. Do you think Leya would be up for it?"

"Has she got any choice?" Jude didn't seem convinced.

"No, in a nutshell. Look, we need to act fast. We have to speak to Leya today and get this plan into action." Callum was already scheming.

"What about Natalie?"

"I'll speak to her. Let her know enough, but not everything. You know she will blab to the world and his wife."

"And Manna?"

"One step at a time, Jude. Let's nail Cherry first then worry about Manna. Leya is the key in all of this. Oh, and by the way, am I forgiven?" Callum dared to pose the question.

Jude wrapped her arms around his waist, tipped her face up to his so that their lips were millimetres apart, and whispered, "If you mess up again, Jacobs, I will personally cut off your bollocks and hang them from the nearest tree. Get the hint? Oh, and... yes, I forgive you!" she added and promptly kissed him.

Chapter Seventeen

Three weeks later at Littlebridge Stables, Manna had finished packing the lorry.

"That's everything! Are you ready to go, George?" She slammed the groom's door firmly shut. Blenheim International Horse Trials were now only a matter of hours away. This was a massive competition for Manna and her career.

"Yep, all ready, Mrs J. Ready when you are." George appeared from the other side of the box, smiling. He was carrying a bag which contained three bottles of wine and numerous packets of nibbles and biscuits.

"I'll tell Callum we're off. That is, if I can find him." Manna looked briskly about her.

"Er, he's over there, Mrs J." George pointed in the direction of the house where Callum was standing to attention.

Manna took a few steps forward and called out, "I'll text you when we get there, you know, just to say we made it!"

Callum called back, "Good luck!"

Manna felt awkward.

"Right, yes, thanks. See you next week then."

She shrugged her shoulders, turned on her heel and walked to the horsebox. George climbed into the driver's seat and adjusted his seatbelt. He revved the engine into life with the anticipation that their very important journey was about to begin.

"Lots of luck, Manna!" Jude called out. She waved frantically at the horsebox. Manna smiled and without a verbal response casually waved back. She climbed into the cab alongside George. The box lurched into action. The sudden jolt caused the horses to kick out at the side of the lorry as it ambled up the driveway.

"Looks like we're alone again, Mr Jacobs," Jude called across the yard.

Callum laughed. "Yes. People will start talking about us."

"Do you care?" Jude came over to Callum and took hold of his hand. He turned to look at her.

"With all this going on? No, not really. But for now we have lots of work to do. Can you ring Leya and go through the plan again with her? Let me know if she is happy with everything and still willing to go ahead," Callum asked.

"Yeah, I just need to finish mucking out then I'll phone her." Jude went to walk off as Callum caught her arm.

"Great. I need to make a phone call too. Someone owes me a favour, if you know what I mean."

"I'll catch up with you at lunchtime then we can compare notes," Jude suggested and made her way back to the line of stables.

"Oh, and by the way," Callum called out with a grin, "did anyone ever tell you that you have a lovely arse?"

Jude stopped without turning around and replied, "Yeah, all the time!" She swaggered off in an exaggerated walk, swinging her hips from side to side.

Callum laughed and walked back to the house. Two of the builders were arguing over some tools in the doorway. Callum interrupted their disagreement.

"Now guys, this house has to be finished by the time Mrs Jacobs returns next Tuesday. Because, if it isn't, well… you know what women are like. I will let her deal with you!"

He left the builders looking bemused but unperturbed as he barged into the house. One of the builders made a rude gesture behind Callum's back. He continued to talk as he walked, his voice echoing within the bareness of the rooms, "Believe me, the wrath of a woman scorned!"

"We get the idea, gov. Don't worry, we'll be done by then. Can't have the lady of the house upset now, can we?" They roared with laughter between themselves.

"Glad to hear it," returned Callum, unaware of the joke.

He went upstairs to his study and reached for the phone. He dialled a number. As it rang he sat down on the edge of a chair and waited for a response.

"Hi Jim? It's Callum Jacobs. Yeah, good thanks. Look Jim, I need a favour from you." He spoke about his plan. "Yes, that's it, Cherry, Darius Cherry – right – perhaps you can give me a ring back later. I appreciate that. Thanks!"

Callum replaced the receiver, looking thoughtful. He hadn't heard Jude walk up the stairs. She was now standing in the doorway.

"Going to plan?" she casually asked.

"God, Jude! Don't creep about like that! My nerves are on edge enough as it is!" Callum quickly recovered.

"Sorry babe. Look, I've spoken with Leya and she is okay with things. She isn't mad about the arrangement to set him up but when I explained again that it could be his downfall, she seemed happy to oblige. But it will have to be split-second timing or it could go terribly wrong!" Jude folded her arms.

"I know," replied Callum. He stared at the papers on the desk. "That's why I've called in a favour from a friend who owes me. He's ringing back later. Hopefully it will all go as we hope."

"When's this all going to happen?" Jude placed her arms around Callum's shoulders and kissed the top of his head.

"Tomorrow. I have suitably informed my source. We need to have that chat with Leya to confirm everything."

"Okay. Have you spoken to Natalie about all this?" she added.

"No, I've decided I want her completely out of the picture, so she doesn't blow it. I can't have her knowing too much or she won't seem genuine if Cherry makes an unannounced visit to her."

"Okay, so where is this all going to take place?" Jude sat on the desk in front of Callum.

"At Leya's house, but we need to make sure that she's alone. Can you take her mum and dad out, down the Sheep or somewhere?"

Jude nodded. "It shouldn't be a problem. I'll arrange it now."

oOo

Leya made her way to the front door. As arranged, Darius Cherry was on the doorstep. He was amazed to see Leya open the door wearing a dressing gown.

"Hello Mr Cherry, how are you? Come in. Would you like a coffee?"

She let him into the house. Cherry accepted and she escaped to the kitchen. She filled the kettle with water. She discreetly took her mobile phone out of her gown pocket and dialled Jude's number.

"Jude! He's here! Keep Mum and Dad busy. I'm really scared! I'm not sure I can do this!" she hissed.

"Calm down, Leya. Callum has got his contact ready and has it all under control. Don't panic, just try and stay calm and act normally. Don't worry, I promise you'll be fine! You can do this! Keep the phone on to record everything."

"Make sure you're right, Jude! Got to go, bye."

Leya placed her phone back into her pocket. The kettle had boiled and she poured the water into two waiting brown mugs. She returned to the lounge and placed the coffee down on the table. Darius Cherry was lounging on the sofa.

"So, Leya, what's this all about? Its midday and you're not dressed!" He tapped his leather briefcase with his car keys.

Leya took a deep breath. "Mr Cherry, I wanted to see you because I'm not sure about the hearing. It has been really worrying me, especially with all the anxiety it's causing everyone around me. Look, to be honest, I'm not sure I can cope with the stress of it anymore."

Cherry slammed his keys onto the table, slopping the coffee on to the surface. He was furious.

"Leya, how many times do I have to tell you? It's only a matter of weeks and you will be looking at a sizeable bank balance and a complete change of lifestyle. How can you be unsure at this crucial stage? I seriously advise you to think very carefully about your decision!" he barked at Leya, making her feel uneasy.

"I really don't want any aggravation. I'm feeling much better now and the physio says I am improving. I have feeling back in my arm and it's getting easier each day. So it really looks like I will be able to go back to work again."

"You would be a fool to back out at this stage. You would be throwing away a life-changing opportunity. How would you feel seeing Manna Jacobs get away scot-free? Surely you must accept that justice has to be done?"

"Well," Leya sat down on the sofa beside Cherry, "I thought you might react like this, so I wondered I could make it up to you. Would you um… like a bite to eat? Or something else?"

Leya let her dressing gown slip open. It revealed a seductive black negligee. Cherry thought for a while.

"It's too early for lunch, but I'm quite happy to consider something else," he slyly remarked.

"Fine. But you haven't finished your coffee yet," Leya pointed out. She suddenly felt a cold sweat creeping over her body and her nerve was rapidly fading.

Cherry smiled again. "Yes, I quite like this offer of a bit extra. Oh, and please, call me *Darius*."

Leya nodded slowly. "But you are my lawyer and perhaps you shouldn't be thinking along those lines."

Cherry moved closer to Leya and placed his arm around her shoulders. He held her firmly and his face was inches away from hers.

"Do you want me to start the proceedings, Leya, because I can, you know."

Leya froze. "No! Erm, I don't need that sort of reassurance, Mr Cherry. Please, let me go!" Leya felt sick.

It had all been clear in her mind what she had to do but now the moment was upon her, she couldn't go through with it. Cherry was almost on top of Leya as he hissed in her ear, "Don't deny me, bitch! I will reassure you enough so you will *have* to go ahead with the case!"

He started to forcibly kiss her neck, face and throat and thrust his tongue awkwardly into her mouth. Leya was terrified as Cherry began to grind his hips against her. He had climbed on top of her and she desperately tried to wriggle free.

"Leave me alone! Please! Leave me alone! I don't think this is appropriate behaviour for a lawyer!"

"But I do," Cherry panted.

He grabbed Leya and forced her into the kitchen. He held her against the work surface and fumbled with her dressing gown. He still held her tightly.

Leya screamed, "Get off me, you pervert! Or I'll call the police!"

"Oh, I don't think you will. Who are they going to believe? A sniffling little girl perhaps? Or a trusted and respected lawyer? No contest, is there? So shut your pretty little mouth and just do as I say!"

He ripped at Leya's dressing gown. Leya tried to fight him off but he was too strong for her.

"Come on! You know you want me! After all, I provide a personal service for *all* my clients. Why should I treat you any differently, Leya?"

Leya trembled as Cherry swept his hands around her thighs and tried to force her legs apart.

"Lighten up, Leya, its playtime now!"

Leya found an inner strength and freed her hands from behind her back.

"No, you don't! Back off and leave me alone!"

Cherry looked at her in annoyance.

"Hmmmm... feisty little filly, aren't you? But I do love a bit of rough!" he hissed and kissed her roughly on the mouth. Leya bit his lip hard, making him wince.

"Rough? Yeah, I can be rough too, Mr Cherry!"

"Well, that suits me just fine!"

Leya glared at him. "Well, it doesn't suit me!" She swiftly lifted her knee and caught Cherry a direct hit in the groin. He fell to the ground in agony. "Is that rough enough for you... Darius?" she shouted.

"You little bitch!" he spat, hardly able to breath. "I don't give up that easily!"

"Neither do I, *Darius*. I suggest you leave immediately or I will call the police."

"Don't threaten me, girlie. You have no idea who you are dealing with. You'd be on very dangerous ground. But I'll have you, don't you worry. I'll give you the reassurance that you crave. Reassurance with this!"

Cherry rose to his feet and grabbed Leya's legs, making her fall on to the floor. He forced himself on top of her as she tried to escape. He held onto her hair so she couldn't move.

"Come on, don't be shy. I'll look after you, little virgin. That's right, isn't it? I'm always right. I can smell a virgin a mile off. I won't hurt you... much!"

Cherry's demonic grin was inches away from Leya's face as she shut her eyes in desperation. Where *was* Jude with the backup?

Cherry ripped open Leya's negligee and exposed her breasts. He kissed her violently as he fumbled with his trousers. Leya continued to fight against him. There was no way she was going to become one of his statistics.

The doorbell rang out shrilly.

"For God's sake, get rid of them! I'm exploding here!" Cherry yelled.

Leya scrambled to her feet: her arm was really hurting. Cherry grabbed her ankle.

"Get rid of them now! And no screaming! Remember, I'm a very dangerous man if you become my enemy! Understand me?"

Leya nodded in silence and composed herself. She clutched her gown to her body and stumbled to the door. Outside on the doorstep were two uniformed police officers.

"Where is he?" demanded one officer and Leya pointed to the kitchen.

They rushed in to see Cherry sprawled on the floor, trousers around his ankles in a very precarious now.

"I am arresting you for attempted rape. You do not have to say anything which you may rely on in court." The officer swiftly clasped handcuffs onto Cherry's wrists and dragged him to his feet.

"Oh, brilliant! Clever girl!" Cherry exclaimed. The arresting officer turned to Leya.

"We had a phone call from someone who'd heard screaming. Do you know this man?"

She swallowed hard and replied. "Yes, he is Darius Cherry, my lawyer."

"At least let me put my dick away!" Cherry protested. "My reputation—"

"Your reputation, Mr Cherry, leaves a lot to be desired. Come on, down the station now!"

Cherry was furious. He glared at Leya as he was dragged away.

"You're not clever! Not clever at all! You need me! You told me so, Leya!"

"Out now, Cherry. I hope you have a good brief," the officer remarked with a smirk.

"Oh, don't you worry. You haven't heard the last of this. Be afraid Leya—"

"That sounds an awful lot like a threat. You wouldn't be threatening this young lady, would you, Cherry? Come on out now!"

Darius Cherry was led away to one of the patrol cars outside the house. Leya shivered. She straightened her meagre clothing. A female support officer directed her back into the house.

"Did he actually have intercourse with you?" she enquired.

Leya shook her head. "No, but I think he was about to when you turned up. I was really scared."

"Why are you still wearing your nightclothes at this time of the morning?" asked the PC.

"I was still in bed. I haven't been well, you see, and Mum and Dad have gone out. He woke me up by knocking on the door. He forced his way indoors." Leya started to cry.

"I will have to take a statement from you. I need you to come down to the police station to do that and undergo a few tests. Are you happy to do that?"

"Yes, of course, I'm more than happy to do that. I don't want that parasite putting anyone else at risk!" Leya sobbed.

"So you would like to press charges?" the officer calmly asked.

"Yes, I would, without a doubt," Leya confidently replied.

Callum drew up outside Leya's house. He saw Cherry being driven away in one of the patrol cars, protesting all the way. Callum got out and walked over to the other police car where a plain-clothed officer stood talking on his radio. He turned and acknowledged Callum.

"Thanks, Jim. That bastard needed nailing before he really did rape someone."

Jim finished speaking on the radio and nodded. "No problem Callum. I think it will be a long while before he's back at screwing people… in the legal sense!"

"I owe you, Jim. Pint at The Black Sheep?"

"Yeah, mate. I just need to interview Miss Martin. I knock off in an hour or so. I'll meet you there," Jim returned.

"Great, thanks once again." Callum patted Jim's shoulder.

Callum caught Leya's attention as she was leaving the house. He waved at her to come over to him. Leya made her excuses to the female officer and walked over to him, clutching her arm.

"Are you all right, Leya?"

"I will be," she replied and looked distant. "Now I know what Cherry is capable of, I'm more than happy to drop the compensation case. He needs to be locked away. He is really dangerous. I wouldn't want anyone else to go through what just happened to me. I know it could have been so much worse… It's just, well, I feel sick to the stomach."

Callum managed a weak smile. "I'm sorry you had to go through that ordeal. But we are truly thankful that you did. You were so brave. If you need anything, just ring me, okay?" he offered.

Leya nodded.

"Yep, okay, I will, thank you. Look, I must go to the station; they need a statement from me. Oh, and just one thing…" she added, "I would like to have my old job back: that is the thing I need most. Okay, my arm isn't quite right still, but I'm willing to give it a go. It might speed up my recovery."

"Of course," Callum nodded. "That won't be a problem."

He climbed back into his car and drove back to Littlebridge with a look of satisfaction and relief on his face.

Chapter Eighteen

Manna's horsebox reached the formidable gates at Blenheim Palace amidst a buzz of excited anticipation. Manna gazed across to the vast expanse of the lake and to the bridge; its reflection in the water made it look like a ring. It was breathtakingly beautiful, like a landscape painting. A flock of birds flew majestically across the water, seemingly skimming the surface with their wings.

George applied the handbrake. They were in a queue of horseboxes which had all arrived at the same time, waiting to be shown where to park and unload the horses. There was a vast array of marquees dotted amongst numerous equine shops, and the stabling arrangements were at the other end of a very large, immaculately groomed field. They drove on and drank in the sights. Manna breathed in the atmosphere.

"This is it, George. This is what it's all about. The ultimate!"

George nodded, "Yep, that's right, Mrs J. Now all you've got to do is to focus on your horses. Shut everything else out and concentrate on the task in hand!"

"Yes, you're right. Keeping calm is the key. Focus and stay calm," Manna muttered.

"Which is what you do best, Mrs J. Ariel knows she has a job to do. So does Othello. Quite something, isn't it? Both of them qualifying for Blenheim."

Manna smiled and looked at George. "Thanks for that."

George looked puzzled. "For what?"

"Just being there, reassuring me. Thanks." Manna leant across and planted a kiss on George's cheek. "Other people have an army of grooms but, well, I'm not that fortunate. Either that, or I don't have enough good friends around me."

George was flattered.

"We'll park the box up, get the horses settled in and then we can have a wander around so you can get your bearings. Check in with the organisers and drink it all in, Mrs J."

Manna smiled fondly at George. "You can call me Manna, if you like, George. Mrs J sounds so formal."

"I'd prefer to stick with Mrs J, if you don't mind. I don't feel comfortable calling you by your first name." George's cheeks were on fire.

They arrived at a very large, superior stable block. The horses unloaded calmly and walked slowly down the ramp. Manna led them to the allocated stabling. Ariel and Othello looked around in excitement as their hooves touched the alien grassy surface. They were keen to investigate their new surroundings.

The dressage phase was due to take place the following day with the cross-country and show jumping on the subsequent two days. Manna was very excited and shivered as she caught sight of one of the perfectly carved cross-country jumps in the distance.

"This is just amazing!" she breathed. She was motionless, frozen in time as she scanned the grounds into the distance, with the palace in the forefront. George closed the stable door behind Ariel and arranged her hay net. He glanced across at Manna, who was still standing in the same spot.

"Something else, eh, Mrs J? It's another world, ain't it? Lucky old Winston Churchill living here." He didn't receive a response from Manna. He closed Ariel's stable door and added, "Why don't you go and check in. I'll stay with these two until they've settled down."

"Good idea, George. I'll take my phone with me. I'll catch up with you later."

"Righto, you go on now, Mrs J." He coaxed Manna away with a gentle shove.

oOo

At Littlebridge, Callum and Jude were relaxing in the caravan. An opened bottle of white wine stood on the kitchen work surface with two tumblers close by. Callum had his arm lazily draped around Jude and she was snuggled close to him, her head in his lap. They listened to the radio, completely oblivious to the outside world.

At length Callum spoke.

"Fancy another glass of wine?"

Jude nodded. "Yeah, why not? What time do you want to eat?"

"Oh, we'll get a takeaway, shall we?" Callum shut his eyes as he spoke.

Jude frowned. "No way. You know what happened last time we had takeaway: the bloody house burnt down. I think it's a bit of bad omen, don't you?"

Callum and released himself from Jude's head, got up and poured out wine into the two tumblers. "What else do you suggest?"

"How about… really getting the tongues wagging and eat at the Sheep?"

Callum thought for a moment. "Are you serious? I've only just come back from there after meeting Jim. And you had lunch there with Leya's parents! Do you have a death wish? We would get slain in our shoes! Not one of your better ideas!"

Jude shrugged her shoulders. "It was only a thought."

"Yeah, I know, but we *have* to be careful Jude, after all that's gone on with Leya. We don't know how long they will hold Cherry for and whether he gets bail.

We can't jeopardise anything, not at the moment. Not until the dust settles and I get my head around telling Manna."

Jude conceded. "Perhaps you're right, and we don't need any more stress. How long do you think it will be before we hear anything about Cherry?"

Callum handed a tumbler to Jude. "I'm not sure. What would be great news would be that he has been charged with assault. We now know Leya's definitely going to drop the compensation case. She even asked me for her old job at Littlebridge. She seems really keen to come back. I hope Manna will be kind enough to ease her back in, even if it's only a couple of days a week to start with. " Callum drained his tumbler of wine.

Jude took a slug. "What about Natalie? She needs to know what's going on. She must be going insane about Cherry and whether he will drop her in it."

Callum smiled. "I'll phone her later and tell her the news. In fact, I'll do it now, whilst you get the dinner on!"

Jude frowned. "So I cop doing the cooking after all, do I?"

Callum grinned lovingly at her and bent forward to kiss her hand.

"Sorry, darling, afraid you do since you don't want a takeaway. Oh, and for your reward, I will make beautiful, sensual love to you!"

Jude placed her tumbler on the floor and expectantly moved forward to embrace Callum. He held her at arm's length.

"Oh, didn't I mention? After dinner. It will be your treat!"

Jude playfully slapped him across the cheek, held his chin in her hand and landed a sloppy kiss on his nose.

"You, Mr Jacobs, are going to pay for that! Hear me?"

Callum pretended to have selective deafness and stared out of the window. Jude smiled to herself, got up and started to search through the freezer for a suitable culinary delight. Callum looked at Jude when her back was turned and smiled warmly at the sight of her backside that was protruding pertly in her black breeches.

oOo

Manna walked from the officials' marquee clutching her numbers and certified entry form. Tomorrow was the beginning of the most important few days of her life. George had remained with Ariel and Othello to ensure they settled in. Manna had wandered around a small part of the course. She would walk it officially next morning.

She found George leaning against Othello's stable in the large American barn complex. He was talking softly to the horses. Manna stopped to listen.

"You hear me, you make sure you both behave. No funny business Ariel, no throwing your mum off. Just do your best and, most of all, come back in one piece. Now, get on and eat that lovely haylage. It's part of the deal, you know, only the best. I'll come back and check on you later."

Manna moved forward, pretending that she hadn't heard George's advice.

"Everything all right here, George? Are they both okay?"

George turned and smiled at Manna. "They're just fine, Mrs J. Calm as cucumbers and happy. It shows, cos they're both tucking into that haylage. Look! Nice it gets provided for them, isn't it?"

"Yes, but it's costing me one hundred and twenty-five quid each a night, so I expect something good for my money!" Manna exclaimed. "Come on, let's get something to eat ourselves and then an early night. We need to get rest as well as the horses. You okay sleeping in the box, George?"

"Of course, I wouldn't want to be far away, Mrs J. Like to keep an ear out, you know, in the night." George tapped the side of his nose.

"I've just received a text from Natalie, wishing us good luck. I still haven't heard from Callum though. Perhaps he'll ring later on."

"Maybe he'll come and see you in person, Mrs J. He might surprise you."

Manna smiled, unconvinced. "Or maybe not," she muttered under her breath.

oOo

Jude had cooked a hearty meal of chicken and chips accompanied by peas and carrots. Callum was delighted and tucked in. Jude watched him as he ate.

"Nice, is it?" she commented. The response was a brief nod and raised eyebrows. "Good, glad you are enjoying it! I don't often cook, unless it is for a special occasion."

Again Callum nodded as he continued to shovel chips into his mouth like someone who hadn't eaten for a week. Jude decided against any further conversation until after they had finished. Callum clearly couldn't multi-task. Jude finished her food, picked up her colourful plastic plate and aimed it in the direction of the circular sink. It was a direct hit. The plate and cutlery clattered against the stainless steel. She looked at Callum.

"Pudding?" she asked, and waited for the response.

Callum thought for a moment and replied, "Yes, I'd like a piece of you, please."

"I can't believe you. You'll get indigestion, Callum! Why don't you let your food go down?" Jude was amazed at Callum's sexual urge.

"I'd much rather let you go down... on me! I just love spontaneity, don't you?" he grinned. He got up and placed his plate carefully into the sink.

Jude gazed at him. "Yes, but I do prefer sex without wanting to reach for the antacid stuff at the first moment!"

"That's what I really love about you, Jude. It's your motherly instincts that come out, just on those odd occasions. I love to be mothered, dominated... you know?"

"I get this feeling," said Jude, "that you are a bit of a kinky devil on the sly." She placed her hands on Callum's shoulders and stared into his eyes. He was smiling in a very boyish way.

"You know me too well, Jude. Bit like reading a book, so I've heard."

Jude reached down for Callum's hand. "Come on," and she guided him towards the bedroom. She flicked at the duvet to check that Tag wasn't beneath the covers and then closed the door.

oOo

Manna dialled Callum's mobile number. She was in her room at the guesthouse. She had spent the evening with George and picked at her meal. They had talked tactics and Manna had gone through a recital of some of the more complex dressage moves until she was confident she knew them.

George had left the guesthouse to spend the night in the horsebox back at the stabling complex. Although there was adequate security on the site, George felt it was his duty to Manna to be close to the horses in the event of any problems arising. He also felt it was vital that Manna got an undisturbed night's sleep so she was alert and fresh for the vet's inspection the following morning, and also to walk the course, which was close on four miles long.

Manna had tried to phone Callum throughout the evening without success and, with mobile phone in hand, she tried again. This time, she left a message.

"Hi, just to let you know we arrived safely, horses have settled in. Perhaps when you get this message you could ring, please? It would be nice to hear from you. Okay, bye."

She put the phone down. She was bitterly disappointed that Callum hadn't wanted to speak to her. Callum had changed since the fire and their relationship had become even more strained. She'd tried to put her feelings to one side and concentrate on the competition.

She slowly undressed, carefully placing her folded clothes into a chest of drawers. She pulled her nightdress over her head. Climbing into bed, she turned off the bedside lamp and snuggled down into the depths of her pillows and drifted off into a dreamless sleep.

Chapter Nineteen

Darius Cherry stood up from the table where the tape machine was recording. He ran his fingers through his hair in despair. Jim Denholm remained seated at the table. A uniformed officer stood by the door of the interview room.

"Mr Cherry has got up from the table," Jim announced and logged Darius's actions on the interview recorder. "Interview ended at 18:00 hours," he concluded and switched off the machine.

Darius sat back down and heaved a sigh of relief. He had been interviewed for the past three hours and was exhausted.

Jim looked towards him. "You've got a situation here that you need to resolve and soon, Mr Cherry. What you have to think about is your reputation. How will all this affect your status as a top lawyer? Particularly if word gets out to the press, which inevitably it will. You are accused of sexual assault: attempted rape. That is not going to look good now, is it? How do you think that young girl feels, particularly with her injuries sustained from her riding accident, at being let down by her lawyer?"

"She was offering it to me on a plate," growled Darius. He folded his arms in defiance. "How is a bloke supposed to react?"

"With decency and with respect. After all, you are supposed to be acting on her behalf, for God's sake, man! You must have remembered that, surely? You could have psychologically scarred her for life, that is if you haven't done so already. Didn't you think of that?" Jim was amazed at how calm and calculated Darius was.

"Suppose so," Darius mumbled.

Jim Denholm got up from his chair and nodded towards the officer at the door.

"Take Mr Cherry back to his cell, please." He turned to look at a horrified Darius. "We'll speak again in the morning."

"But I can't stay here! I can't. I have things to do..." he spluttered and rose to his feet.

Jim looked at him, his head on one side. "But, under the law, which I assume you must be aware of, you are under arrest and I am able to hold you for questioning. Good night, Mr Cherry, and have a very pleasant evening!" He looked to the officer and nodded for Darius to be led back to his cell.

oOo

Leya Martin listened to her statement as it was being read out by the police liaison officer. She nodded her agreement.

"Could you sign here for me, Leya, to confirm you agree that this is your statement?" The officer handed Leya a pen and she duly signed.

Leya sighed in relief. It had been a long afternoon and she was very tired. Her arm was aching and she felt nauseous.

"Thank you very much." The officer shuffled the papers together and placed the pen back into her bag.

"What's going to happen to Mr Cherry now?" Leya asked.

"He will probably be charged with attempted sexual assault then be bailed, pending a court case."

Leya thought for a moment and then spoke. "There is a slight problem in all this. Mr Cherry is defending me in a case where I am suing my employer. Presumably, if he is sentenced, then he won't be able to act for me, will he?"

The liaison officer thought for a moment. "That has put a different light on things. I would strongly advise you to have separate legal counsel. But, when Mr

Cherry came to your house, you told me you were intending to drop the case anyway, weren't you?"

"Well, I asked Mr Cherry for a meeting to discuss all of this. That was until he, well, you know, tried to…" She broke off as her voice faltered.

The officer continued, "It is entirely up to you on how you wish to proceed, Leya. I know it is a difficult situation to be in and somewhat complicated. The crucial thing for you to decide is if you definitely wish to press charges against Mr Cherry."

"I need time to think things over and be completely clear about all of this," announced Leya.

"Well, here is my card with my direct telephone number. Ring me as soon as you can to let me know, since we can only hold Mr Cherry for a maximum of forty-eight hours."

"Thank you." Leya took the business card and glanced at the telephone number. "Give me until tomorrow and then I will let you know," she added.

"I'll show you out."

The officer led Leya to the reception desk and quietly closed the door behind her.

Mr and Mrs Martin were anxiously awaiting Leya's version of events. They were in the main reception area of the police station, ready to take her back home. However, they made the journey in silence, and as soon as they arrived at the house, Leya climbed the stairs to her bedroom. She was holding her mobile phone. She closed the door behind her and dialled Jude.

Jude answered quickly. "Hi, Leya, how are things?" she asked.

"Horrible. I feel exhausted after giving my statement. Trouble is that I have a bit of a problem, about Cherry. If he is charged, then he won't be able to defend me and the case will drag on and on. I'll have to find a new lawyer."

"I thought you'd decided to drop the case against Manna?" Jude was shocked at Leya's indecision. "That's what today was all about. That's why we set Cherry up, to get back at him, through his wallet."

Leya blinked away a tear. "Yes, I know, I know..."

"So you drop the riding accident case, he is charged with sexual assault and is jailed—"

Leya interrupted Jude.

"But I'm thinking about the money, Jude. It won't be such a bad thing to gain something out of this, will it?"

Jude reflected for a moment. "Look, don't say anymore now. Let me speak with Callum, see if he has any solution to this. And I'll phone you back. But promise me, please, don't make any rash decisions."

"Okay," Leya agreed. "I told the police that I would let them know in the morning, about the charges and all that."

"Right, well, get some rest and I'll phone you back later on tonight, okay?" Jude reassured her.

Jude turned her phone off and sat back down on the sofa. Callum was watching TV.

"We have a dilemma. That was Leya. She's having second thoughts about everything! She's thinking about the money she could get if she carries on with the court case."

Callum groaned, closed his eyes and placed his hands over his face. He picked up the TV remote and pressed the mute button. He thought for a while and eventually spoke.

"I need to phone Jim Denholm and get advice on this. I can see that Leya is torn. If she does go ahead with the case then Cherry can't defend her. I don't know. I'll phone Jim."

"The other problem is that Leya has told the police that she'll give them her decision in the morning, so it's getting a little urgent now." Jude had to press Callum for action.

Callum phoned Jim Denholm's mobile phone.

"Hi Jim, yeah, have you got a minute?" Callum continued to brief Jim about Leya's situation.

Jim listened and then spoke. "Well, Leya could always drop the charges against Cherry and settle out of court, so that would solve her financial dilemma. But that means Cherry will be released. We could arrange enforcement on him to prevent any form of contact. But that would mean she would also have to drop the court case to sue the riding stables. How much would she settle on? It would have to be a substantial sum to hurt him, financially. I don't know where he'll get that sort of money from. Trouble is, we still have a pervert on the loose. This might frighten him enough, however, to keep his brain in his head and out of his trousers."

Callum nodded his head. "I bet he'd try to get money from Natalie Roberts. He knows about her inheritance. She'll want something in return, knowing Nat. I'm sure they'll work it out somehow together."

Jim frowned. "I hope they won't get together too closely..."

Callum didn't understand. "Why not?"

"Cos… let's just say I have a vested interest myself in Natalie."

Callum was surprised. "You mean…? You old dog! Well, I never, Jim! Anyway, I'll phone Leya to tell her the situation. I'll get some idea on how much she would ask for. I'll ring you back. Thanks for the advice and your news!"

Callum ended the call.

"Well, it can be sorted out," Callum placed his arm around Jude's shoulders. "Depends on how much Leya wants. But I would say," he thought for a moment, "a hundred grand would damage his wallet, don't you?"

Jude raised her eyebrows. "A hundred grand would certainly make him wince! Does he have that sort of cash?"

Callum smiled knowingly. "Someone like Darius Cherry would have access to any sort of cash he wanted."

"Then I think Leya should think about it seriously. That would get you and Manna off the hook and then she would receive a tidy sum and get Cherry off her back for good."

Jude dialled Leya. "Hi, how are you? Are you okay to talk?"

Leya sighed. "Yep, what do you want?"

Jude took a deep breath. "Callum and I were talking about everything that's gone on and have a suggestion."

"Okay." Leya didn't sound that interested. "But I did say I needed time to think things through."

"I know, but I think you will like what I am going to suggest."

"Go on." Leya twiddled with a strand of her hair.

"How do you feel about settling out of court with Cherry? What do you think about asking him for money rather than go through the stress of a case? It could go on for ages and you know how sly Cherry is. He could have a lawyer on his side who takes you to the cleaners and makes you look like the guilty party."

Leya shrugged. "I don't know. What sort of money are we talking about, here? It's got to be worth my while after all that I've been through."

Jude briefly paused before she spoke. "What about one hundred thousand pounds?"

Leya was silent. "Is that all?"

Jude frowned. "That's a lot of money, Leya. Serious, life-changing money. You could do so much with that. Don't forget that you haven't thought about whether Manna may want to sue you over the loss of Del. You seem to have glossed over that. You never know with Manna, she may spring something on you from a great height. You need to have some sort of financial back up in case she does one day decide to confront you."

"But it was her fault. She made me drive the lorry. I didn't want to drive it!" Leya was indignant.

"Yes, but it wasn't Manna's fault that you and LB had an altercation that caused the crash. That was definitely your fault, Leya, and don't you forget that!" Jude snapped.

Leya was silent at the other end. She felt tears pricking her eyes as she remembered poor Del in the lorry.

"Okay, point taken," she eventually replied. "I get it."

Jude persisted. "Right, so I'll ask you again. Will you be prepared to accept one hundred thousand pounds as an out of court settlement from Cherry?"

Leya nodded. Yep, okay, I'll accept."

Jude was visibly relieved. "Good. If it's okay with you, I'll ask Callum to phone the officer dealing with the case, Jim Denholm. I think you know him; he was at the house when Cherry was arrested."

"Yes, I know who you mean. Please, let me know what they say."

"Great, I'll ring you tomorrow, bye." Jude ended the call. She smiled at Callum, "Leyn has agreed to our hundred thousand demand to drop the charge. Now we need to let Cherry know his fate!"

"I'll ring Jim and give him the news. I think I need a drink after all this!"

Callum dialled Jim's number and relayed the information.

oOo

Darius Cherry woke from the worst night's sleep in his life. His whole body ached from the hardness of the bed and the chill of his cell. He lay in his shirt and boxer shorts with a rough grey blanket covering his body. There was someone at the cell door speaking to him. He could just make out a face at the trap door as he blinked to focus on who was talking.

"Wakey, wakey, Mr Cherry. Get up, I need to speak with you!" Jim Denholm stood patiently at the door. "Now would be good, Mr Cherry. I have a busy day ahead of me, catching villains!"

Darius Cherry rubbed his shoulders and sat up on the bed. His head ached and he felt dirty and in need of a shower. He glanced at the undignified stainless steel toilet facility that lurked in the corner of the room.

"Let me have a slash, then I'll get dressed!" he croaked.

He rose and walked to the lavatory. He took one look at the bowl and closed his eyes in disgust. He aimed without opening his eyes.

"I'll be waiting, Mr Cherry!" Jim closed the trap on the door and paced about in the corridor.

Cherry was led back to the interview room where Jim Denholm was sitting at the table. He looked disgruntled.

"Oh God! Not another questioning session! I can't bear this!" Darius complained as a uniformed officer ushered him to sit down at the table.

"Believe me, you will want to listen to what I have to say to you." Jim encouraged Cherry to take notice of him. "I have been informed that Miss Martin has decided to drop the charges against you. This is very disappointing news for me, Mr Cherry, very disappointing indeed. But, before you go out and celebrate with your favourite tipple, which I am sure you will, there is a big *but...* which you need to know about." He signalled to the uniformed officer. "Get us two coffees, please." The officer left the room.

Cherry looked at him and shook his head. "I don't understand, what big but?"

Jim lowered his voice. "Well, it seems that Miss Martin would like to settle out of court with you."

Cherry nodded. "Right... so?"

"She would like you to pay her some money, Mr Cherry. How do you feel about that?"

"Well... how much *money* does she want?" Cherry exclaimed. He appeared to be upbeat.

"How does one hundred thousand suit you?" Jim probed.

Cherry looked disturbed. He swallowed slowly to take in the amount. Jim continued.

"One hundred grand to keep your reputation, your good name and your job. Seems like a fair amount to me. That is, unless you want to be charged. Cos she could always change her mind, Mr Cherry. It's entirely up to you!"

Cherry's face turned pure with rage. He put his hands up in defence.

"I don't have a choice, do I? I'm getting fleeced whatever I decide. Right, okay, I'll settle out of court. Provided this puts an end to things and the charges are dropped."

"As you wish, Mr Cherry—"

Cherry interrupted Jim. "Course it isn't what I wish, I can't win!"

"Think of the alternative, Mr Cherry. Sexual assault does attract quite a long spell in prison. Not to mention the special treatment you could expect from your fellow inmates."

"Yes, all right! Tell her I'll settle. Oh God! I need to get away from all this!" he shook his head. "Can I go now?"

"Yes, you're free to go, Mr Cherry. But please take my advice: don't mess up again. We have you on our records now. Just a foot out of line and we will be on to you like a ton of bricks. Get my drift? Oh, and a further piece of news for you. Miss Martin is not pursuing her claim against Amanda Jacobs either. So it looks like you're off the case!" Jim smirked.

Cherry was seething as he got up from the table and was escorted to the front desk to collect his personal belongings. Jim made a phone call to Callum to confirm Darius Cherry's agreement to pay up.

Cherry staggered out into the fresh air. He breathed a sigh of relief as he reached for his mobile phone. He dialled Natalie's number.

"Hi, yeah, it's me. Need to see you now, Nat! Pick me up from outside Malsham nick, will you? And don't ask!" He thrust his phone into his pocket and paced up and down outside the police station waiting for Natalie to pick him up.

Natalie's 4x4 arrived twenty minutes later with a concerned driver at the wheel. Darius Cherry looked suspiciously around him as he climbed into the car. Natalie was shocked at his appearance.

"Christ! Have you spent a night on the tiles or what, Dar?" she joked. She had no idea on what had previously gone on.

Cherry was not amused. "Just drive, will you! Back to your place. I will explain then…" He broke off as he relived Jim Denholm's words. They were ingrained in his mind: one hundred grand.

Natalie parked at Heyrick Heights. Darius Cherry swiftly got out of the car and strode with intention to the house. He stamped impatiently on the vine-encrusted porch as he waited for Natalie to open the door.

"Come on! Come on!" he roared. "I need to get inside!"

"Keep your pants on!" Natalie remarked as Cherry virtually threw her through the doorway and into the kitchen. She laughed without realising what he had experienced. She added. "Do you need me *that* urgently?"

"Shut up! I am *not* in the mood for sex!" he snarled and leant against the Aga. "Listen to what I have to say. Long story short, I need money, Nat. Now! I am in deep shit and I need you to bail me out!"

Natalie was taken aback. "But you've got the partnership. Surely you have enough money invested there. What sort of amount do you need?"

Cherry was still fuming. "I need one hundred thousand. Like… yesterday. Or I will lose everything!"

"Sounds serious, Dar. What have you done?"

"Business stuff, you know. Let's just say I need to borrow the cash until I get straight again. I know you have it. You've got that pay out from Sam's estate, haven't you?" he urged. He paced up and down the kitchen. His suit was creased and unkempt.

"Yes, but it isn't going to leave me with much, is it Dar? When will you pay me back?" she asked, uncertain as to his intentions.

"Soon, I promise, Nat. I need that money. Believe me, I need that money!"

Natalie pondered for a moment. "Tell me what it's for and I'll consider it."

"Christ, woman! Okay! I've been set up by Leya Martin and her cronies. She wants one hundred thousand pounds from me to drop the charges!"

"What charges? What are you talking about?" Natalie continued to probe. After all, she felt entitled to know what she was bailing him out for.

"She has accused me of assault. When I went to see her yesterday, she came on to me and set me up. Made it look like I was raping her!"

Natalie shook her head. "Now why doesn't that surprise me? I knew your dick would get you in hot water sooner rather than later."

"I didn't rape her! I didn't go that far!" he spluttered. "I need a drink!"

"So *my* money is bailing your *dick* out of trouble then?" Nat confirmed with distaste.

"If you like, yeah." He wiped his face on his suit sleeve and looked at Natalie. "Please, help me, Nat. I will be forever in your debt!"

Natalie wasn't convinced and she was amazed to hear of Leya's actions. She thought things through for a moment, frowning.

"Okay, I will *lend* you the money. But remember you owe me, Dar. You *do* owe me and I would like to think that you would pay me back sooner rather than later. I have debts to pay on this place." She mused further, then spoke again. "In fact, I have a proposition for you."

"What?" he growled.

"I lend you that money and I get to keep the farm. You sign Heyrick Heights over to me. Deal?"

Cherry was desperate. He briefly thought about Manna's involvement in the partnership, but, he concluded, as she wasn't aware of Sam's will he could quite easily alter the paperwork. With pursed lips he nodded.

"That's blackmail, woman! But yeah, okay."

"I need a contract drawn up to state that this is a binding agreement or you don't get the money." Natalie was being realistic and, for once, wise.

Cherry nodded, trying to pacify her. "Yeah, I'll get a contract drawn up. But I need that money now, Nat. Seriously… now! When it's sorted out, I'm going away for a while. Beat a retreat, so to speak. Got friends in the Caribbean. I'll stay with them."

Natalie nodded her approval of his plan but narrowed her eyes. "You'll get your money when I get my contract. I need to be satisfied you won't set me up and I need to be safe in the knowledge that you won't steal my home from me. Do it and you'll get your money, Dar. Oh, and do you want company on your trip? I could do with a break too."

Cherry looked at her condescendingly.

"No. Sorry Nat. Can't have my style cramped, can I?"

Natalie felt disappointed but nevertheless walked to the fridge and selected a bottle of chilled wine. She uncorked the bottle and poured two glasses. She handed one to Cherry. "Here's to little our arrangement. Cheers!"

Cherry gulped his wine, made a face and looked defeated. Natalie smiled to herself, she was elated with her victory.

Chapter Twenty

Thursday dawned into a typical summer morning. It was seven o'clock and the birds had begun their chatter. Manna was taking a shower when her prearranged wake-up phone call came. She grabbed a towel then dashed to the bedside cabinet to reach the phone.

"Thank you, I'm awake already!" she announced and replaced the receiver back on to its cradle. She caught a glimpse of herself in the mirror and whispered, "This is it, do or die. Do they pass or not?" She was thinking of the impending vet's inspections.

She returned to the shower to rinse the remaining shampoo from her hair. She climbed into a bathrobe and dried her hair. She walked into the bedroom and checked her mobile phone. There were no messages. She threw it on the bed in disappointment. Why hadn't Callum phoned? Surely he would, to wish her luck? He knew how much this meant to her. She cast her mind back to when she saw Callum leave Jude's caravan, but she convinced herself that Callum was as loyal to her as her horses were.

Her mobile phone rang; she jumped and hurriedly picked it up. It was George.

"Good morning, Mrs J. Are you up?" George's soft voice blew across the airwaves like a summer breeze.

"Good morning, George. How are the horses?" Manna sounded deflated.

"All is well, Mrs J. But, we do have a problem." George hesitated.

Manna stopped towel drying her hair. "What? What sort problem?" her voice quavered.

"Well, I've just had a visit from one of the Organising Committee people and he has told me that the competition is oversubscribed. Apparently they only allow one hundred and twenty horses to compete and they have five more than that. So, they are only allowing you to compete on one horse. The other problem is that they need to know immediately who you are going to scratch."

Manna shook her head in disbelief. She pursed her lips and closed her eyes.

"Uh, Mrs J, are you still there?" George's voice seemed distant to Manna, like he was on Mars.

"Oh shit, shit, shit! Oh, I don't know. They both have their good and bad points. Ariel is spot on with her dressage, but Othello is a bold jumper in cross-country and he doesn't get fazed. Ariel has the stamina... I can't decide! When did you say they needed to know by?"

"Um, now, Mrs J. That's why I'm calling you. The OC person is standing alongside me, as we speak."

Manna frantically tried to weigh up each horse's pros and cons and then blurted out, "Othello! I'm scrubbing Othello! Tell the man, George, will you? And I am coming straight down to the stables. I need to walk the course and then get ready for the vet's inspection."

"Right, I'll tell them it's Othello that won't be competing then, shall I?" George confirmed.

"Yes, just do it, George. He's the lesser qualified of the two horses in dressage, and if I don't choose then the OC will check up on his qualifier details. Much as it breaks my heart not to give him a chance to show his worth," Manna was fighting back the tears. "I'll see you shortly."

George duly informed the official and returned to the stabling complex where Ariel and Othello were looking over their respective stable doors, the picture of innocence and wonder. It put a smile on George's face.

"Hello, my beauties! Listen, I got news for you Othello, my old mate. You've got the next few days off. It's just you, Ariel. Now you gotta really do your best, hear me? Perform like you ain't never performed in your life. But, and most importantly, stay safe. Get round in one piece."

George ran his hand down the mare's neck as she softly whinnied and drew her head close to George's so their eyes met.

"And no flirting neither!" He patted Ariel's cheek and she gently nudged his arm. "Don't give me those soulful eyes, Ariel. Get your rest and play fair. No shying or napping or bolting off. Do you job, right? Your mum deserves that at least," he added thoughtfully.

He recalled the mess back at Littlebridge. The fire, the court case, Callum's lack of support — Manna was up against the odds and George hoped she could put all her worries behind her and enjoy the realisation of her dream to compete at Blenheim International Horse Trials.

oOo

Manna arrived at the stable complex half an hour later. She had taken a buggy ride from the guesthouse, which was only a short distance from the grounds of Blenheim Palace. She met George at the horsebox where he was sipping a cup of tea and balancing the *Racing Post* on his lap.

"Damn shame, that, Mrs J! Such a terrible job to decide — I know you must be really upset."

"Well, it's done now, George. I can't dwell on it. I need to think forward now. Have the horses been fed?"

"Yes, about an hour ago. Gave them what you said. I also took them both out for a stretch of legs beforehand over to that exercise paddock place. The OC bloke said it was okay as long as I kept them on lead ropes. So they've both had a good quarter of an hour to wander and eat. Much of the time they spent whinnying for each other! Silly animals! I made sure I was in sight of 'em too! I couldn't manage to take both of 'em. So I took Ariel, then Othello."

"That's great, thanks George. Right, fancy a walk? I've picked up the course layout, all forty jumps, might I add! Apparently there is a bit of a change to the course but it doesn't make any difference to me, seeing as I've not been around it before. I hope you've got plenty of energy. It's a long walk!"

George pointed at his stout walking boots.

"I'll be fine, Mrs J. If we'd have thought, we could have brought young Tag with us: she would've loved this walk."

Manna nodded and thought of the excitable Jack Russell.

"Perhaps I should have asked Jude to come along. You know, as groom."

George shook his head. "No need, Mrs J. She's running your yard. You need that stability, when you are away. That girl is worth her weight in gold when it comes to horses. Ain't much she don't know, is there?"

"Yes," Manna nodded in agreement, "perhaps I don't appreciate the fact that she's always there, no matter what. Particularly when the fire happened. If she hadn't have been there, perhaps Callum might not be alive today." She paused in reflection and nodded to herself.

"Come on, Mrs J. We've got a course to walk. Have you got that map? I'll navigate whilst you sort out your striding and approaches firmly in your mind."

He trundled off towards the first fence, remarking out loud how large it was and how Manna had to be careful to get over it as it would settle Ariel straight away for the rest of the course.

Manna was in a world of her own. She walked up to each fence, gauging her approach, the striding into the jump, the exit out and approach to the next jump. It was such a beautiful setting with Blenheim Palace majestically overseeing the occasion, providing the backdrop to the dressage arena. Manna shivered in excitement and nervousness as she passed each fence and memorised her route. She mentally imagined herself on Ariel in a steady gallop – hunting pace – making her way over the course.

They passed a couple of well-known riders who were in deep discussion with their trainers at one of the water jumps. George nodded as they walked past and received a similar reciprocation.

"Do you know who that was, Mrs J?" George whispered excitedly.

"Of course I do, George," Manna laughed.

"Well?" George queried.

"Well, what?" Manna responded.

"Cos I don't know! Who were they?" he answered in all innocence.

Manna's laugh was hysterical. "Oh, you're so funny, George. Heaven help us! Look, I won't bore you with the details! You'd forget anyway!"

George frowned. "Well, it looked like that nice chap with the double-barrelled name!"

"And you'd be right, George. Well done! There's hope for you yet! Come on; let's get a coffee and a cake from the shopping village."

Manna linked arms with George and they walked over to the vast array of trade shops and stands that adorned a large part of the park. Manna stared at the Blenheim Flyer brush and ditch fence that was positioned close to the entrance to the trade stands. 'Scary!' she thought to herself but nodded in determination, 'I can do this, I *really* can do this. I'll show everyone that I can! Everyone!'

oOo

Later on that morning the first vet inspections were underway. Each competitor had to have their horse completely checked over for fitness, soundness and capability. When it was Manna's turn to trot Ariel up and down for the inspection, she was clearly delighted when the mare passed with flying colours. She patted Ariel's neck in appreciation.

"Good girl. Well done! That's it now! We're definitely on. Right, George, can you tack Ariel up for me and I'll do some schooling. I've been given my time for the dressage tomorrow so I can breathe for a few more hours at least."

George ably tacked up Ariel and handed the reins to Manna.

"Thanks, George. I'll be about half an hour. I just need to run through a couple of moves for the dressage. She's a bit sticky on a couple of the paces halfway through the test."

"Right, Mrs J. I'll muck out the stables and I'll walk Othello out if you like."

"Yes, that would be good. Keep an eye on the big guy for me!"

Manna mounted Ariel, adjusted the girth straps and picked up the reins. She walked Ariel to the entrance to the exercise paddock and began with a collected walk, first on one rein, then the other. There were other riders who had the same idea and were quietly schooling their horses. It was blissfully silent with only the soft thud of hooves lightly touching the springy grass and the occasional chink of a bit. All the riders were focussed on their schooling and the prospect of their job in hand. Manna was so engrossed that she didn't hear the rapid approach of a galloping, loose horse that had jumped the paddock gate and was frantically kicking up its heels in the knowledge it had escaped. There was a stifled yell of "Loose horse!"

Manna looked up at the last minute to see a large, dark bay horse with rippling muscles and wide eyes suddenly turn behind her, giving a huge buck with both hind legs off the ground. Manna urged Ariel forward to escape the inevitable connection, but it was too late. The back hooves connected with Ariel's hind leg and there was a sickening thud.

Ariel lunged forward in terror as the loose horse continued to buck and kick out at her. Manna rode Ariel out of further harm's way as the crazed horse moved on towards its next victim further down the field. Manna stood up in her stirrups and bellowed, "Loose horse, loose horse!" to warn the other riders, who instantly stopped schooling and got out of the way of the galloping horse. For a brief moment, the horse seemed familiar to her.

Manna dismounted and hardly dared to look at the injury. She checked Ariel's hind leg to see the imprint of a half shoe shape with broken skin and grazed hair. A small amount of blood had started to ooze from the wound. Manna shook her head. The new wound was only inches from the one inflicted a few weeks ago when Leya had had her accident. This was terrible news for Manna.

"Oh no! Please, no!" Manna wailed. She shook her head in disbelief. "Why me? Why now?"

She walked Ariel up and down but the mare was clearly distressed and showing signs of lameness. The cut had started to swell. Manna phoned George to ask him to fetch the duty vet. George quickly reached Manna just as the loose horse was being recaptured and led back to its stable by a young, red-faced groom. Manna was seething.

"Keep an eye on your bloody horse in future! You've ruined my chance of competing tomorrow!" she screamed.

The girl looked devastated but kept on walking with the horse without saying a word.

"Oh George! This is terrible! She's lame! Where's the vet, for pity's sake?"

"On her way, Mrs J. She's coming straight over. Looks like there is some heat in that wound."

"I know, George! I'm not stupid!" she snapped.

Moments later the vet hurried up to her.

"Please help me – that wretched animal kicked my horse when I was schooling. I want to know whose horse that is and get it disqualified!" Manna blurted out to the vet, who was trying to assess the seriousness of Ariel's wound.

"With respect, you need to see someone on the OC, madam. I can't make that decision. But it appears it was an accident."

"That groom should be more careful! Especially at somewhere as important as Blenheim! It's my first time here competing and look what's happened! Stupid, stupid little bitch!"

"Right," the vet had made her assessment of Ariel's hind leg. "I am afraid this horse will not be able to compete tomorrow. She has a deep tissue wound and swelling. She will need box rest. I'm sorry but your mare will have to be withdrawn from the competition."

Manna was furious. With angry tears welling in her eyes, she snatched the medical certificate from the vet's grasp and stormed off to the OC marquee, leaving George and the vet to treat and bandage Ariel's leg and get her back into her stable.

Manna reached the marquee and slammed her entry details onto a table in front of one of the organisers.

"Firstly, I would like to complain about the sheer incompetence of one of the grooms at the stabling complex. She is totally incapable of looking after her horse, which got loose from her supervision and kicked my horse so badly that she has just been withdrawn from the competition by the vet! Who can I speak to about this?" Manna demanded.

The OC rep calmly advised Manna to have a seat and provide Ariel's entry details so they could check her on the computer.

"Do you have another horse, Mrs Jacobs? It says from my information here that you do."

"Yes, but only my mare passed the vet's inspection. My other horse hasn't been vetted as I had to scratch him from competing due to the over-subscription of entries." Manna's mind frantically churned over as her chances of competing at Blenheim were slipping away.

"I can arrange for your second horse to have a vet's inspection, Mrs Jacobs and if it passes, then you will have my authority to substitute your injured mare with your second horse. I cannot do any more than that."

Manna was in shock. "Thank you so much. I appreciate your cooperation but I really would like to have that other horse withdrawn from the competition. It is a liability."

"I'm afraid that's not possible, Mrs Jacobs. However I'm sure that you are aware of the need to have at least third party insurance and public liability insurance, which applies to all competitors to cover their horses in events such as these." The OC rep was methodical and calm in his explanation.

"Yes, of course I do," Manna snapped. "It's the principle."

"It was an accident, Mrs Jacobs. An accident, and you know as well as I that these things do unfortunately happen."

Manna got up. She was still furious that she hadn't been able to get her own way with the official, but she was determined to get revenge on the owner of the loose horse.

"Oh, Mrs Jacobs," called out the official. "The vet's inspection will be in half an hour. In the same place, so if you would like to bring your horse over?"

Manna waved her acknowledgement without turning around and strode back to the stables. She met George standing outside Ariel's stable holding Othello's rein.

"How's Ariel?"

"A bit bruised but comfortable. She's had a painkiller and I'm about to give her the first packet of antibiotic powder. I've mixed it up in a bit of feed, so she won't know it's there."

"Do you know whose horse it was that got loose? I didn't have the opportunity to see where it was stabled."

George was silent. Manna stared at him intently.

"You know whose it was, don't you?" she quizzed and folded her arms in annoyance. "Tell me! Whose horse was it?"

"Erm... well... it was... him." George slowly pointed in the direction of Othello.

Manna looked in disbelief. A cold realisation began to creep over her.

"Don't be stupid! Who *was* it?"

"It was Othello, Mrs J. When you went, he got over-excited and when I went to get him out of the box, he bolted past me to get to Ariel. He cleared that gate with at least two foot to spare."

"I don't believe you. I don't... Othello? How could you be so stupid?"

"It was an accident. He was too strong for me. I couldn't hold him!"

"What about that groom who was leading him?" Manna was still in denial.

George swallowed hard. "She helped me: came to the rescue and caught him. She was in the box next door and saw what was happening. She saw Othello clear the gate with no problem. Then she ran after him! Caught him for me."

Manna looked crushed as the realisation hit her. She spoke in a hushed whisper. "I thought he looked familiar and... Oh no! I've just chewed that poor OC person's ears off complaining about that groom and the horse. I'm going to have to eat humble pie forever. Oh, but there's no use to keep moaning about it. Can you get Othello ready for the vet's inspection? They are allowing him to be inspected and, if he passes, he'll replace Ariel. I need to be over there in about twenty minutes. Hopefully this will be the saving grace to this nightmare!"

oOo

Callum stared at his mobile phone. He was in the tack room at Littlebridge. His finger was poised to dial Manna's number but he withdrew it. He had noticed that there were three missed calls on his phone from her. He felt strangely guilty for not calling his wife. He left the tack room and watched Jude place the feed bowls over the door of each stabled horse. She was so engrossed in her work that she hadn't seen him. Tag was playing with a pebble and kept dropping it in front of Jude in the hope that it would encourage her to throw it for her to fetch. Jude obliged and threw the pebble to the end of the stable block with Tag in hot pursuit. The game continued until Jude had finished feeding the horses.

Callum smiled to himself and walked back to the house. The workmen were collecting their tools; they were finished for the day.

"How's it going, lads? Can I move back in yet?" Callum waited for the usual answer but was pleasantly surprised.

"Soon, gov. By the weekend, I reckon," the foreman replied as he closed his toolbox.

Callum was flippant. "Which weekend is that then?"

"This one, gov. In fact, I reckon this time tomorrow you can break open the bubbly and get that lovely wife of yours carried back over your brand new threshold!"

"Oh that's brilliant! Great news!" Callum's spirits were lifted.

"We'll see you in the morning then, gov. You only got one more night under the canvas!" The foreman laughed and waved his goodbye. His colleague smiled and walked towards his van.

"Yes, right, good. See you in the morning then, lads," Callum reached for his mobile phone. He checked that Jude wasn't nearby and then phoned Manna. He stood to attention as the phone began to ring. There was no reply. It went straight to voicemail.

Callum didn't leave a message but decided to try later in the evening. He headed over to the house to see for himself how the work was progressing. He was really encouraged. The workmen might have spent a lot of time bickering over their tools, and drinking tea, but the job they were doing was certainly of a very high standard. Callum couldn't wait to move back in.

Kier was sniffing the ground in the front garden. Callum called him to his side and they both walked towards Jude's caravan in the meadow. Callum paused when he reached the gate, leaned on it for a while, deep in thought. Kier gambolled through the high grasses making a brace of pheasants fly up right in front of him. Callum knew he faced an important decision: a decision that needed to be made very soon.

Chapter Twenty-One

Manna woke up from a deep sleep. She could hear her mobile phone ringing. She reached out into the darkness and tried to focus on who was calling her so late. By the light emanating from the phone, she could see it was Callum. She sat upright in bed, still in the dark, and answered it.

"Cal? Hi! Do I have some news for you!"

She proceeded to tell Callum of all the events and happenings: of Ariel and Othello and how Ariel had been kicked by a loose horse, which turned out to be her own animal! She spoke excitedly without taking a breath. Callum smiled to himself.

"It could only happen to you, couldn't it? One of your own horses getting loose! You wait till I speak to old Randy!" he joked.

"Old Randy? Who, George, do you mean? How come you call him old Randy?"

"It's what Jude calls him: Randy the Handyman. I think it's hilarious, don't you?"

"Well," remarked Manna, switching on the bedside lamp and rearranging her tousled hair, "I hope he doesn't live up to his name!"

"Listen Manna," Callum wanted to get his point across, "do you want me at Blenheim? Look, I've not been myself these last few weeks and I would like to make it up to you. What do you say?" He held his breath tightly for the response.

There was silence then Manna spoke. "I would *love* for you to be here. Can Jude cope on her own?" Manna asked, still trying to push hair from her eyes.

"Yes," Callum reassured her. "Jude can cope. I'll be there in the morning. It should only take an hour or so to drive. What time's your test?"

"Half ten. Oh, and by the way, Othello passed the vet's inspection!"

"That's great. I'll see you in the morning. I'll give you a ring when I'm close to Blenheim, take care… bye!"

Callum walked from the shadows of the yard to the caravan. He had excused himself from Jude's slumbering advances on the pretence that Kier needed to relieve himself. He had suddenly found himself feeling remorseful about his affair with Jude and, after speaking with Manna, had come to the conclusion that he in fact needed to be with his wife. After all, Blenheim was a major event to be competing at and the only support Manna had was George.

Callum made another phone call before it got much later. It was to Leya.

"Hi, it's Callum, yeah… I know it's late but, after all that's happened, I know you want to get back to work again, don't you? How about tomorrow morning? Yes, I'm going to Blenheim to watch Manna compete and I think she needs a decent groom behind her. How about it? Yeah, that's great. No, Jude's staying at the yard. Right, I'll pick you up at about seven thirty at your place. Be ready. See you tomorrow, bye."

The arrangements made, Callum's duty was now to do the decent thing and tell Jude. He felt she wouldn't be best pleased so he prepared himself for the expected uproar.

"You're what?" yelled Jude. "I don't believe you! Why? Why now?"

"Because," began Callum, "I think it's only fair that I go and support her. I feel—"

"Oh don't tell me! Guilty… the old guilt thing! You are unbelievable, Callum! What about me? What about us?"

"We're okay, aren't we? Surely you don't mind me going to see Manna do you? She's—"

"Yeah, yeah, your wife! I know, typical! And I thought you were different, Callum. How stupid can I get? Blokes! You're all the bloody same! Next thing you'll say is that we're over. I'm right, aren't I? Callum?"

Callum looked at the floor, like he always did when he found a question difficult to answer.

"I don't know. It's been bloody difficult lately, what with all that's gone on. And I really appreciate what we've got. What you've done for me, saving my life; helping me with Darius Cherry. For standing by me."

"Spare me the lecture. I think you'd better get out, Callum. I need some space. I think we both do. Go and stay at Natalie's; she might make you see some sense. Just go!"

Jude pointed to the door. Deep down she was seething with rage at her naivety over Callum. How could she have let herself be taken in by false promises? And for a second time, no less. She should have realised that married men never leave their wives and that they always want the best of both worlds and act the innocent party. She was angry that, yet again, she had been duped into thinking the relationship was something to hold on to. Someone to share her life with, but she never learnt. It never happened for Jude. There were always complications.

She slammed the caravan door behind Callum as he left and locked it. She gathered a sleeping Tag from the sofa, cradled the Jack Russell in her arms and burst into tears. She sobbed relentlessly into Tag's thick coat. Tag lay helplessly in Jude's arms but fully understood the hurt her mistress was feeling and she reassured her by licking the tears from her cheeks.

oOo

Manna's early morning call rang out for the second morning running. This time at six o'clock. Manna leapt up out of bed with a start. This was it! It was *the* morning. She quickly showered and grabbed a coffee and made her way to the stabling complex. She called out to George who was preparing the horses' morning feed.

"Good morning. Here we are! Dressage day! By the way, George, Callum is coming up to watch. He will be here about ten. He phoned late last night. I can't wait to see him!"

"What wonderful news, Mrs J. Good of him, don't you think? Not long after recovering from the fire too! Good on him!"

Manna's mood had been lifted by the news of Callum's imminent arrival. Ariel had settled too. She'd had a good night and was happily eating her morning feed. Manna was able to clear her mind and focus entirely on the dressage.

She started to prepare Othello by washing his legs thoroughly and then giving him a bath. Time ticked on relentlessly and it wasn't long before Manna's phone rang and Callum, keeping to his word, phoned to announce his arrival. Manna took the call with soapy, wet hands as Othello shook to relieve himself of all the shampoo.

"Hi Cal, we're at the stabling complex. Park up in the public car park and I'll meet you at the entrance to get you through security. See you in ten minutes, bye!"

Manna threw her phone into the tack box. "Can you finish rinsing Othello off and then rug him up to keep him warm? Then start towelling him off. I'll be back in a minute. That was Callum. He's here!"

She dashed off into the direction of the public car park and saw a familiar figure striding across the grass. Manna suddenly stopped. Callum wasn't alone. She wasn't sure at first who his companion was, but as they drew closer, she felt a twinge of anxiety pulse through her body. Confused, Manna walked cautiously up to Callum. Callum held out his arms.

"Hi, love. How are you?" He embraced Manna who reservedly held on to her husband but never took her eyes off Leya.

"What is she doing here?" spat Manna, with a venomous look.

"It's okay. Look, we need to talk. Leya, can you give us a while? Go and find George and give him a hand, there's a love."

Leya smiled without speaking and walked off to the complex to find George. Manna was still fuming.

"I said, what is *she* doing here? I need to know, Callum. What the hell is going on?"

"It's all right. Leya is working for us again. I managed to sort out the court case and she's dropped the charges. Look, it's a really long story, which I will tell you about after the competition, but, believe me, it's okay."

"And what about us? Are we okay too?" Manna needed to know as Callum protectively held her in his arms. He thought for a while, of Jude, of the argument the previous night, and spoke. "We've had our difficulties, but I now know that we'll be okay. I promise. I want us to have a new start. But for the time being, you need to relax and concentrate on doing your best. I believe in you, Manna. Truly I do. That's why I'm here. I want to be here. I want us to get back to where we were, if not better. What do you say?"

Manna considered Callum's words. "I think we need to talk things through but, for now, you're right, I need to be focussed. I must get back to Othello and get myself ready. Will you help me?"

"Course I will, Manna. Just tell me what to do," Callum reassured her.

"Go and get me a cake, I'm famished!" she replied with a smile. She pecked him briefly on the cheek and ran back to the stabling complex. Turning as she ran, she called out, "You might as well get loads of cakes for the troops. We've got a competition to win!"

oOo

Back at Littlebridge, Jude had finished her morning chores and was heading to her caravan when she saw a 4x4 draw into the yard. She waited until it approached. It was Natalie. Jude watched as she parked, got out and waved to her.

"Hi, stranger! Haven't seen you for a while!" she called out.

"Hi, could say the same to you. Look, Jude, what's the score with Callum? He spent last night at mine." She noticed Jude was close to tears.

"Well, the lovely Callum has gone to watch his wife competing at Blenheim. Dropped the bombshell last night and, get this, he's taken Leya with him as Manna's groom! Can you believe it?"

Natalie was clearly shocked. She shook her head in dismay.

"Wow, Leya's gone with him? I put so much effort in towards that girl and what the hell was Darius playing at? Just can't help himself, can he?"

Jude nodded. "But why does Darius Cherry bother *you* so much?"

Natalie smiled mysteriously. "Well, let's just say he was a bit more than my brief. In fact, he was in my briefs, if you get my meaning. When he wanted to, you know, a quickie here and there. Nothing serious at first, then, well he got... let's say... what he wanted."

"Oh, I see. Another conquest?" Jude nodded thoughtfully.

"Yeah, but he could be a bit rough, you know. Well, you know me, I like a bit of rough every now and again," she nervously laughed. "But, he meant it, Jude. He was harsh and unkind."

"What, sexually or mentally rough to you?" Jude looked very concerned.

"It's not for me to say. Not here. Look, you haven't got a drink to hand have you, Jude? I could do with a swift one."

"Yeah, come back to the caravan. I've got some wine, but it isn't like your usual fancy stuff, it's only a cheap bottle from the supermarket. It's not even a cork job, it's a screw lid. I bought it for Callum last night until he decided he wanted to be with his wife."

"Jude, if it's wine, I can drink it, wherever it came from. I don't care, lovie." Nat put on a brave face.

They walked to the caravan where Jude found a couple of glasses, unscrewed the lid and poured two large servings of red wine. Natalie gulped half of hers in one slug. She closed her eyes and thought.

"So what did Cherry do to you, Nat?" Jude probed.

"It's all to do with Sam's estate — the will and the business partner he had. I had no idea that the partner was Cherry. I was absolutely gutted. He told me to keep my nose out of his business. The will had said that the partnership owned Heyrick Heights and he threatened to evict me from the farm. Then…" she hesitated, "he forced me to have sex with him."

Jude was furious. "You mean he raped you?"

Nat took another huge gulp of wine and nodded. There were tears in her eyes.

"I didn't mean for it to happen, but he forced me to do it, taunting me all the time. I was scared, really scared. I had to go along with it, because of the farm."

"Well, perhaps Callum's police friend should know about this. He can't be allowed to get away with that." Jude was furious.

"What would that look like? I'd be laughed out of the court. I know what he's like. I've consented to sex with him on a few occasions so no one would believe me that this time was different. I'd be labelled the slapper from Heyrick Heights. It wouldn't be worth my while getting involved. He would only threaten me again and take my home from me. Scarring me mentally, without any physical force. I couldn't cope with that. I don't want to spend my life looking over my shoulder in fear of him. Living off anti-depressants and suffering the consequences of being mentally unstable. It's hard enough without Sam, but I can't lose the farm. However, the saving grace in all of this is Leya dropping the charges and asking for a pay-out. Money that Darius hasn't got but, thanks to Sam, I have. I'm going to lend him the money and he has promised to sign Heyrick Heights into my ownership. He's going to the Caribbean for a while." Natalie blinked away a tear and smiled bravely.

Jude took in all that Natalie was telling her. Natalie indicated for Jude to refill her wine glass.

"Nat, you have to make sure he signs some sort of contract before you give him any money," Jude advised.

Natalie nodded. "Don't worry, already arranged. And I still vow that one day I will get Manna back for her involvement in all of this. When I had the letter from my solicitor saying I had some money to come from Sam's estate, I thought it was the ideal opportunity for payback time because at last I could afford to see her squirm. I know it was a terrible thing to do but I needed closure on this whole, horrible mess. It was the only way I could get my revenge. And now, with Leya going back to work for her and the case dropped, it isn't going to happen. But I can't worry about all that now. However, I'm telling you, Jude, one day I will get even, I truly will." She drained her glass and stared into space.

"Seems like we both have been dumped on, so to speak," sighed Jude. "I've lost Callum, and you've lost your opportunity to get even. Looks like Manna has the upper hand."

"Yeah, maybe, but I'll get to keep the farm. I can bide my time over Manna. What goes around comes around, so they say… I won't be beaten."

"We make a good team, don't we," joked Jude.

"What? The losing team?" laughed Nat. "Yeah, I suppose we do. Hey, when I get things sorted out, I'll have a few quid left. How about you come and work for me at Heyrick? Get the farm back to its former glory? I'll get some new event horses with rich owners, turn things around. What do you say?"

Jude nodded thoughtfully. "Can I have a think about it? But it does seem like it could be fate, don't you think?"

Nat nodded and swigged at her wine. She looked at her glass. It was empty.

"Could well be fate. I am a firm believer. Damn shame the bottle's empty… but, I suppose, all good things do come to an end," she concluded.

oOo

Chapter Twenty-Two

Manna was warming Othello up in the collecting ring. Her dressage test was due in fifteen minutes. She was smartly turned out in black cut-away dressage jacket, black hat, black boots and gleaming white breeches, whilst Othello shone like highly polished mahogany against the morning sunshine that had spilled over the grounds. Manna was inwardly nervous but outwardly in control. She kept an eye on her watch and continued to school Othello until it was their turn in the dressage arena.

Callum, George and Leya had taken their places in the spectators' enclosure. Leya checked her phone for messages, George had started to bite his fingernails and Callum was staring into the far distance, his mind clearly focussing on other matters.

Manna continued her warm up, going through the test in her mind and keeping Othello supple and moving. His fine-toned muscles rippled as he trotted in a good, forward pace around the collecting ring. Suddenly her number was called and she was directed in by a steward. Manna took a huge breath and rode Othello towards the dressage arena.

As they arrived, her supporters called out their *good lucks* and waved frantically. Othello, wide-eyed, nostrils flared, walked quickly and with purpose. The test was about to begin. Manna moved Othello up into a canter outside the arena and they began. Othello took on the role of performer directly he set foot within the arena boundary and completed an encouraging test, with only a few faults where he had been a little over enthusiastic at "A". He had caught a glimpse of some flowerpots, which he thought might come to life and attack him. Manna had tried to catch him before he attempted his nap but missed the timing and he took a couple of side strides. Otherwise, it was a good start to a promising test. Manna was ecstatic and, at the end of the test, patted Othello's neck with her soft, white kid gloves with vigorous enthusiasm and relief.

She made her way back to the collecting ring. Her mission was underway and now she had to wait until the following day for the long-awaited cross-country phase.

"Manna, that was superb! Well done!" shouted Callum. "He went like a dream! Well done, Othello! Clever lad! You must be elated!"

"Yes, I suppose I am. He was a good boy." Manna dismounted and handed the reins to Leya, who swiftly ran the stirrup leathers up and loosened Othello's girth. She led him round to cool off and placed his cooling rug on over his saddle.

"Great exhibition, Mrs J. You worked wonders there!" congratulated George. He was brimming with pride over Manna's performance. "You surely must have got some good marks there. I'll be very surprised if you ain't!"

"We'll see, George. Right, let's get Othello back to the stables, walk him around and cool him down. Are you all right with him, Leya? Can you manage?" Manna called out.

"Course, Manna. I'll look after him for you. You take a breather, great test!" Leya smiled and continued to walk Othello round. She had her injured arm in a narrow sling.

"Come on, let's grab a coffee. Those two are capable of looking after your steeds. We need some time together, don't we? Let's go to your room." Callum put his arm around Manna's shoulders.

"I think that sounds like a proposition. Lead on," Manna smiled and held Callum close to her as they walked away from the gathering crowd.

oOo

Later that afternoon, Manna awoke from a deep sleep to find Callum holding two cups of coffee. He had a towel wrapped around his waist. He smiled at Manna as she slowly came round. He perched on the edge of the bed next to her.

She looked at him. "I think we did more than talk, didn't we?"

"Yes, I believe we did. And I have to say that it was the best conversation I've had with you for ages. We didn't have to say a lot, did we? I think the actions spoke complete volumes." Callum grinned.

Manna sat up in bed, took her cup of coffee and sipped thoughtfully.

"I think the time apart has done our relationship wonders, don't you?"
Callum nodded. He drank from his cup and spoke frankly. "It's funny how you can be around someone for such a long time, then spend time away and suddenly realise how much you actually missed them. I have done some serious soul-searching and I know where I want to be. I want to be back at Littlebridge, with you there. The house is just about ready. The builders have done a cracking job this week. I'm sure it's better than before. And after the weekend, we can get back to living again. What do you say?"

"I say... yes. It seems like a complete nightmare, all of it, doesn't it? And now suddenly it's all gone away. I'm prepared to give us another go and I promise to make more time for us... but not just yet. I need to get tomorrow and Sunday over with. You understand what I am saying, don't you?"

Callum leant over and kissed Manna's forehead. "Course I do. But, before you get back into your focussed mode, how about me wishing you lots of luck in my own special way?"

"You mean... oh Callum! You have definitely changed. You're suggesting sex mid-afternoon? Well, things are looking up! What happened to Mr Serious?" She giggled and placed her coffee cup on the bedside cabinet just as Callum leapt astride her and began to kiss her neck and whisper in her ear.

"I think he's still here and I just *love* spontaneity, don't you?"

oOo

At six pm Manna attended the rider's briefing for the cross-country phase. It consisted of a health and safety demonstration, the rules and regulations and the importance of the second vet's inspection that would be held first thing in the morning. Manna was dazzled by the array of top riders whom she was sitting amongst. She blinked many times to make sure she wasn't dreaming.

After the briefing, she made her way back to the stabling complex where George and Leya were watching TV in the horsebox and drinking wine from plastic cups. Callum had gone off to book a table for an evening meal at a local restaurant. Manna joined her team and slumped down to watch the television.

"I can't wait till tomorrow. I feel like I have a million butterflies in my stomach. It's weird: I feel excited, nervous, nauseous, everything. But above all, I can't wait!"

"It must be amazing to think that you are going to be competing against all those famous riders," dreamed Leya. She thought of her favourite pin-up rider and sighed. "I would love to compete against him. Not that I would come anywhere, but just to say that you were in the same trial as him, oooh, what a dream!"

George and Manna went into hoots of laughter as Leya was in a trance.

"Good job you ain't competing, Leya. You'd be there on your horse, gazing into the distance with not a clue as to where you had to go or where you had to jump the next fence!" joked George. "You're only jealous you aren't a competent horse woman like Mrs J. She can handle anything life throws at her."

Manna nodded in silence. George got up.

"I'm going to check the horses before we go out to dinner. I'll be back in a tick. Oh, and help yourself to wine, Mrs J, there's plenty!"

He left Manna and Leya alone. Manna seized the opportunity to have a chat.

"So, are you glad to be back working for us again, Leya?"

Leya nodded enthusiastically. "Yeah, I really am. I didn't want to go ahead with all that legal stuff, it's not my bag."

"Wise words for one so young, Leya," Manna began to probe. "So what made you decide to drop the case?"

"Well, after... the problems I had with my lawyer, Nat... I mean, *I* felt that it wasn't right for me to go ahead with the claim. He was a horrible man. I didn't like him."

"Uh, did you mention Natalie just then? What has she got to do with all this?"

Leya fell silent and her face reddened. She bit her lip.

"Has Natalie got something to do with this?" pushed Manna. Manna needed to know and she felt her blood begin to boil but she remained outwardly calm.

"Erm, well, Natalie suggested I sue you, to get the compensation. She said she would help me and not to worry about you, as your insurance would pay out," Leya stumbled.

"Did she now? Oh, right." Manna was controlled. "How would she have helped out then?"

"By paying my legal costs if I didn't win. She got this Darius Cherry bloke on the case, top lawyer. She asked him to act for me but instead he turned out to be a pervert and tried to rape me. That's when Callum called the police and got him arrested. Callum was brilliant. He got this friend of his, who's a copper, to catch Cherry to get him for sexual assault. Well, he didn't actually do anything, but he came close to it."

Leya took another swig of wine. She had become very liberal with her explanations and Manna's eyes lit up with disbelief. Still she remained calm.

"So Callum was a great help to you?" she continued to question.

"Oh yeah, him and Jude, they were brilliant. Got things sorted out well good. They even stayed with Natalie a few times when things got bad. When the fire happened. Jude was like a godsend to Callum — nursing him, visiting him at the hospital. She looked after him. He thought a lot of that, I know for a fact."

"Right," Manna spoke in a low voice. "How *much* did he think of her?"

"Well, they spent a lot of time together when you were away. Oh, perhaps I shouldn't have said that, sorry. It's not for me to say. It must be this wine." Leya looked to the floor in embarrassment, fearing she had said too much. She clutched her arm and readjusted her sling.

"No, course not, Leya. Anyway, I'd better get back to the guesthouse and change. Mustn't be late for dinner, must we? I'll see you back here at seven."

Manna didn't rely too heavily on the information from Leya as she had clearly drunk a few too many glasses of wine. But she was very interested to learn of Natalie's involvement with the court case.

Manna returned to the guesthouse and found Callum lying on the sofa watching the news channel. He got up to greet her.

"Hey, I was wondering where you were. Look, is it okay if I stayed the night? I was hoping to watch you and Othello at the cross-country tomorrow."

Manna smiled and walked towards the bedroom. "Yes, course you can stay but, if you don't mind, can you take the sofa? I need to have a clear head for tomorrow. You do understand, don't you?"

Callum nodded. "Course I do. Oh, and the table will be ready for half seven. I've booked one for four people. That's right, isn't it?" he called out.

In the bedroom Manna pursed her lips and then cheerily called back, "Yes, that's fine. They deserve a treat for looking after the horses." She gazed into the dressing table mirror and looked perturbed. "As long as Leya keeps her mouth shut," she uttered under her breath.

oOo

Manna's overnight dressage score was encouraging. She had thirty penalties and was currently lying in a very creditable eighth place.

The next morning dawned with steady rainfall. This was not good news and Manna was apprehensive. She gazed out of the bedroom window. She called out to Callum who was taking a shower.

"Cal, it's raining really hard. What a bloody nuisance. I'm going straight over to the stables to check on Othello and get any information I can about the going."

"Okay, I'll grab a bit of breakfast and meet you there," replied Callum from the shower. "I expect George will have found out all you need to know though," he added.

"That's what I'm hoping for." Manna drew back the shower curtain to reveal her naked husband. He leant across and kissed her on the cheek, leaving her face wet.

"See you in a while," she smiled and closed the curtain. She wiped the water from her face on to her sleeve.

At the stabling complex George and Leya had given the horses their morning feed. Leya was attempting to muck out the stables with one hand. George had rugged up the horses and had tethered them alongside the horsebox where they were each devouring a net of haylage. The weather forecast wasn't promising for the day. Rain for the morning and sunny spells in the afternoon. Manna was drawn to ride at two pm.

The vet's inspection was scheduled for half past nine and Manna was confident that Othello was sound to compete in the cross-country phase. She arrived at the complex as Leya was briskly sweeping the yard apron.

"Hi Leya, how's your head this morning?" breezed Manna with a huge grin on her face.

"Ooh, could be better, Manna, thanks for asking. The horses are tied up at the box, but I'm nearly ready for them to come back in now. Oh, and the stables are nearly clean."

"Good! Can you get Othello ready for the vet's inspection? Give him a good brush all over and wash his tail for me. I'm just going to have a quick chat with George."

Manna walked off in the direction of the horsebox. George met her halfway.

"Morning, George. I need your thoughts. Have you heard how the going is on the course?" she asked searchingly.

George plunged his hands into his coat pockets and shrugged his shoulders.

"The folk I've spoken to so far this morning aren't too happy. Especially the ones who are down to ride first thing. Talk is that parts of the course are pretty slippery, so make sure you got the right studs in, Mrs J. Othello will be fine. Just ride him steady into the jumps, particularly the drops and the in and outs. Anyway, it's only supposed to rain this morning. By the time you ride, it should've cleared up," he said in reassurance. "It's important that you think positive both for yourself and for Othello. He needs to know that you have one hundred percent faith in him and stay calm. Just go out and enjoy it!"

Manna smiled and kissed George on the cheek. "Thanks, that's what I wanted to hear," she whispered next to his ear. "I'm so glad you're here. I'll make a horseman out of you yet!"

George was practically bursting with pride but he managed to stay calm.

"I'm just telling you how it is, Mrs J. That's all," he remarked. "I'll help Leya get Othello ready for the inspection. Shall we keep his rug on?" he added.

"Yes, put his lightweight rug on; it's not cold, is it, just wet." Manna walked over to Ariel's stable and patted her neck. "How's her leg this morning, Leya?" she asked and ran her hand over the mare's withers.

"Getting much better. I've managed to change the dressing and the wound is healing well. I think she'll be ready to trot up later to check the lameness."

"That's brilliant," Manna continued to pat Ariel's neck. She fed her a mint. "You get plenty of rest now, girl, hear me?"

Leya and George got Othello ready for the vet's inspection. Leya washed his mane and tail and groomed him until he shone. Manna led him over to the inspection enclosure at nine-thirty. Othello, fresh from the dressage test, was on his toes. He looked all around him with wide eyes and flared nostrils, snorting and side-stepping as he was led.

Manna hissed at Othello to stop. "And you can cut that out, matey! Behave yourself, you hear me? Just be good for another half an hour and then you can get back to Ariel."

Othello seemed to take notice of Manna and began to walk in a sensible fashion, with only the occasional shy at non-existent hazards. He nudged Manna's pockets in search of Polos as they walked.

"You can have one after you've had your vet inspection, otherwise I know you will spit it out when she's checking your mouth!" Manna warned him.

The inspection went well and Othello was declared fit to compete. There was a riders' briefing meeting called directly after the inspections to run through the condition of the course and make everyone aware of the health and safety issues arising from the poor weather.

Some horses had been scratched from competing in the cross-country owing to lameness or from owners' concerns for their horses' welfare. Manna was secretly delighted as it opened up her chances of getting a better placing in the overall marks. She clenched her hands into fists and began to feel encouraged and positive.

Callum met her outside the debriefing area.

"Everything okay, love?" he asked and placed a protective arm around her shoulders.

"Yeah, great. There are a few competitors who haven't qualified for the cross-country, so that'll help me hopefully get a better score. I should move up on the points board now."

"Right. But you're happy to go ahead, despite the debrief?" He wanted confirmation from Manna that she was happy with her decision.

"Definitely! More than ever. I am *really* looking forward to it. Apprehensive? Yes! Scared? Yes! Determined? Well, you know me!" she chuckled.

oOo

It was a quarter past one and Leya had made her finishing touches to Othello. He was gleaming from head to hoof. She had, with George's assistance, plaited his mane and tail and he looked dazzling. Othello knew something exciting was going to happen, particularly as he was being plaited, and he quivered with anticipation whilst snatching small mouthfuls of hay and staring out of his stable.

Manna had changed into her cross-country colours. She was wearing bottle green and white checks with matching skullcap, cream breeches and brown leather riding boots. She was fastening her spurs to her boots when George tapped her on the shoulder. He handed her the medical card and she shook her head.

"I'd forget my head if you weren't here, George!" She inserted it into the clear pocket on her shirtsleeve. This was a vital piece of equipment that she had to carry in the event of an accident to assist the first aid officials. Without it she would be disqualified.

"Have you got your stopwatch, Mrs J?" George asked.

"Heavens, no! I think it's in the horsebox in one of the cubbyholes. Can you get it for me, there's a dear?"

She paced around the yard apron, checked the fixings on her skullcap and picked up her riding crop. The rain had stopped and there was the smell of freshness in the air. The sun was trying to come out. Eventually the course was bathed in weak sunshine.

Callum walked around the stabling complex, talking on his mobile phone.

"Nat, I feel so guilty about everything. I needed to be here with Manna. It's such a huge deal, not just any old eventing competition, is it? No, I haven't spoken to Jude since Friday evening. We decided we both needed some space. Yes, I will speak to her after the weekend. Manna? She seems fine. We had a bit of a chat the other night. It's going to take time. Yes! I do know you think I'm a shit. But, I don't know… I'm so confused at the moment. Anyway, I'd better go. Manna's on in half an hour. It's being televised on Channel 2. Look out for her! See you… bye!"

Manna mounted Othello and adjusted the girth. He was very excited and wouldn't stand still to have his tack checked. He promptly received a slap from Manna's stick on the hindquarters.

"Stand up, Othello! Just a few more minutes and then we'll warm up," Manna yelled and Othello promptly stood to attention. His neck was arched and he appeared to have grown a few more hands in height.

Leya fastened his brushing boots and checked the breastplate.

"Okay, Manna, all set. Good luck. We'll stand in the enclosure. I'll bring the grooming kit and sweat rug for you when you've finished. Go for it!" She patted Othello's neck.

"See you at the finish!" Manna smiled anxiously and pointed Othello in the direction of the warm up arena.

Callum slapped Othello's neck enthusiastically.

"Go for it, Manna! I know you can do it! Good luck and be safe!" He squeezed Manna's thigh in reassurance.

George watched from a distance. Manna looked across at him and he nodded without speaking. She knew what he was thinking. He didn't need to say anything.

Othello walked in forward fashion around the warm up arena with his head and tail raised very high. He was excited about the prospect of being at a completely new venue with lots of other horses and smells around him. He walked with purpose and settled into his warm up. Manna moved him forward into trot, rounded and collected. Figure of eight canter work followed in twenty-metre circles. Manna took him over the practice jumps to keep him warm and his muscles supple. A few minutes later her number was called.

"Competitor 224 to the start, please!" a voice boomed out over the PA system. Manna nodded to herself, moved Othello into a trot and made her way over to the start.

The starter indicated for Manna to prepare. She had Othello's tack checked by one of the stewards. There was no turning back now. She trotted Othello in a circle. The countdown began. " Five... four... three... two... one... good luck!"

They were off! Manna clicked her stopwatch to the on position and asked Othello into a settling pace as they approached the first fence. Othello cantered sideways towards the jump. His eyes were fixed on it and the decorative flowerpots placed either side of the wings. He almost came to a standstill. Manna thought of what George had said previously and what she always told other people: "It's so important to get him over the first fence, then he'll settle in..." She growled at Othello, urged him with her leg firmly on and gave him a sharp reminder with her crop. He lifted up like a gazelle and cleared the fence with feet to spare. They were on their way.

Manna upped the pace to a steady gallop as Othello, who was still trying to nap, headed on towards the second fence: an upturned boat with telegraph poles over the top. This time he didn't hesitate but took off over the jump with a perfect landing on the other side. Manna patted his neck and drew a breath. It was the first time she had breathed since the start. Her nerves were calmer and she was now able to set about the task in hand. They headed towards the third – the in and out. She noticed how much the ground had been churned up by previous competitors but Othello was oblivious to that fact and was on a mission to get over it. Again he jumped it well, bounced the in and out, gathering speed as they continued on through the course.

They reached the woodland section and galloped into the dark green shadows of the cover to clear two more upright fences. Next was the water jump. Manna collected Othello to wake him up to the fact that he was about to attempt the *bogey* fence. Many previous competitors had slipped here and had ended up getting a ducking, much to the delight of the immense crowd that was gathered either side of the lake. The TV cameras were set up nearby to record the action.

Othello began to tense as they took the approach out of the wood into the bright sunshine that reflected off the water. Manna kept her leg on and gave him a brief jab with her spur to keep him forward. She felt him gather himself up on the take off. It seemed as though they were in suspended animation as she slipped the reins to full length in mid-air.

Callum, George and Leya were watching a large TV screen at the collecting ring and were yelling like banshees in encouragement.

"Go on Manna! Go on!" they yelled in enthusiasm. Leya grabbed George's arm and hung on with grim determination.

Othello launched into a huge leap, cleared the fence and landed safely in the lake with a huge splash. Othello tripped momentarily, launching Manna on to this neck but she quickly gathered the reins back up, corrected her position and they cantered out of the water towards the thatched roof fence and jumped safely back on to the course. A roar of delight from the crowd and much applause raised Manna's spirits and she kicked on.

Othello continued to gallop as they approached the awesome oxer. Manna's concentration had a brief lapse. She was, for some reason, suddenly thinking about Littlebridge. Othello sensed she wasn't fully in control and decided to refuse the fence. Manna woke up from her drifting thoughts and turned Othello back to the jump. This time, although hesitant, he cleared it. She had unfortunately gained her first penalties. She was angry with herself and she collected her concentration back as the next jump loomed towards her. It was the quarry where she had two steep step jumps down and an upright on two steep steps up. Unfazed, Manna approached the quarry like a pro and performed a faultless display of concentration and harmony with her horse. She was back on track.

There was a section of open ground which Othello steadily galloped along, closely followed by a film crew on a quad bike. The route was lined by many spectators, who all clapped and urged them on. Manna checked her watch and noticed they were a little behind on time due to the refusal at the oxer. She pushed Othello up a gear to make up time.

They were three quarters of the way around the course. They cleared the next few fences with ease and the home straight lay in front of them. Just the infamous Blenheim Flyer brush and ditch fence near to the entrance to the trade stands stood between them and home. Again Manna moved Othello onwards. She could feel he was beginning to tire but with one last boost of energy they cleared the fence and galloped gallantly on to the finish line. Manna slowed Othello into a canter and clicked her stopwatch off.

Leya ran across to meet them and deftly threw a sweat rug over Othello's hindquarters. Callum was the first to congratulate Manna.

"Bloody brilliant, Man! Absolutely bloody brilliant! He jumped so well. What a star! Well done!" he yelled with a huge grin on his face.

Leya patted Othello as Manna brought him to a walk and then stopped. She hopped off and hugged Callum.

"Oh! That was so great! I can't explain – he was a star! All the way round. I can't speak!" she gasped and tightly held on to Callum.

Leya ran up the stirrups on Othello's saddle and loosened his girth. "Well done, Manna! Excellent work! Oh and don't forget you've got to weigh in and Othello has to be checked again by the vet. Over there!" She indicated to a corner of the ring.

Manna nodded without speaking and obediently untacked Othello. Leya moved his sweat rug over his body and fastened it. She continued to walk Othello round as he was still blowing hard.

Manna weighed in without any issues and Othello was checked by the vet and passed fit. Manna collapsed in a heap on the grass. Callum knelt by her side. He held on to her shoulders.

"You did so well, Manna. You rode your heart out, didn't you? I am so proud of you and Othello! You rode it so well and were a great team!" He kissed her on the cheek.

George reached the party and was smiling broadly. Manna got up and threw her arms around his neck.

"Oh George! Can you believe it? Little old us competing at Blenheim. Can it get any better?" she asked.

"Well, Mrs J. It may well do. Got to think positive cos sadly you got twenty penalties for that refusal, but on the plus side, no time penalties so… at the moment, that puts you in seventh place! Loads of horses had problems on the course, what with the conditions. So, yep, it can get better! Well done!"

Manna shrieked in disbelief and let go of George. She stared up at the leader board and saw her name in seventh position on the list. She was astounded and so delighted that she grabbed Callum and leapt around him like a child who had just been presented with her first pony.

"Oh… my… God!" she exclaimed, time and time again.

"You are unbelievable!" Callum shook his head in pride. "This is ground-breaking! Manna, do you realise you are up with the pros – you and Othello! If you can go clear tomorrow in the show jumping , you stand a wonderful chance of being placed. Do you realise… you are on the brink? This is truly amazing stuff. I am so glad I came. This is brilliant!"

He held Manna close to him and she felt his heart beating rapidly against her body. She didn't let go of him for a long while. Not until a TV presenter and crew interrupted their embrace for an impromptu interview on live TV!

"This is Amanda Jacobs, rider of The Storyteller, or Othello as you call him. Amanda, how did you find the going? Was it as bad as predicted?" asked the presenter, who thrust a fluffy microphone under Manna's nose and nodded for a response.

"Oh, uh, it was a little hairy in places, but now the rain has stopped – it made life easier," Manna responded and tried to make sure her face was clean as the camera zoomed in for a close up.

"I understand this is your first time at Blenheim. What are your thoughts on the course layout?" the presenter probed.

"It is a wonderful course, it rode really well. A credit to the course builder, fabulous!" she gushed, still out of breath.

"And you are currently lying in seventh place. Do you think you can win Blenheim?"

Manna considered for a while and responded. "It's a dream just to compete here. To complete a dressage test with the Palace as your backdrop, it would be a dream to win but, well, we'll have to see what happens tomorrow."

"Amanda Jacobs, thank you very much and very good luck. I'm sure all the viewers at home will be watching the show jumping phase tomorrow with bated breath!"

"Thank you," Manna gasped as the TV crew reassembled and swooped on their next unsuspecting interviewee.

"Wow! Talk about pro! TV interview! Jesus, how cool is that?" remarked Leya. "You're really famous now, Manna. Everyone at home will be watching. This is *so* exciting, I can't wait!"

Manna let out a huge sigh. "I feel completely spaced out now! I can't think straight. Anyway, we'd better get Othello back to his stable and cool him down. He really deserves it!"

"We'll look after him, Manna," said Leya. "Won't we, George? And Callum will look after you, won't you?" Leya looked across at Callum who was flushed.

"We'll go and have a coffee and let Manna get her mind back on track. We'll meet up with you two guys, say, in an hour?" Callum held on to Manna's arm.

"Yeah, we'll be done by then. Do you want me to walk Ariel out for you, Manna?" Leya tentatively asked.

"Yes, but leave the trotting up until I get there later on," Manna instructed. "I want to see her moving first."

oOo

Callum bought two coffees and placed them on the table in front of where Manna was sitting. She had loosened her stock from beneath her chin. She sipped her coffee in silence. They were in the competitors' hospitality marquee.

"You're reliving the course, aren't you?" surmised Callum. He smiled as he watched Manna, who sat expressionless opposite him.

"Yes," she smiled. "I still can't explain how exhilarating it was. The jumps are massive and they seem to come up so quickly. Othello did so well; he really jumped his heart out. I couldn't fault him."

"What about the refusal?" Callum felt he should broach the subject.

"Entirely my fault. Do you know, I was thinking about the yard and he knew I wasn't in control. That's why he refused. Cos I didn't ask him to jump. Such a terrible and costly mistake!"

"But at least you got him over it the second time," Callum sipped his coffee.

"I was determined to. I had to get over it and I'm so glad I did," she returned.

"Yes, because if you'd panicked, you would have blown it."

"I had to keep in control. I'm ecstatic, Cal. All I have to do is to go clear tomorrow, and who knows."

"If you want it badly enough, Man, you will get it. Anyway, I think," he added and took hold of Manna's hand, "that we need to celebrate, don't you?" He looked lustfully at her.

"What, really? But where?" Manna quizzed in surprise.

"I think we can take time out and go back to the guesthouse. You need to get changed, don't you?"

"Yes and have a shower. I'm covered in mud," Manna concluded and stared at her spattered clothes.

"And I can soap your back for you." Callum looked over his coffee cup and raised his eyebrows.

"I think that is a wonderful idea. Come on, we've got an hour!" she laughed.

oOo

They arrived back at the guesthouse. Manna peeled off her riding clothes as Callum ran a shower for her. She removed her bra and panties; Callum was standing in the doorway watching.

"I've missed you," he announced. "I really have missed you."

Manna smiled in acknowledgement and placed her bathrobe over her shoulders. She walked up to him. "I'm glad." She kissed him gently on the lips. "Wait here, I'll only be a few minutes," she whispered.

"Can I join you in the shower?" Callum's eyes were leaden with lust. He looked serious.

"Yeah, why not?" Manna led him into the bathroom and closed the door behind them.

Callum was still confused over his feelings and, as he closed his eyes to kiss Manna, he thought of Jude. They began to explore each other's bodies, delicately kissing like two love-struck teenagers. Their flame rekindled as their reserve diminished and they passionately made love in the shower. The water cascaded over them as they rose and fell against the shower's tiled walls in a crescendo of lust. They collapsed on to the freshly laundered bed and held one another close; neither dared to let go.

Manna sighed in contentment. "This has to be one of the happiest days in my life…"

oOo

Chapter Twenty-Three

Manna trotted Othello around in the warm up arena. It was Sunday afternoon and the final phase of the three-day event, the show jumping.

Othello, although tired from the cross-country of the previous day, was still able to find the energy to shy at a dog in the crowd. Manna scolded him and moved him up into a collected canter. He had passed the final vet's inspection that morning and was eligible to compete.

Leya and George stood next to the practice jumps and indicated to Manna that it was clear to start jumping. She collected Othello into the canter and, with leg on, put him over the first jump. He jumped from a virtual standstill but cleared it with inches to spare.

Manna circled him once again and took the jump off the other rein. Othello jumped better that time and he was clearly listening to Manna's aids. Leya and George altered the jump's height and Othello jumped again with ease. Manna remained focussed. She knew how crucial it was in this phase to go clear.

There were two more competitors before it was her turn to jump and Manna decided not to engage in any conversation before she competed. Callum had opted to watch from the viewing arena. He realised that Manna needed a clear mind. Leya and George only spoke if they had to, knowing that they would not receive a response from Manna. She continued to canter over the practice jumps in silence. All that could be heard was the rhythmical thud of hooves on grass as Othello took off and landed on the other side of the jump.

The PA called Manna's number. Manna raised her eyebrows, crossed her chest in a religious fashion and trotted into the ring.

The entire show jumping ring was packed with spectators. There was a sea of faces and a deafening applause as Manna and Othello trotted to the centre, stopped and saluted the judge. The bell rang to start and the large digital clock began to count the seconds.

Manna rode Othello forwards into canter and headed towards the first jump, the upright. They cleared it well and cantered on to the second. As she rode around the arena, the commentator explained to the crowd how well Manna and Othello had performed in the cross-country phase and that the revised overnight scores indicated that they were currently lying in fifth place! The commentator went on to say how the course had been quite testing for all competitors. She felt a warm glow as Othello clipped the third fence. She heard the clatter and glanced back – the fence was still intact. She sighed in relief.

The spread loomed in front of them and Manna gathered Othello up and urged him over. Again the fence was rapped and the crowd groaned, but yet again the fence hadn't been dislodged. Manna breathed. They moved on to the double. Othello was hesitant and got behind the bit. Manna managed to move him on forward and he cleared it with inches to spare.

Two fences from home. The oxer and then the treble. The crowd were on the edge of their seats as Manna turned the corner to face the oxer. Othello took a hasty glance at the jump and decided it wasn't going to upset him and cleared it. Just the treble remained. Othello cantered on the spot, his head held high as they made their attempt as the clock ticked on. The first element rattled heavily, the second was close and, at the third element, Othello's body moved upwards. Manna felt him take off as they glided over safely! A clear round! The crowd erupted into uncontrollable cheers and applause as Manna cantered round, wildly slapping Othello's neck in praise. She punched the air with a white-gloved hand and the crowd roared again, all standing and applauding her achievement.

Othello took in the atmosphere and bucketed around the ring. He gave a celebratory buck, which unseated Manna momentarily. She laughed and brought him back to a trot and exited the ring. It was a momentous occasion. Manna leapt off Othello, red-faced, straight into Callum's arms where they openly embraced, just as the TV crew and presenter were armed ready for the instant reaction interview.

"Sorry to interrupt, Amanda, but we would like a quick word. Well done, by the way, that was a tremendous round. How did he go?"

Manna was tearful and pink-cheeked but managed to squeak a reply. "Fantastic! Bloody fantastic! Oops! Sorry to swear. It was great, he is a real performer!"

"And that clear round has now put you in fourth place overall. What are your feelings?"

oOo

"I can't watch this anymore." Jude got up from her chair in the living room. She was watching the television with Natalie at Heyrick Heights.

"Oh Jude, don't get upset. He's not worth it!"

Jude was in tears in the kitchen. "I know, typical bloke. Yeah, I know. I just feel so cheated. I really… Oh, I don't know! I can't keep on saying the same old things. Looks like we're definitely over, judging from that snog they just had on national TV."

"It's probably the heat of the moment. You have to give it to her; she's done really well. It looks like she is going to get placed. Actually in the money!" Natalie tried to reason.

She poured another glass of wine and handed it to Jude. Jude took it without acknowledgement and took a gulp. She wiped her tears away.

"I can't help it, Nat. I still really love him and I don't want to let him go."

"Well," Natalie sipped her wine, "then you are going to have to show him what he is missing. Give it time, Jude. Play your cards close to your chest, but just give it time. Come on, let's see what the final placings are."

Natalie threw herself back on to the sofa in front of the TV and squinted for the results.

"Blimey! That posh bloke has got twelve penalties, you know, Thingy! And there's only the leader to go. So that means, with him going down the leader board, that Manna's guaranteed second place! That's so amazing!"

Natalie leapt up and down on the sofa, scattering cushions on to the floor. Jude managed to summon up the dignity to watch the last competitor as he performed a winning clear round. A roar of the crowd indicated the end of the competition and Manna had been placed second.

Jude shook her head. "I can't believe it, Nat! She's got second place!"

"Well," Natalie got up from the sofa and held her arms out to comfort Jude. "Things are probably going to change now that Manna has hit the big time. You've got to ask yourself, do you put up and shut up or, for want of a better way of asking, do you want to come and work for me? What do you say? Have you had any more thoughts about it?"

Natalie's voice was a distant haze in the background. Jude watched Manna being presented with a beautiful trophy, rosette and prize money. She watched as Callum planted a kiss on Manna's cheek and embraced her. She watched as Manna was interviewed on live TV *again*. After a few moments she answered, still staring at the television.

"If, if it means one day we get her back for our weyuudyluys, for what Callum did to me, then, for the chance of a stable life, I am prepared to give it a go!"

Natalie embraced Jude and refilled her wine glass in celebration gesture. She chinked her glass against Jude's and announced a toast.

"Well, here's to new beginnings and here's to *stability*. Here Jude, is to… stability!"

oOo

Printed in Great Britain
by Amazon